THE GEORGIA EXPRESS

A Tale of the Civil War

Phillip Urlevich

Burning Bulb
PUBLISHING

The Georgia Express
By **Phillip Urlevich**

Burning Bulb Publishing
P.O. Box 4721
Bridgeport, WV 26330-4721
United States of America
www.BurningBulbPublishing.com

Cover illustrated by Melissa St. Giles with the following photographic elements from Unsplash, Leon Skibitzki (front cover) and Chris Chow (back cover).

First Edition.

Paperback Edition ISBN: 978-1-948278-60-7

CHAPTER 1

Big Shanty 1862 - The "General" locomotive- The"General" crew - The Lacy residence - The train stolen- Refreshment delayed-The raiders-The man with a tall hat and big beard-Bill Fuller-Anthony Murphy-The engineers give chase—Useful suggestions-Hootin' and hollerin'

The day at the Big Shanty train station started as did most spring Georgia days. Nothing unusual, rather dull. The air was filled with the sounds of the train whistles. Either signaling their arrival or the departure. The crowd swarming and milling about, ushers calling for the passengers to board. Were they listening? Probably yes, or possibly no. It would be just another day, albeit a cloudy and rainy one. However, there was only one thing out of place, the large presence of men in grey uniforms wielding rifles, guarding the little train station against foes. Just across the tracks, there was a large encampment with more men in grey. They had both young and old ones, training for the day when they would leave their camp for a distant field of battle. As the sun rose, a sentry was doing his paces. Walking back and forth, making sure there wasn't any shenanigan afoot by the enemy he was guarding against. Right now, his greater enemy was boredom. He stopped to adjust his greatcoat closer for warmth, a typical way to kill time (read: a few seconds). He found himself gazing at the sky. The air was cool and wet; rain was attacking everyone at the station mercilessly. People ran for shelter, while some actually enjoyed the beat down. The sentry's attention was diverted by the sharp whistle of a steam locomotive. He looked to the south to see the familiar plume of smoke billowing into the not-so-clear sky.

He had seen this sight before. Plenty of times! He went back to his paces, not paying attention as the great locomotive eased into the train station and stopping perfectly in sync with the wood platform. The locomotive let out a loud hiss. It looked like it announced its arrival

1

when it came to a complete stop. It was an impressive piece of machinery. The color of the main engine was dark green with reddish orange accents, adorned with a long cylindrical boiler. On the boiler was stenciled the number 39. On the main engine located right above the wheels, in gold-lettered plaque, was the engine's moniker, 'General.'

"Twenty minutes for refreshment!"

With that call, the station suddenly started to fill with people. They flooded out for relief from the cramped quarters to the promise of food and open-air, if only that was for twenty minutes. Everyone followed a pathway that led to the nearby place, Lacy Hotel. Once they made it past a duck pond filled with muddy ducks quacking angrily at them, they were greeted by the beautiful white two-story building, with a tall columned porch, complimented with green shutters. Mrs. Lacy's home cooking was the stuff of a legend. As everyone made their way to the hotel was told, they couldn't wait to try it and judge for themselves. Mr. Lacy sat outside, waiting for the breakfast crowd. He made pleasantries with everyone there. Mr. Lacy had a bag of silver for change in his lap. He expected to make good money, I suppose. In exchange for twenty-five cents, a traveler could get a fresh hot breakfast of eggs, grits, and biscuits with gravy, sorghum, and flapjacks with butter and hot coffee to wash it all down. Among the crowd were the General's crew: engineer E. Jefferson Cain, foreman of the Western and Atlantic Railroad Anthony Murphy, fireman Andrew Anderson, and engineer Bill Fuller."

It was only a brief respite for these gentlemen. They had been working for a while that morning. Anderson fed the fires with cordwood to keep the engine running. Cain would stand next to him, and as a result, both had black hands and nearly dark faces. The crisp and cool air was a welcomed change of pace than the cramped, smoke-filled cab. Anderson, leading the group, was particularly eager to wash up and see what smelled so good up ahead.

"Step lively gents," Anderson exclaimed. "For if we are to be late, all the good food will be perished by our fellow travelers." He looked back at Cain. "That goes for you, too. Cain."

Cain was long and frail, tubercular. He coughed and said, "I will just help myself to your portions."

"Only after I shit it out", chuckled Anderson.

Murphy snapped. "There are ladies about Anderson. Be still. We only have a short while before we get it again. I'd rather eat in peace without hearing you hallooing about."

They had to break from their conversation as several ducks darted in front of them. Anderson broke the silence.

"Well, what do you say, Bill? Do you think the weather will grant us fair passage?"

"Hard to say," Fuller replied. "Regardless, I will keep on schedule. I will not allow the rain to slow us down. It should not. If the rumors of the federals taking Huntsville are true, then we need to get the fighting men to Chattanooga to join Beauregard. He can drive them out of Alabama and Tennessee."

Fuller looked considerably older and more mature than his twenty-six years suggested. He worked his way up to becoming a conductor and earned every bit of it, completely. Fuller ran a tight ship, expected nothing less from his crew that he would put in his share of the burden. He looked every bit the chief conductor with his uniform checkered pants, black boots, and a dark indigo coat, which covered a plush vest topped with a large gold watch.

"It's all too well that you stayed on as conductor, Bill", Cain said. "We would have been at a loss if you heeded the call of Jeff Davis to join the fighting men. I mean it."

They arrived at the hotel and waited in line. It was tiresome but seemed worthy.

"Governor Brown needed some more railroad men more to run the locomotives," Murphy said. "That's why we're here. In Anderson's case, we could spare him."

All of them chuckled.

"Say," Anderson said, as he slowed down to fall in with the others. "What have you heard? There was a fight up Tennessee way, weren't there?"

Fuller said, "Just rumors from our boys, there was a scrap at a place called Shiloh. It was a great victory for us, as the federals turned and scattered home, is what I heard."

"That'll teach 'em!" Anderson whooped.

"Hush!" Murphy exclaimed.

Anderson simmered. "They ought to learn to stay out of our land by now." He impressed his statement.

"The Yankees are slow learners." Cain said, "They took a whuppin' at Manassas and still came around now, causing mischief in Virginia. Can you believe it?"

"If need be, we can teach them as many lessons it takes until they decide they had enough," Anderson replied.

They reached the front door, where Mr. Lacy was sitting. Mr. Lacy was a pleasant-looking fellow without an ounce of meanness in him.

"Hello, gentlemen," he said. "How are you this morning?"

"We are well, but hungry," Anderson replied. "We heard this is the place to come to for some good southern hospitality."

"Indeed, you heard correct, Seh," Lacy replied. "For twenty-five cents, my wife has the best cooking in all of Big Shanty. Although I must ask you to wash up first. Mrs. Lacy will be saying grace before we eat. We have soap and water on the front porch"

"For the host and the good Lord, I will Seh."

While Anderson and Cain dealt with the transaction. Murphy fell in with Fuller.

"Bill, I noticed you had them hawk's eyes the whole time it took to get up here. What is it you're looking for?"

"When I was collecting the tickets, I noticed a group of men. They weren't wearing our grey, and they looked a bit out of place. I have not seen where they've gone."

***

Just as the station was full of people, it was empty just as quickly. However, save for the lone bored sentry. The General steamed and hissed as if it was rearing to go again. A tall figure walked through the steam like an apparition. A cinematic entry. Walking casually along the track, he cut an impressive figure with dark slacks, a vest with a gold watch chain hanging across. He wore a handsome Prince Albert coat, and a stovepipe hat to top it all off. He walked as if he had all the time in the world, and he used it to take in his surroundings. Following him was another fellow. He was watching the tall man with rather intent interest. The tall man looked at the first three boxcars. Then he motioned to them.

"Mr. Knight, uncouple the first three cars, please."

Mr. Knight, Will Knight, nodded. "Yes, sir."

The tall gentleman turned. He walked to the end of the engine. He looked out at the railroad tracks towards the wilderness of Georgia and beyond. Knight walked to the third car and the mailbox car. He sidled up to the coupling pin and was just about to pull it out when he saw the sentry right there, about ten feet away. The sentry had his back towards Knight, he seemed to stop for something, but then continued his patrol. The train hissed. Knight was startled, which shook him out of his trance. As gently as he could, he pulled the pin out, yet it still scraped against the metal. Knight stopped, waited, and when he didn't hear the sentry, he yanked the pin out and laid it gingerly on the drawbar. He peeked around the corner of the mail car to see the sentry at the far end of the platform. As if he had every right to be there, Knight strolled leisurely back towards the main engine. He passed the tall man and gave a slight nod. It was to approve of something. The tall man shifted the saddlebags as he passed and walked to the passenger coach. He climbed the steps, and opened the door, said something, and climbed back down, heading towards the engine. Behind him came eighteen men all out of the coach. They looked determined as they walked. Not running, just keeping an even, determined step. The tall man motioned to the third boxcar, and everyone went single file to clamber in. The tall man watched and motioned for one.

"Mr. Wilson, please assist Mr. Knight."

Mr. Wilson, John "Alf" Wilson nodded and, without hesitation, moved to the main engine. He was followed by Wilson Brown. The tall man watched as the last man filed in. Then he looked around and found no commotion, no one yelling, "Stop!" The few people and soldiers were milling about and paid them no mind. Sentry was walking back towards the main engine now. He looked bored and didn't even look at the tall man's direction. Wilson climbed into the main engine. Knight looked at him and judged Alf immediately by his size and build.

"Are you here to lend a hand, Alf?"

"Yes, sir."

"Very good. When I say so, engage that gear with your hands. Use your foot for the brake to slow the train. I also need you to work the handbrake tender." Knight commanded.

"Yes, sir," Wilson said, hoping he could remember to do so when the time came.

Right then, the tall man came aboard. Everyone faced him, waiting for the order on what to do next. James Andrews gave the command.

"All right. Let her go."

There was a hiss. Knight pulled the throttle.

Nothing happened. Everything was as it is.

It felt like an eternity to the men in the engine.

Suddenly there was a loud engine hiss. The engine lurched forward, jerking the men inside. The General moved slowly at first but started to pick up steam and chug its way out of the station.

***

Fuller sat at the end of the dining table with all the other passengers - Cain and Anderson on his right. Murphy on his left. All of them had their heads bowed in prayer with the passengers. When the final "Amen" was said, everyone raised their heads and started eating. It was an awaited moment. Anderson was quiet, not that he suddenly dropped out of character, he just didn't have much time to waste with idle chatter. He wanted to eat in peace. Fuller was just digging into his eggs when he suddenly heard a loud chuff of an engine. In the dining room, there was a window that showed the train station. Right now, it showed a train departing.

His train.

Fuller almost choked; that was his train. His train was leaving.

"Someone is running off with your train!"

Murphy's cry snapped Fuller out his stare. He got up immediately and ran for the door. Everyone heard the commotion and headed for the window to watch in astonishment as the train that took them here was leaving without them. Murphy pushed his way through to join Fuller as they exited the hotel and headed towards the station. They ran but in vain.

"Who do you think it could be? Those men you thought suspicious?"

"I do not know. They all had tickets to Big Shanty or elsewhere. They could well be deserters," Fuller said as he ran. They were panting, too. He went straight to the nearest sentry he found.

"Excuse me, soldier. Did you see who took my train?"

The sentry, who looked young, looked back at him with scared eyes. "Uh, yes... sir... It was a group of men... There was a big man with a black hat and a cape who was the last one on."

Fuller tried to remember such a man and continued. "You did not think to prevent them from doing so in any way??!!"

"They...uh...did not give me... any reason to."

Fuller sighed. This wasn't going anywhere. Murphy appeared. "I just spoke with a Mr. Kendrick. The train had left, and they couldn't do anything about it. I told him to grab a horse and ride down to Marietta and telegraph the superintendent in Atlanta on what has just occurred."

"It could very well be deserters from Camp McDonald," Fuller said. "The yellowbellies could have stolen it just to get away." Fuller turned to watch the train go. He then quickly broke into a run.

Looking north, Fuller could see the last car disappear beyond the trees. From the hotel, he heard the sound of laughter from everyone gathered outside of the hotel. Fuller didn't think it was funny. Someone stole his train. His livelihood. His responsibility. It was not at all funny. He decided right there on the run that he was going to chase it till his legs gave out. He didn't look back but Murphy, and Cain, in a coughing fit, were behind him.

Anderson was back at the hotel. He watched them run after the train before he slunk away. "To hell with this shit. I didn't sign up to fight no train thieves, I am out."

Fuller's only concern was the train, and nothing else. He tried to tune out the laughter and jeers from the onlookers. Even ignored the random helpful suggestions.

"Grab a horse!"

"Telegraph for an engine!"

Someone yelling this thought stuck out, though.

"Are you really going after that train on foot?"

Fuller shot back, "Yes!"

"What a damn fool," was the reply.

CHAPTER 2

*Before then-John "Alf" Wilson-Humble beginnings-Haskins-Town
pride-Hunting trip- Rumblings of war -Friends- Rumors - An
interesting idea-The secession - Call for volunteers- Friends off to
war- A father's promise Summer Tidings- A promise fulfilled.*

John Alfred Wilson, or "Alf," as he preferred, was at some
considerable distance from home in Wood County, Ohio. The hamlet
of Haskins was where the family farm was at. His father, Ezekiel,
uprooted him from Worthington to Haskins when he was just
seventeen years of age. His mother had passed, and Ezekiel needed
him to tend to a patch of land that belonged to them... Growing up,
he attended his lessons at the local schoolhouse, washed up for church,
and worked the land with his father. He didn't mind the arrival of his
aunt, who was living with them nor by the arrival of his little cousin
Daniel. Wilson had a nervous temperament but the determination of
steel when it came to getting the job done. He would endure long hours
toiling in the earth, sometimes long after dark, when the moon was the
only source of light. Either the crop was sown or harvested. He would
get it done... With his bluish-grey eyes peering from under blondish
hair, he became a crack squirrel and bird hunter. In the summers, he
would venture to the Maumee River with his friends, two good friends
Jedidiah Willard and Martin Hopkins. They would camp, fish, and
hunt. In the winters, they often would venture out and hunt deer.
Other times, they made use of the piles of snow and built snowmen.
Even though Wilson loved the outdoors, there was nothing better than
to come walking down the forest trail, rounding the bend, only to see
Haskins come into their view. Sure, the farm was home, but there was
also a strong sense of community; how all the shops, farms, and
churches came together. Maybe it was the school lessons on how
powerful countries maintained their power because they stood

together. Or the many lectures of the churches on faith and community. Either way, he hoped nothing would change ol' Haskins.

***

It was December 1860. Wilson, Willard, and Hopkins were coming back from a hunting trip, empty-handed. There were no bucks out today. The snow was on the ground, whilst the day turned slowly to night. Along with the temperatures, cold to freezing. They were bundled up in heavy wool and could have stayed out longer, but the appeal of a warm fire and the dinner table sounded too comforting. Willard moved his scarf so he could speak easier.

"It is alright, fellows, we should have better luck tomorrow. I feel the weather will take it a li'l easy on us, and we should be able to fill our smokehouses much easier."

"You said the same thing yesterday Martin," Hopkins said. "It is perhaps because of your foul tongue the Good Lord decided to keep the deer in the protection of the snow."

"I will be proven right, Jed," Hopkins replied. "Someday."

They all giggled. "Is Mrs. Willard doing a fair job on the smokehouse?" Wilson asked.

"She is quite a capable woman," Willard said. "I am very fortunate. When will you two scoundrels finally let up and marry a woman that will make you honest?"

"I am sweet on that Helen Roedel," Hopkins said. "But she is too strong. She has made a demand to not marry a man who resides with his mother and treats her decidedly better than a potential bride."

"She is right," Wilson said.

"You should not speak Alf." Hopkins snapped. "For you have no sweetheart."

"Perhaps because there is none to be had. They are all taken. The ones who are left fell on to the two of you," Willard chuckled. "Pay him no mind, Martin, he is sweet on his farm and the town. Why, look at him now! He is as giddy as a damn fool when he sees it."

Wilson laughed. He couldn't help it; he knew it's the truth. He never wanted to leave Haskins.

As they rounded the final bend of the forest, Haskins came into view. Nearly the whole town had gathered in the Main Square near the church.

"What is going on? It is not Sunday." Hopkins said.

"Let us find out," Wilson said.

As they worked their way through the crowd, they heard murmurs and people speaking aloud.

"The traitors!"

"Whatever will happen to the country?"

"This could very well mean war."

Wilson could only surmise at what had happened.

Finally, he spoke out. "What has happened?"

An elderly gentleman turned to him and informed, "South Carolina has seceded! The union has dissolved!"

Wilson was shocked. "How could that be?" he asked.

Another elderly fellow spoke. "They claim its right; a result of Lincoln elected as president."

Wilson didn't know what to say. Right then, his little cousin Daniel appeared by his side.

"Uncle wants you to come home."

***

The fire warmed Wilson, and the stew his Aunt Fanny prepared went well with it. Yet there was a cold feeling around the table. Ezekiel sat at the head of the table, while Alf at the other end. Everyone ate in silence. Finally.

"I can hear your finger tapping the table, John," Ezekiel said. "You can kindly state the reason why or cease."

"Have you not heard the news, father? About South Carolina?"

"I have."

A silence.

"Well, what do you think?"

Ezekiel took another mouthful of stew before he continued, "Listen, I am just a simple farmer, John. I do not pretend to know the ways of the world. The folks down south believe they have rights, rights to live the way they choose, and the rights to own slaves, which this family does not and will never condone. It is not righteous to own another person. We have always taken care of our own and never needed anyone else to keep this place. Always remember that."

"Do you think it will lead to war?"

"I certainly hope not," Fanny said.

"I do not know, John," Ezekiel said. "I do know there's plenty of folks who want to fight on both sides. You remember the way folks reacted when we went to war with Mexico. All the young fools ran off. The ones that came back – many were not the same as they were before, some came back without an arm or a leg, while some did not come back at all. Is that what you want, John? Do you want to end up like those men?"

Wilson spooned his stew. It was cold.

"No, sir."

"Then let us speak of this nonsense no more."

***

The winter snow thawed, perhaps because of the passions of the townsfolk weathering the secession crisis. Alf Wilson lived day by day, focusing on the progress of everyday events. Talk of the secession crisis inevitably made its way in every conversation. It did not help Ezekiel any when he and Alf were working the land, and a neighbor or a of Alf's friends would come running up with some new information. Ezekiel could see the excitement and anger boiled upon his son's face.

Indeed, when the news was that Georgia, Florida, Mississippi, Alabama, Texas, and Louisiana had joined South Carolina in seceding from the union, old Ezekiel knew there was no stopping it.

***

The month of April had now begun.... The ground was still muddy because the last of the snow was melting. Wilson, Willard, and Hopkins were collecting squirrels; they felled with their deadly aim.

Hopkins led the conversation.

"I heard of Bill Withers claim to be the father of poor Miss Jenny Olson's child."

"I do not care to hear the details of that damned scoundrel," Wilson said. "Jenny Olson is a sweet girl. She did not deserve to be treated as such... What happens to her now?"

"Her family is moving away," Hopkins said. Willard, "That is too bad, her mother's pies were the only reason I had to attend the church social."

"What has happened to Withers? The hangman's noose is not too kind a fate for that scoundrel." Wilson asked. "A posse has formed to bring him to justice under Mr. Olson. Word on the street is Withers has stolen a horse and made his way to the Maumee, paid for a ferry, and made his way up north to Michigan. That's the last I have heard."

"Let us speak no more of that nasty little cuss," Wilson said. "Since Jed has mentioned pie, and Mrs. Willard said she'd be baking a fresh one this afternoon. Martin, I propose we go down to his house and get at it before he does."

"I accept!" Hopkins whooped.

Hopkins and Wilson broke into a run. Left behind was Willard and his cry of "Wait!" Despite the fact that these men were pushing thirty, they could not help but go back to their childhood. They ran into the village square. There was another crowd this time gathered at the church steps. On the steps were two men, one dressed in a fine coat and a top hat. The other wore a crisp blue army uniform. The three ran up towards the edge of the crowd. The man with the top hat read loudly from a sheet of paper.

"Once again, this is a call to arms. The southern states are now in open rebellion. Fort Sumter has fallen. The rebels have seized it along with our men at arms there."

The crowd erupted in a fury. Wilson felt a blow in his stomach. As the crowd turned to rage, the man in the uniform spoke up. "Men of Ohio, President Lincoln has called for seventy-five thousand volunteers to put down this insurrection of the southern states. Who among you will join us to restore the union?" The crowd erupted, yet again.

***

Wilson didn't make it home until after dark. He saw his father sitting in front of the fire as usual, in his easy chair. Wilson made his way to his father's side. His father said nothing. After a brief pause, he said, "I know all too well what you are going to say, son. You want to enlist and fight the good fight to save the union."

"Father, the rebels fired on us. If it takes a fight to settle whatever our differences are, then by God, we'll let them have it!"

Ezekiel sighed. Wilson toned it down.

"Everyone says the war will be over in three months of time. Martin and Jedidiah have enlisted. Jedidiah's wife encouraged him."

"I can only hope this war will be over by that time," Ezekiel said. "I know I cannot stop you from enlisting. I can only ask that you stay until August after the summer planting. I suppose Daniel is ready to take up your mantle."

That was enough for Wilson. Four months. "Yes, father."

***

Spring turned to summer. All of Haskins seemed rather quieter, which was especially hard for Wilson as he really missed his friends. He was excited when he finally received letters from them. They told their tales of Washington DC and about the many northern men

12

massing an army. All the while, more news came of Virginia, Arkansas, North Carolina, and Tennessee seceding, thus forming the Confederate States of America, its capital in Richmond. Hopkins and Willard boasted that when the army would finally move, there will be a clash indeed and that they would whip the rebs, conquer Richmond, and come home to glory. Wilson bemoaned the fact that he would miss it all.

It was the end of July. Finally, the news came off a great battle that had occurred at a stream called Bull Run in Virginia. It was a disaster for the Union. The troops routed by the Confederates were poorly trained. All talks of a three-month war had stopped. Wilson, like many others, was hit hard by the news of the defeat. It did, however, boast his resolve to fight and willingness to see it through the end.

He was coming home from the general store when it happened. His father and aunt were in the yard, feeding chickens. Willard's wife, Emily, walked from the opposite side of the fence.

"Emily!" Wilson cried out, "Are you well? Have you heard from Jedidiah?"

She stopped, lowered her head and sniffed.

"Oh, Alf," she said softly. "I have received the news. He has fallen at Bull Run. He is no more."

The shock of hearing his childhood friend being killed was worse than anything he had ever felt before. Before he could say anything, she turned around and left. He didn't see his father approach him from the side. "You want to enlist still?"

Wilson looked at him with pain in his eyes. "Yes."

August came. He did his end of the bargain and left home. It was a big step. This was the first time he truly left Haskins. He packed up, bade farewell to his family, and took a stagecoach to Perrysburg. There he enlisted and soon became a private in Company C of the 21st Ohio Volunteer Infantry.

CHAPTER 3

*A year later-Gone to soldier-Picket Duty-Camp life Walking back-
A warm fire-The Englishman-Poker game-Boredom-Talk of
movement-The sergeant-Meeting the colonel-A mission-The plan-
Accepting the mission-What to expect-Relieved-A Fistful of Dollars-
The captain's furlough.*

It was in April 1862. Nearly a year had passed since the firing on
Fort Sumter. The 21st was encamped near the village of Shelbyville in
Tennessee. The air was both cool and wet. The ground was of pure
mud. In the middle was a sea of white pitch tents that went as far as
the eye could see, dotted by men who wore blue uniforms. As the sun
started to settle and dusk approached, Wilson wore his overcoat to
keep warm as he walked back to his tent. He was on picket duty, as
alert and ready as he could be in the cold weather, waiting for the
enemy. No one ever came. The walk back to his tent was arduous, with
the mud sucking at his shoes. He had to walk quite fast so his shoes
wouldn't sink. He slung his Enfield rifle-musket over his shoulder. He
had enough of holding it all day and rubbed his hands together to keep
warm. Fanny had knitted him a pair of mittens, but he had lost them
and sheepishly written her for another. She wrote back she would, and
sent a new scarf, so he had something to wait for, at least. His legs
ached from the extra effort from walking. He had been alert all day,
and now his mind had begun to wander. His eyes hurt. Occasionally
amongst the tents, there was a fire blazing with a group of soldiers
huddled around it. The heat was a welcomed diversion for Wilson,
especially the smell of brewing coffee and salt pork cooking. Around
one such fire, there was Ebenezer Wade, Michael Shaffstall, and Mark
Wood. They sat on logs, playing a rousing game of poker. Wood was
dealing the next hand. He was not a native Ohioan. He was born in
Nottingham, England, and immigrated to the States when he was

seventeen. He was twenty-three. He had made a decent living as a machinist in Toledo. He was now a soldier in Shelbyville.

"Quite right, Ebby, your trio of kings would defeat Shaff's pair, but I'm afraid I have to disappoint all parties involved as I have a full house and therefore claim victory." Wood said.

"Aw hellfire," Wade grumbled.

Wood gathered up the cards and began to shuffle. He noticed a figure trudge by and made his face by the glow of the fire.

"Why, if it isn't our glorious soldier of the guard. 'Ello Alf! What's the good word? Have you been keeping the wretched enemy at bay so we may engage in games of vice?"

"If you mean boredom is an enemy, I give an unconditional surrender and am now paroled to go home," Wilson replied.

"There is the valiant spirit that keeps this army a step away from annihilation! When we face Johnny Reb on the field, we might perhaps 'ave enough sense to care. Alf, once you are settled, do join us. We have fresh coffee if it entices you."

Even though he craved sleep, the lure of coffee was enough.

"Sure, Marky, I'd love some."

Wilson went to his tent, knelt down to crawl in. He took the bayonet off the stock of the rifle, sheathed it, and set his rifle down on the rubber blanket set down on the mud. Wilson removed his overcoat, took off his strap. He felt for his knapsack in search of a new pair of socks. He took his shoes off, switched socks, and then returned the shoes. There was a time when Wilson was cleanshaven and stocky. The combination of hard work and a home-cooked meal. Now months of soldiering, he was wire-thin and had a goatee. The result of a diet of hardtack, salt pork, and occasional vegetables. Wilson crawled out of his tent, stacked his rifle against everyone else's, and rejoined his comrades.

Shaffstall spoke.

"We should have been in Grant's or Buell's army. They are advancing much faster than we are, hell you've heard the rumors about the fight at Pittsburg Landing. All the while, we sit here in the mud."

"I've heard a rumor of us finally advancing to Huntsville just as soon as the weather breaks", Wade said.

"When would that be? Many of our boys have taken ill in our company alone. We are not at our full strength." Shaffstall replied.

"Come now; when the time is right, our beloved general Old Stars Mitchell shall make a glorious advance. Which will be 'never'. Shall I cut you in, Alf? Or are you too righteous to play?" Wood said.

"As long as it is not for money," Wilson replied.

"Oh, come now, your maidenly virtue will have you succumb to the vice of the army. As if now, we have gathered the best 'ardtack without weevils, and that is what we play for." He grabbed a piece from Shaffstall's pile,

"Say!"

"Oh, bugger off."

Wilson grabbed a log and rolled it over. "Count me in."

Before the game could continue, a big booming voice called out, "Attention!" The soldiers stood up immediately and snapped to attention. From the darkness came forward a determined figure, it was the company first Sergeant Asa Spafford.

"At ease, men. Private Wilson, the company commander, and commanding colonel wish to have a word with you."

"Yes, Sergeant", said Wilson. He was unsure why.

Spafford led Wilson to the colonel's quarters. Unlike the rest of them, the colonel had a generous place to live. A quaint little cabin that might have been a quarter for slaves. It was now abandoned until Colonel James Norton slept in it. Spafford led Wilson to the front door. He knocked, waited for the affirmative reply, and then entered.

He stepped back out and said, "The Colonel will see you now."

Wilson entered with Spafford behind him. The cabin was small. One side held a wooden bunk bed. The other held a small blazing fire pit. The little space in the middle was occupied by Norton, who sat behind a wooden table covered with papers regarding the operation of a regiment. Norton was a stoic man with a look of determination. To his left was the company C captain, Arnold McMahan. McMahan looked less serious, yet the ideal person to lead men into battle. Wilson entered, snapped to attention, and saluted.

Norton returned and said, "At ease, private."

Wilson's mind was still wandering. He had never been this close to the colonel before. He had only seen Norton mostly during regimental reviews or when Norton made a speech, while he was on his horse some distance away. McMahan, though, had given him direct orders many times. Wilson had a personal audience with McMahan when he had requested and received a Christmas furlough last winter.

"Private, you are probably wondering why you were brought here. Rest assured, it is not for any disciplinary reason. General Ormsby has given orders of a secret raid into the heart of Dixie commence. This will happen before the division moves onto Huntsville. The raid is being led by a scout named James Andrews. Have you heard of him?"

"No, sir."

"He approached General Orsmby with his plan. The general approved and sent a request to the brigade for the ablest of soldiers. Captain

McMahan here says you are an excellent breed of soldier, in good health. Sergeant Spafford spoke of you in high regard."

"Thank you, sir."

"Now, I am not ordering you to go. This is voluntary. If you go, you will adapt civilian attire and go on an expedition to the heart of the enemy's country. If you are successful, you will strike a blow to the Confederacy. If you are caught, you will hang, if not be killed outright. Would you be willing to go?"

"Yes, sir."

"You have time to think about it."

"Thank you, sir. I am willing to serve my country. If this raid assists our cause and increases our chance for victory, then I am more than eager to go. No matter what it takes."

Norton nodded. "Very good. You have made the right choice. Do you possess any civilian clothes?"

"No, sir."

"That's alright. Captain McMahan will grant you furlough to Shelbyville. You may procure any items you need to conceal yourself as a civilian to the enemy."

He sifted through his papers and picked up a stack of currency that looked odd to Wilson.

"The local stores use our greenbacks, as Shelbyville is a union town. This should cover your expenses." He handed a generous handful to Wilson. "After you secure your articles, meet with Mr. Andrews and the other volunteers on a farm right outside Shelbyville. The farm owner's name is Holland. An ambulance wagon shall fetch you outside my quarters tomorrow just after dark. Spafford will procure a revolver and some spare ammunition from the quartermaster for your protection. Now then private, I believe I have said plenty. Do you have any questions?"

"No, sir."

"Very well." The colonel stood up. "I wish you all the best on your endeavor."

"Thank you, sir." Wilson saluted. The colonel returned it. McMahan handed Wilson a piece of paper. "Your furlough private. That is all. You are relieved." Wilson took it and saluted again. Then he walked out. His mind was too busy to sleep through the night.

CHAPTER 4

The pistol-Going to Shelbyville-The general store-A welcome accomplice-New clothes-Mailing a letter-Saying goodbye-The wagon-John Porter-Meeting the Ohioans-The valley-James Andrews-The plan-Wilson and Wood-Rain-The Adventure Begins-More rain

The next morning Wilson rose with reveille and enjoyed a hearty breakfast. Soon after he was done, Spafford came to fetch him. He took Wilson to the quartermaster, where he procured him, an 1858 Navy Colt revolver and a cartridge pouch.

"You ever fired one of these?"

"Yes, sergeant, back home," Wilson replied.

It was the previous winter when Jed's father had bought a revolver. Jed invited Wilson and Martin over to shoot it. Suddenly, Wilson felt a sense of remorse remembering that.

"Private?" Spafford was in Wilson's face.

"Yes, sergeant."

"If you are ready to listen," said Spafford.

"Yes, sir." Responded Wilson.

"You are not to tell anyone of your intentions or your destination. Do you understand?"

"Yes, sir."

"When you come back to camp, see to your belongings and say your goodbyes. It may be sometime before we see you again."

"Very well private, you have your leave. Good luck."

"Thank you, sir." Wilson raised his hand to salute, but Spafford offered his hand to shake. Wilson shook back.

***

In town. Wilson and his friends had been here before on a day pass to purchase some goods. It took him a moment to adjust from the visuals of a landscape of tents to actual buildings and people of all shapes and sizes who wore different colors as opposed to soldiers in blue. There were a few ladies about too. A few caught his eye, but they didn't pay him much mind. Wilson strolled onto Main Street. He spotted the general store he was seeking and made a beeline for it. As soon as he entered, the clerk behind the counter smiled and said with energy.

"Hallo there! What can I do for you?"

This clerk obviously had not seen Wilson before, but the eagerness in his eyes suggested he knew a potential sale had just walked in.

"I am looking for breeches, coats, and hats for outdoor work."

"Right this way, seh!", the clerk said.

He made his way behind the counter rather quickly and begun to show Wilson men's clothes.

"Here you are, seh. If you require anything else, let me know."

"Thank you."

While he went through the clothes, he noticed several other soldiers walking by carrying parcels. They exchanged nods as they walked past. Wilson figured that these men were also volunteers for the same expedition.

"Oh, there you are. The provost guard is looking to place you under arrest for desertion, and for being Alf Wilson."

Wilson turned to see Mark Wood standing there.

"Marky, what are you doing here?"

"Oh, you are not the only one the commanding colonel hard a word with... He asked if I should like to go on an expedition to smash Johnny Reb right good, and of course, I said yes. If you are to go, I could give this sort a better visage."

"Let us hope that wit of yours can be of some use then," Wilson smirked.

"It has so far."

***

In the end, Wilson just picked out the attire he was familiar with, just as if he was back on the farm. Sturdy boots, heavy wool trousers, and a thick wool coat, with a slouched Stetson hat to top it all off. He traded union blue for plain black. He also grabbed some pairs of socks, a canteen, and a knapsack. Wood gathered similar type of clothing, but of a smaller size and in a light brown color with a derby hat to top it off.

When they approached the counter to purchase, the clerk's eyes were glittering.

"You boys in blue are going to make me close early. There's been quite a few of you in here today buying up all my clothes and wares."

Before Wilson could respond, Wood piped up. "The devil has beset once good men in my regiment and turned their righteousness, including this one 'ere'', he said, pointing to Wilson. "Now they are drummed out in disgrace, not before they dig for us a few latrines. I, however, am going home to my sweet Annabelle for a spell and must look my very best."

The clerk's grin faded. He looked at Wilson.

"Well, seh, good luck to you on your endeavor."

Wilson didn't know whether to laugh or to scowl. He ended up saying thanks and paid. Wilson waited outside while Wood paid. His clothes were wrapped up nicely in a parcel package. Wood eventually came out, and the two fell in step.

***

"Perhaps that could have been handled a little better."

"My little fib 'ushed him up now, did it not?"

"It did. Let's go back to camp and ready ourselves."

"Why? We have our leave and are not due until dusk. Come along and let us find a tavern, for I am 'ungry and thirsty."

Wilson couldn't argue. He felt the same way.

***

When the two arrived back at camp, the whole company knew these men were going away on a secret mission. They all turned out to see them off and offer their wishes, jeers, or both. By the time they made it to their tents, they had seen almost everybody, including soldiers they had not known. Wilson ducked into his tent. He went through his personal items and gathered them. He set aside his army issue canteen, tin cup, and rifle and cartridge box. He then changed into his civilian clothes. He put his spare socks, ammunition pouch, and blanket into his new knapsack (he kept his pistol in the waistband of his pants) When he stepped outside, Shaffstall and Wade were waiting for him.

"Well, boys, this is it," Wilson said. What he was about to do began to sink in.

"Good-bye, Alf," Wade said. "I wish you luck and Godspeed on your come back. I aim to get you in a game of poker someday solely so I can take your money."

Wilson chuckled. "I have a serious request if you could see my effects until I return."

"Of course, Alf."

"Thank you." He exhaled deeply. "Well, my brave men, until we meet again."

"So long, Alf."

"Good-bye, Alf."

Wilson walked off. He wasn't really done yet. He went to the regiment postmaster and fired off a letter to his family. He also mailed cash from his pay, a watch belonging to his father, and a jar of dirt. This was his piece of Haskins he brought with him, now sent back. He mailed all of it home. Satisfied, he went and secured himself some food, as he did not know when he would get to eat again. He got some salt pork, hardtack, and some deer meat as some deer were killed by the pickets and were now tonight's fresh dinner. Satisfied, he met Wood at the edge of the camp perimeter.

"Come along now, Alf, the war ain't got all day."

"It can. But I am ready now, so let us be off on this adventure, a bloody good one that ends with us reaping glory and earning praise from the generals as well as the kisses from the ladies. Then there is the obvious: hanging from a tree. Either way, it shall be jolly good. Off we go then."

The two fell in step and started walking up the dirt road back to the colonel's quarters. They were stopped by a voice calling from behind them.

"Wait up, boys! I am to come along!"

They stopped to turn and see John Porter, a rather boyish-looking soldier, trying to catch up. He had nearly reached when he tripped and fell. He quickly picked himself up and caught up with them.

"I am coming along with you two," Porter said breathlessly. He was barely twenty.

"You are invited but are merely a babe separated from his mother."

Wood huffed. "The colonel requested I go." Wood and Wilson looked at each other.

"Well, all right then, pup, if you can keep up with us," Wilson said.

The night had begun to appear when an ambulance wagon came creaking down the road. As it neared the cabin, the horse team pulled to a stop. The driver was illuminated by a hanging lamp at his perch. He was a grizzled looking driver, chewing tobacco. He just looked at this pair, leaned over to spit, and motioned with his head to the back of the wagon.

The trio went to the back, where a horse was tied. Wood went first. Wilson slowed a bit as it had slowly begun to sink in what he was doing and couldn't bow out. No, he made up his mind to go face the unknown and risk certain dangers. It was his decision, and he planned to keep it... He took a deep breath, exhaled, and climbed up into the wagon. The lantern had a faint glow that barely illuminated the wagon's interiors. Wilson stepped carefully to get in. When he looked deep into the wagon, he saw a bunch of unfamiliar faces.

"Hallo", Wilson said. There was a small open space towards his right. He moved to it, but the wagon lurched forward, almost throwing Wilson off balance. He made his way to the open spot and wedged himself in.

As usual, it was Wood who did the talking.

"My, this is exciting. All of us from Colonel Sill's brigade, you are all from Ohio?"

"Yes"

"Yea"

"Yes sir"

"Yes 'um"

"And 'ere we are, all looking to give Johnny Reb a good walloping. Say, does anyone know what it is we are to do?"

"No."

"No sir".

"No."

"Oh."

"We will discuss the particulars when we come to arrive."

"Who is that?"

"That's James Andrews. The leader of this expedition." A deep voice said.

"Say, Mr. Wood, that is a peculiar accent. Where do you hail from?", asked someone in the dark.

Before Wood could answer, Wilson did.

"My friend comes from England, he is trying to be an American, but as you can see, he does a poor job."

That drew some laughs.

Wilson could relax. "I am Alf Wilson. That is Mark Wood, and the young one is John Porter. We are from Company C, 21st, Ohio."

So it went, going down the line, everyone said their name: Bill Campbell, civilian scout, and associate of James Andrews.

From the 2nd Ohio:
 Marion Ross - Company A,
 Perry Shadrach - Company A,
 George Wilson - Company B,
 Bill Pittenger - Company G,
 Jamie Smith - Company G.
From the 21st Ohio:
 William Knight - Company E,
 Wilson Brown - Company F,
 Bill Bensinger - Company G,
 Robert Buffum - Company H,
 John Scott - Company K,
 Elihu Mason - Company K.
Because all the other men from the 21st were from different companies, so this was the first time Wood and Wilson had met them.
From the 33rd Ohio:
 Martin Hawkins - Company A,
 William Reddick - Company B,
 John Wollam - Company C,
 Sam Robertson - Company G,
 Sam Llewellyn -Company H,
 Jake Parrott - Company K,
 Sam Slavens - Company K.

The ambulance dropped the men off at a knoll outside Holland Farm. Wilson was closest to the end of the wagon and hopped out first with his knapsack in tow. It was dark now, stormy clouds paved in, obscuring the moonlight, which made it hard to see. Wilson ambled over to a grove of trees and waited for the others to fell in around him. Besides Wood, Wilson could barely make out their faces, let alone match their names.

"This is something, is it not?"
"Who is that?"
"Daniel Dorsey. You are Alf, right?"
"Yes, sir. So, what have you been before the war?"

"A schoolteacher. I taught all the necessary subjects to the children."

"Poor bastard. You are brave. When I was a lad, my schoolmates were full of mischief and often let the schoolmaster have it." Wilson said. "I have a few children every now and then that are unruly, I tend to use my wits as to not let them get the upper hand. If I am to be overrun, then I will use the rod as a full measure", Dorsey said.

"Say, I am a schoolmaster as well-"

"Who is that?" Wilson asked.

"Bill Pittenger! I taught astronomy. I have always had a passion for learning, particularly about the stars. But never am I harsh with my subjects. 'Spare the rod and spoil the child' is my personal belief. You fellas enjoy the stars?"

"Yes," Wilson. "On warm nights, I will find myself staring at them."

Dorsey looked at the black mass he spoke to. "What did you do, Alf?"

"Oh, I am nothing but a simple farmer, unlike you two learned men."

"Thank you."

Pittenger beamed in the darkness.

"Attention!" Someone shouted. The cloud broke momentarily as the valley lit up. The ambulance wagon was rolling away. A tall, stocky gentleman with black hair and a long black beard walked towards them, leading the horse that was tied to the wagon. Everyone parted out of his way and closed around him so he could be in the center of the crowd. They heard thunder... Somewhere in the valley, a dog barked loudly at some unknown intermittent danger. Through this noise, spoke Andrews.

"Once again, I am James Andrews, I am responsible for the undertaking of this raid, and have gained the approval of General Ormsby himself. Now, my brave lads, you have been chosen by your officers to perform a highly significant service, which, if successful, will change the whole aspect of the war and materially aid in bringing an early peace to our country. Chattanooga is the objective point. It is the central location of the rebel's railroads in this region and the gateway to the Deep South. Our purpose is to cut it off without any supply or reinforcement, to leave it vulnerable to General Mitchell. We are to achieve this by journeying south into Georgia, to the town of Marrietta, and seizing a locomotive."

He had said a lot, so he took a pause to let that part sink in before continuing.

"After we secure the locomotive, we shall proceed north to Chattanooga, tearing up the tracks to prevent any resupply and reinforcement, and tear down the telegraph wires. This will cut off their communication and burn the bridges. When we arrive at Chattanooga, General Ormsby will have taken it and will receive us. God willing, the rest of the confederacy will fall shortly thereafter." The excitement started to build amongst the men. This could work! This was a bold raid that could cripple the whole confederacy! Or at least this was worth volunteering and risking their lives.

"Now, there are inherent risks. We will be moving into an enemy country. It is important not to draw attention to yourselves. We will move into small groups. We will proceed on foot to Chattanooga, then by train to Marrietta, Georgia. We shall stay the night at a hotel there. The very next morning, we shall seize a locomotive and begin our journey. I have prepared maps for us and will furnish you all with confederate greenbacks for food, assistance with your journey, or anything else you need."

"What if we are caught or questioned?"

"If you are caught or questioned, you ought to say you are from Flemingsburg Kentucky and are journeying south for enlisting purposes. If you are pressed further, then you may enlist to avoid suspicion. At some point, if that does happen, you should desert at the best opportunity. The difficult part is not getting in the rebel army." He paused again to let that sink in.

"What if we make it southbound, but are unable to make it to the return train?" Pittenger asked.

"All of us shall cling together. We will come through together or die together. Now, it is the seventh of April. We have four days as the last train for Marrietta leaves from Chattanooga at five in the afternoon. Be sure to catch it as I will be on an earlier one. Good-bye till then."

That broke all of them up. Wilson let it all sink in for a moment until he got interrupted by a dark form with Wood's voice.

"Jolly good, right? Smash up Johnny's train tracks. Sounds good, yes?"

"Yes. This will be my first trip on a locomotive."

"Say you there, Mr. Wilson. Mr. Wood. Would you like to join our group?"

It was Pittenger.

"How many," Wilson asked.

"Well at least four thus far." "A large hunting party often frightens away the deer. Thank you, but my companion and I will make the journey ourselves."

"As you wish."

Another burst of moonlight came through the clouds. Shining a light on the makeshift groups that were now filing away.

"Such savagery, butchering of those poor critters." Wood said. He was much further from Wilson than he had realized.

Wilson replied. "You still eat them."

"Only after someone else has done the dirty work." Wood said, then sighed.

"All right then. If I am to go into the 'eart of Dixie with anyone of this lot, I suppose I can't go in worse company than you."

Wilson chuckled as he fell in line. "Come along, Marky, for we are off on a bloody good adventure."

"That's the spirit, Alf!"

It was his turn in the line now. Andrews nodded and gave him a thick handful of greenbacks with a sheet of paper, followed by a handshake. "Good luck."

"Thank you."

There it was. The two dozen men split off into the countryside. The cloud cover returned. This was much bigger than any hunting trip. They were going off into the wild and the unknown, where the danger lay everywhere, and the end result was uncertain. Despite this, Wilson was in high spirits. He was on the move, and through it all, they thought they could do it. They could pull it off. He didn't think anything could go wrong - then it began to rain.

CHAPTER 5

Rain-The journey begins-mud-Staying in a shed-Rain-In enemy country-Dorsey and his group-Wrong pants-The Kentucky story-mud-Cumberland mountains-Two groups team up-Rain-Andrews help-The Farmer-The colonelChattanooga-Just plain unlucky.

The rain fell in sheets, the droplets were thick as it nearly obscured Wilson's vision. He pulled his coat tighter and trudged along. He moved to the side of the road, which was the best, so he and Wood walked on the grass to avoid the mud. Yet several times Wood or Wilson would slipp while the other helped. They said little during the walk, neither could think of anything as they walked through the dark Tennessee countryside. They had no idea of how far they should go before stopping to rest. Wilson would tell himself just a little further, and would keep going. They both knew they had over ninety miles to go, plus another hundred miles by train, so they pressed on hard. They wound up on the road again, and the mud kept sucking their boots down into the ground, making them work much harder to walk. Wilson's eyes began to get heavy. Moonlight made its way through the dark clouds, and Wilson spotted some a dilapidated shed at a distance.

"Say, Marky, are you there?"

"Where else would I be?"

"There is a shed up ahead that seems comfortable, I say we bed down in here."

"Fine by me, Alf."

They made their way to the shed. Sure enough, the shed was old and it smelled, but there was room for two, and the roof kept the inside dry.

Wilson threw off his knapsack. It felt good to have that off. He opened it and fumbled through it in the dark until he felt his blanket. He spread it on the ground as best he could, removed his revolver, and sat down. That felt good, too. Wood also brought his blanket and sat next to Wilson and spread his blanket out so it would cover them both. Wilson took his hat off and laid down.

"Perhaps when we awake, the rain will stop."

"That would be too kind."

Wilson closed his eyes.

***

When he opened them, it was daybreak. Not much of daybreak, the sky was grey, the air humid, and it still rained. Wilson stood up to stretch. His back was stiff. He was habitual of sleeping comfortably in his own bed or in his tent. Sleeping on the bare dirt was a new experience, Wood gathered himself up and started to stretch his joints. "I had the most 'orrid dream, I dreamt I slept in mud. Now it is all I see."

"Yes, Marky, that's our fate. Let us have some breakfast and be on it again. We have quite a way to go today."

Wilson brought out his deer meat, tore it into strips, and gave some to Wood. Wood managed to get some onions and carrots from the regimental quartermaster. He split an onion and gave half to Wilson.

They ate their food cold.

"So, glorious map holder, which way do we proceed?"

Wilson unfolded the map, which was partially wet but still readable.

"We keep on pushing on this road. Eventually, we shall reach a river and will have to find a way across it."

"Splendid."

They finished, packed up, and began to slog through the mud once more. During the day, the rain would let up for a while before it came down hard again. The one advantage was that the pair could actually see. They stayed again on the side of the road to try to avoid mud, but the progress was slow. They stopped to eat lunch in the afternoon before continuing on with their journey. Strangely enough, they hadn't seen anyone. Besides the rain, it was relatively quiet until finally, they came upon a farmhouse. As if on cue, an elderly farmer came out to greet them.

"Excuse me fellows, but you are on my property without my knowing or permission."

***

Daniel Dorsey had a much easier time. He paired up with Will Knight, Samuel Slavens, and Robert Buffum. They initially stayed with Andrews as they proceeded. Instead of getting rest in the night, they kept moving. While they were ahead, it was by no means an easy pushing through the rain and the mud. Stopping at Wartrace, they found it occupied by union cavalry, and were halted before Andrews had a word with them, and the cavalry let them go as they moved on.

In the clear, Andrews eventually separated from this group to scout ahead and keep track of the other men in the mission. The small group pressed on and stopped for a meal at noon. It was at a farmhouse, where they paid for a wagon to drive them off to the river for a ferry. The wagon was rickety and had no cover. The four men had to squeeze onto two benches that were just not as big enough. And bounce along with the ride, while wind and rain blew in their faces. Eventually, they made it to the river, paid for a ferry, and started again on foot toward the village of Manchester. The men spoke very little, lest they spoke too loud of what they were going to do. Now, out in the open, they were slightly more carefree.

"I've worked in the railroad business for about most of my life," Knight said. "I worked in the running locomotives to Chicago when I was only eighteen."

"That is quite the feat," Dorsey said. "I suppose that is why they chose you."

"Not quite," Knight said. "My captain requested any man who had the locomotive experience to step forward. I had presumed to think it would be a soft snap, like working with tools of some heavy sort. Instead, I found myself here."

"Yeah, well, do not tell anyone else that, for when we do succeed, you can take the lion's share of success", said Slavens.

"That is kind of you to say, Sam," Knight replied. "However, I was speaking to that fellow Martin Hawkins, and he has much more experience than I do. When the hour of our job approaches, he'll take charge, and I will assist him in any way."

"Thank you, Jesus, for providing us a capable, trained man," Buffum said. "But goddamn it all for this foul weather you've bedeviled us with." Everyone cast glances at Buffum, while he stared straight forward.

"So. Our brave Captain Andrews. What have you heard on him? Anyone?" asked Slavens.

"Only rumors. I spoke with Old Stars Mitchell personally, as he had approved me himself. He spoke of Andrews being a scout and gathering information for our forces, and nothing more." Knight said.

"Be not afraid of greatness, some men are born great, some achieve greatness, while some have greatness thrust upon them," Buffum said.

"What did you say?" Slavens asked. Buffum didn't respond.

"He was quoting Shakespeare, I believe", Dorsey said.

"We should be coming up on Manchester soon. Perhaps it would be best if we avoided it altogether." Knight said.

"Hallelujah! Praise the Lord," Buffum said. "The goddamn rebels are most likely to be there."

"You are a strange fellow. You curse and say the Lord's name at the same time." Dorsey replied.

This made Buffum look at him.

"Me? You are the one who wears Yankee blue trousers in the land of the grey rebels."

This was true. Dorsey had bought shoes, a shirt, overcoat, and a hat but wasn't able to find the right pair of pants, so he wore his uniform pants, hoping to find another general store, but had no luck so far.

"Into Manchester, we shall go! And we should be quick about it." Dorsey said.

***

They entered the town and made it straight to the general store. Buffum darted inside, while the other three waited outside as regular citizens hanging around. Buffum came out quite early and handed Dorsey a pair of yellow and white cotton striped pants. Dorsey took it, and the group left the town just as quickly, avoiding casting a second glance.

Once they were away, Dorsey began to unfold the pants. "I need to change that is when we are far from prying eyes. I shall bury my trousers too."

"I would have purchased a black colored hat like mine. Not like your straw hat." Dorsey pushed his hat back while looking at Buffum's white derby. "Your hat is white."

"I humbly disagree, sir. It is black." Dorsey was tired of this weird, pointless exchange.

"Sure it is."

They started down the road. While rounding a bend, they suddenly came across four confederates on horseback. Everything slowed down. Dorsey's felt his heart starting to beat faster. The confederates looked surprisingly at these strangers who came upon them. They all had double-barreled shotguns, which they aimed at the Yankees. Everything seemed to freeze.

Finally, a confederate with Sergeant's stripes spoke. "Good evenin', gentlemen, good evenin'. What yo gentlemen bound for?"

Dorsey felt a lump in his throat. His mind went blank.

"We're bound fo' Geo'gia seh. To Ma'ietta, Geo'gia seh, to jine the confede'ate a'my", Knight said, stepping forward.

The sergeant looked at him. "Whar did ye cum frum?"

"Cum from Kentucky. Flemin' County", Knight continued. "Left that to get rid o' Yankee rule seh.

"Them Yankees are a mighty bad set. They're tearin' things up it's awful. Stealin' everything they can git thar han's on. Runnin' all the niggahs off no'th. An' tryin' to fo'ce our people into their a'my. An' we jis wouldn' stan' it, so we left thar. If we got to fight on ary side, we fight fo' the south. We secesh we are!" Both Slavens and Buffum chimed in agreement. Dorsey swallowed and nodded too.

The sergeant looked at them momentarily, then broke into a smile. "Wal shoot", he said, as he holstered his shotgun, his troops following suit. "We're mighty glad to meet our friends from Old Caintuckey cummin; to jine us in fightin' for our rights. We been fallin' back and lettin' on like we was feared on 'em. But we're jut drawin' em on, gitten' 'em sort 'o scattered out like, but we'll pounce on 'em d'rectly an' whup hell outen 'em."

"One southeneh kin whup 'fo Yankees any day", said one of the troopers. "But why you gentlemen go way down to Geo'gia to enlist? We got a mighty fine company heah, why don't youens jine us? We'll treat you mighty well. Come go back with us to the village an' jine our company." Dorsey noticed one of the troopers cast an occasional glance at his trousers.

Knight shook his head. "Very much obliged to you, gentlemen, but we have our friends in a Kentucky regiment near Mai'etta, and we would prefer to be with them."

Dorsey nodded to the trooper, "A dogon good hoss you a ridin' there seh."

The trooper nodded. "Much obliged for the complimen'."

The sergeant started reaching in his saddlebag. Dorsey slid his hand to his overcoat, where his revolver was kept. The sergeant pulled out a bottle of whiskey. "On this 'ccasion gentlemen, I'd like to propose a drink to Jeff Davis and the confederacy!" He took a hearty swig, dismounted his horse, and passed on the bottle to Knight.

"Heah heah." Knight said.

"When the bottle got passed to Buffum, he broke into tears and blathered, "Success to the Confederacy! Death and defeat to the blue bellied Yankees!"

After some hearty laughs and toasts, both sides parted ways, left feeling as that they had contributed to their cause. As soon as they were clear, Dorsey changed his trousers and discarded his pants under a pile of brush.

***

The group made better of their time as they cut straight through the woods and thus avoided the mud and some of the rain. They emerged to find a lone cabin and managed to buy some whiskey from the owner. They bought the other men their drinks too. On the way out, they nearly walked into another group of men who walked up to the cabin. Dorsey said, "Oh, pardon me sir-" He looked at the man he nearly walked into, and the others. It took him a moment to recognize this man to be Perry Shadrach, and the others as Pittenger, Campbell, and George Wilson.

"It is you!" said Dorsey as they all shook hands. "You all have made it! How have your travels been?"

"Fairly well. It was slow on account of the rain." Shadrach replied.

"We had run into a rebel picket line some distance back. It was fairly dangerous." Pittenger said from the back.

Knight looked up while his face filled with rain. "I don't suppose this will pass on anytime soon." he coughed.

"Are we going to move gentleman or continue to stand around and cluck like a bunch of hens?" Campbell growled. He was quite a large and intimidating man.

"He is right. Well, gentlemen. For now, we are out of immediate danger. We should be able to complete the last leg of our journey together." Knight said.

"That is fine. Let us be on our way." Shadrach said.

Just like that, the nine men were on their way. In front of them were the Cumberland Mountains. A rather steep climb, but beyond it was Chattanooga. Instead of soldiers, they looked like a rabble looking to cause shenanigans. Pittenger fell in with Campbell. "This mountain ought to be quite the feat to climb. Back when I was a lad romping in the woods near my house, I never had to climb a mountain as grand as that. It was just as well, for I have horrible vision and would be terrified if I got lost and-"

"Excuse me." Campbell fell out of step and walked with Buffum.

"What do you have to say?" said Buffum giving him a wild-eyed look. Campbell tried again. He fell in with Dorsey.

"That feller talks too much," Campbell referred to Pittenger.

"Maybe he has a lot on his mind. I noticed you were not in uniform when we all met and never mentioned said what regiment you are in."

"That's 'cause I weren't in any. I never cared for drill or bowing to some officers. I was see'n some friends in second Ohio, and the call for vol'teers for a high adventure went out, I had my own reasons for joining."

"I see."

"You look a little dandy. What did you do before the war?"

"I was a school teacher."

"A teacher? Poor bastard."

***

The raiders started climbing up the mountain. The rain drizzled light, but the mud still sucked in shoes while the grass was still slippery. While every man slipped at least once, no one tumbled down the mountain. When they reached the top of a fold, they found a young confederate who was resting under a tree. They told him the Kentucky story. His story was going home on furlough.

"If that don' beat all, it does me good to see frien's from Caintuck' cummin' down heah to fight for th' cause. If y'all headin'to Chattanooga, I kin show y'all a quicker way on nutha' path."

They took him up on his offer, trusting yet cautious of being led into an ambush, they made sure their revolvers were handy. Pittenger fell in with the confederate while they shared tales of the battle of Bull Run (or Manassas). As Pittenger's regiment arrived on the field, yet only after the union retreat, they laughed at the memory of union troops who ran away in terror. They eventually parted ways with their friendly enemy and continued their trek across the mountain. After three full days of slogging through the mud, they reached the magnificent sight of the Tennessee River and the town of Chattanooga: A mixture of a wild frontier town mixed with heavy industrial railroads, wedged between a ridge and a mountain, all surrounded by the river. The raiders made their way down the river, where they paid for a ferry crossing. Finally reaching their destination after a long, rain-soaked journey. The raiders were of relief that the hard part of the journey was over and wonder as to what came next.

***

"My humblest apologies, seh. My friends and I are Kentucky men on a trek to join the southern army." The old man looked at him with a scowl.

"I care not for the southunn cause, for I am a union man, and not afraid to say it."

Wilson was caught. He did not expect that response, even though he knew of the plenty of pro-union sentiments in this part of Tennessee.

"What my companion and I understand is that individual states have the right to secede. Nowhere is it written that we can't. Especially if merciless Yankees are burning our houses down." Wilson said.

"I can't abide that", the Farmer said. "This union was made t' stand in spite of our differences. We talk it out with words. Not ammunition."

Wilson knew this back and forth exchange would go nowhere. "Well, seh, to each their own. My companion an' I mean to enlist. We mean no harm to you if you will oblige us to cross, we would be most appreciative. If not, we will find another way."

The Farmer still had the scowl. "I cannot approve of your destination. As I am a Christian man, I feel obliged to offer you the passage across the river. It is not far off and must be swollen with all this damn rain. Come along then."

Wilson was astonished. He did not expect this. He watched the Farmer start off. He looked at Wood, and they shrugged at each other and followed The Farmer. Nobody said anything on their short walk to the river. Wilson wasn't sure what to say, so he didn't. After walking for several miles in the rain, which was starting to get heavy, The Farmer took them to a crossing where he then arranged for a skiff to take them across.

"Well, boys, this is the end. This should take you across. I don't approve of your destination, so I can only offer luck, and hopefully, when the war is over, we can be countrymen again." He held out his hand.

"I hope so too." Wilson shook it. The Farmer nodded and walked away. Wilson and Wood shoved off, wading into the freezing water and hopping on to the boat.

Immediately it went with the current, while the Ohioans had a hard time seeing with the rain constantly in their faces, yet they rowed as hard as they could. It felt like an eternity rowing against the wind, the current, and the rain, but they did eventually make it to the other side. After tying up the skiff at the crossing, they made their way up the bank.

"You know Marky, I can't quite get it out of my head, why did that old fellow help us so much."

"He meant for us to drown Alf. That is why he wanted us on the river."

Wilson chuckled. The remaining light of the day had begun to fade. The rain had slowed to a drizzle. Wilson was tired.

"Say Marky, what say we bed down under those trees?"

"I was waiting for you to say so, Alf."

"So be it then."

There was a grove of trees with thick branches. They kept the ground damp below. The Ohioans repeated the routine in the shed. Wilson leaned back against the tree, placed his hat over his eyes, and fell asleep to the sound of raindrops bouncing off his hat.

***

The next morning, they ate the last of the rations they had left. Cold.

"Well, bugger Alf. What are we to do?"

"We need to purchase some rations in the next town we come across."

"Very well then"

"Off we go then, right?"

"Right, right." They set off again. Wilson looked at his map. "This ain't right, Marky. We should be further than where we are now."

"Where should we be?"

"At least a day ahead. Not behind."

"Bugger."

"We'll have to move faster."

***

They reached the village of Manchester near dusk. The air was humid as the rain had slacked off. As they entered the town, there were quite a lot of people who included a column of confederates marching in two's right at them. Wilson and Wood acted as regular Manchester citizens coming back from a jaunt. Right away, though, the citizens questioned the strangers, just as the confederates passed by.

"Who are you two?"

"We are from Caintuckey."

"Where y'all gwyn'?"

"To enlist. Georgia"

Wilson felt everyone's eye's burning into him. He suddenly heard a familiar voice.

"You! Caintuckey, where was it you were headed to?"

He looked up to see a rider on a horse. It was Andrews! Wilson tried to conceal his surprise and excitement. There he was, with a thick black beard. A Soft voice. In the daylight, at least.

"Yes, seh. Gwyn' down south to enlist. Th' Yankees have burned aw homes. Stol' aw livestock and told us they would cut our throats in the bargain. We headed to Geo'gia way."

"Very well, gentlemen. The best way is to pilot over the mountains. It's much dark now, and you'd be better-served beddin' down foah the night heah. There is a large red cabin at th' end of this heah road owned by a colonel who takes kindly to good southern men who wish to fight. Go to it."

Andrews nodded and spurred his horse out of town.

"Thank ye kindly, seh." Wilson said as Andrews rode off. That little act did the trick. The people who had gathered to question them had gone about their business.

***

Wilson and Wood found the red cabin in the dying light. The timing was impeccable, as the rain began to pour. Wilson knocked. The door opened by an elderly man who looked as if he was full of vinegar as he held up a candle holder with a lit candle.

"Who is that knockin' at my door at this houh. State yo' business and be quick about it!"

As the roof has cover, Wilson and Wood took off their hats.

"We are southern men seh. We are on our way to Chattanooga. Seein' as it's dark and rainin' we can't figure gwyn' on like this. We were told this would be a place of shelter."

The colonel eyed them. Holding the candle close to Wilson and Wood. Real close.

"Well shit, any south'un man brave enough to be out in this mess can rest a spell in my home. Come on in!"

There was a fire blazing that warmed and lit the place up, flanked by two rocking chairs. An individual's portrait adorned the wall. It was rather cozy.

"I had my cook prepare a meal. Are you boys hungry?"

The Ohioan's stomachs growled. "Yes, sir."

***

They ate a feast of roast chicken, mashed potatoes, peas, corn, and grits. All eaten by candlelight. The colonel spoke as they ate.

"I don't believe if I have ever seen a Yankee. Never been that far north. You have. They any different?"

"None as far as I have seen, they are no different than you or I," Wilson said between bites. "The next time I see one, I will peer down the sight of a rifle."

"Amen," the colonel said. He got up and walked towards a cabinet. "For you two brave Kentuckians, I shall bring out my best whiskey as you are willing to march all the way down to Geo'gia to fight."

"My compliments to the chef. That was a meal fit for a king", Wood piped up. The colonel looked at Wood, then Wilson.

"Your frien' talks funny. "Never mind him. He is English."

"Indeed, I am, sir. I moved here some years ago and feel as though the south has embraced me as one 'er own. I feel like my responsibility to repay her by taking up arms against anyone who tries to strike 'er down."

"Heah, heah."

As the candle burned to the end, the colonel staggered to his feet.

"Now gentlemen. It is late, I am old, and I am drunk. I am going to bed. I shall have my servants prepare blankets for you. In the morning, you shall be provided with any provisions you may need."

The old man tottered off. Wrapped up in blankets by a fire felt like heaven to Wilson. He slept quite well that night.

***

The next day the pair were on their way to hike up the Cumberland Mountains. After a long walk, they made it to the Tennessee River, where they paid for a ferry for crossing.

"It was a bit thin for a while, but jolly good job piloting the ferry." Wood said to the ferry captain after they made it to the other side.

"Your friend talks funny," said the captain to Wilson. They made it. Wood and Wilson maneuvered their way through the wild town to reach the train depot, where they reunited with other raiders. They did it. Four days. Ninety-five miles on foot. If only they weren't one day behind schedule.

***

Group by group, the raiders trudged their way into Chattanooga. All safe for the pair of Sam Llewellyn and Jamie Smith. It was nightfall when they reached the town of Jasper in the Cumberland Mountains when they got surprised by a Confederate picket line. With a surly looking sergeant in charge to boot. As instructed they gave him the Kentucky story.

"So y'all tellin' me this story." The Sergeant said with a harsh glare. "The two of you aw jus' decided to take a walk from Caintuckey all th' way down to Geo'gia to enlist? In this weather. At this hou'h. Withou' so much as a knapsack? Well, seh, I got a story fo' you. I don' believe you. They are plenty a' good southun regiments heah."

Llewellyn stood firm. "We have frien's in Atlanta whom we want to jine up with-"

"No seh. We have good ones heah. If you mean to jine up, you kin heah. If not, I will arrest you, and you kin tell this story to a militareh judge."

Llewellyn grinned. "Wal shoot. I s'pose y'all right. We kin jine up heah."

He nodded to Smith.

"Can' we, Smith."

"Yes, suh. I'd be aw honou,' too."

Before they knew it, the union men found themselves wearing confederate grey and assigned to an artillery unit in Chattanooga's defense.

Sometime later, on yet another rainy night, Llewellyn stuffed his knapsack with some rations, with a map of Tennessee and where the confederate lines ended, and the unions began. He waited for the first sentry to be out of sight and then made a run for it. He eventually found a union cavalry patrol to surrender too.

He told his story, to many different people, before they took him back to his regiment to verify. They cleared him, and soon, he was back in his company wearing the union blue as if nothing had happened.

Smith, on the other hand, wouldn't desert until sometime later. He made it back to his regiment, yet no one believed his reasoning for waiting so long to the desert.

CHAPTER 6

The train ride-Panicked Civilians-Riding Conditions-Enemies aboard-Cap Andrews- On to Marrietta-Going to the Fletcher House for the night-The Clerk-Sleeping arrangements-Time to go-Final meeting-Marion Ross-The train-Hawkins and Porter-The Ride-Big Shanty

Wilson knew that they were to arrive on the tenth. Waiting at the train depot, it was obvious the way it was filled with fleeing panicked civilians with everything they could carry.

"The Yankees are coming!"

"This will be the end of everything!"

"Oh, lo'd help us!"

He wasn't sure if he should gloat at these people fleeing their homes. After all, they were enemies. Right? The loud whistle of a locomotive pulling out the station disrupted his train of thought. It was true; he had never been on a train before. Never even seen one of 'em. It was an awe sight. It was like a horse but made of iron and steel. Better than a horse, as it went faster, could travel longer, and was smoother than a wagon ride. He felt excited yet nervous.

"Oh, come on now, Alf, your legs are shaking too much. You are making me anxious." Wood said.

"Sorry." Wilson took a deep breath. He looked at his boots and rubbed them against the wood platform to get more of the mud off. They were a good pair at one point in time.

But now they showed signs of being worn. His feet ached. It felt good to sit. Dorsey, Wollam, and Knight sat a few feet away on another bench. Their group had split up. Half were going to Marrietta early to avoid any suspicion. The two groups didn't say anything to each other so that they wouldn't draw much attention.

"Say you there", Wood said to Knight as he sat down. "By any chance, did you inquire about the arrival of the five o'clock train?"

"Yes-sir," Knight replied. "It will be there on time."

"Thank you." Wood looked up at the sky. "Does it ever stop raining here?"

"Can't say."

Wilson sat near the door to the main depot. He overheard someone say, "If it's true that the Yankees are in Huntsville, where on earth is General Johnston or Beauregard? If they had won a great battle, they better come down here quick!"

A loud train whistle blew in the distance.

"That is our train," Knight said.

The giant engine rolled into the station, letting out a blast of steam. Wood and Wilson boarded when the conductor opened the doors. Wilson was the first to go into the boxcar. He stepped inside and immediately ducked his head as he was tall, and the roof was quite low. The aisle was narrow. He went to his seat towards the station side. The 'seat' was really a wooden bench. He sat down and tried to move over as best he could when Wood came and sat right next to him. It was a tight squeeze. On the floor by his feet was a spittoon full of used tobacco juice. He gently pushed it away with his boot. He never cared for chewing. His nasal senses immediately picked up the difference between the cool air outside and the stale air inside, with the aftermath of cigar smoke lingering around. He looked out the window. He couldn't see much besides his own reflection and water running down. Wilson was about to say something when he looked up to see who boarded. Dorsey, Knight, and Wollam were seated. Just getting on was Andrews! Behind him came a line of confederates whooping and hollering. Dorsey and Knight sat on the row opposite to Wood and Wilson. Wollam sat in front of them. Andrews sat in front of Wilson. The confederates, mixed in with some civilians then scattered all over the seats.

"Whoa! Johnstons boys whupped them Yankees good at Shiloh!" The Yankees refused to fight! They turned tail and ran like the yellowbellies they ah!"

Wilson wanted to reach for his revolver. The engineer appeared and begun down the rows. "Tickets, please!" He went down each row to collect tickets. When he was done, he shouted, "Thank you for yo' patience! The five o'clock bound for Mai'etta will be departing shortly."

Wood leaned over. "Now remember, we will hear a loud hiss, feel a light push, then we will be on our way."

"Yes."

Wood looked over at

Dorsey. "It was his first time riding a locomotive."

"Ah."

Sure, there was a hiss. Wilson was rocked forward, and he felt the sensation of the motion. It was slow, but it picked up speed. It started to feel exhilarating. He leaned over and tapped Andrews on his shoulder. He looked back. The light from the lanterns hanging overhead wasn't enough to light the boxcar, so Wilson couldn't see Andrews clearly.

"Excuse me, Cap. I know we're on a tight schedule, but I've begun to doubt the transaction you have made. We are already a day late, and the other party must have made it by now and will be rather crowded."

Andrews nodded. "There was still a good chance to succeed. I believe we can still finalize the transaction as the sellers won't be expecting us in such weather, and with all parties present, sir."

"Alf Wilson." Andrews nodded. "Mr. Wilson, we will be able to slip in, do our business, and get away without anyone wiser. Get some rest, my boy. Do not let your worries bother you. We will succeed."

That was good, but not good enough to satisfy his anxiety. Andrews' calm demeanor was proved enough for Wilson to let it go. Tomorrow. It was still on despite the delays, the harsh weather, and the troops moving down with them. Could it work? They could still steal a train without anyone noticing. They could still pull off a surprise raid and get away. They could still get to Chattanooga to be warmly received by Mitchells forces. They could win. That was enough for Wilson. So, with the sound of the train's wheels scraping the tracks, cigar smoke from some businessmen filling the boxcar, and being wedged in an uncomfortable seat, Wilson went to sleep.

***

"Ma'ietta! Ma'ietta!"

The call of the conductor awoke Wilson and Wood. The conductor was doing his round and was towards the end of the boxcar.

"Excuse me, sir", Wood said, yawning. "Would you be so kind as to tell us the time?"

The conductor checked his watch against the light, which came from the lanterns, which were dying. "Well, seh. It is nigh one minute past midnight. Saturday, April 12.

"Much obliged."

While the conductor went back to his rounds, Wilson felt the locomotive slowing down. He staggered to his feet to stretch, his legs were stiff. His back and rear end were sore. The locomotive came to a final stop. Wilson nearly lurched forward with it. Everyone stood up to file out. Andrews kept sitting.

"So, Alf, how did you care for your first train ride?"

"Cramped seats? Intolerable passengers? I enjoyed it. I cannot recommend it." Wood chuckled. Then he coughed from the cigar smoke.

"Gentlemen. The Fletcher House. Directly west from the train depot. That is where you want to go." Andrews said suddenly, after which he went out the opposite end. Wilson and Wood stepped out to the chill Georgia air. It was still raining. Marrietta was a lovely resort town, even in wartime, but at this hour in the dark, they couldn't tell. Wilson and Wood trudged along, using the lampposts to guide them towards a four-story building labeled 'Fletcher House'. The lobby was rather small. Only a chair and the reception desk with a lone clerk to deal with the large crowd of weary travelers who sought refuge for the night. Dorsey, Slavens, and Pittenger arrived and got in line behind Wilson and Wood.

"Say, we got word cap wants us to meet in his room at the Marrietta Hotel at four. Room # 3. It is to discuss the business deal. It didn't go well, so we will gather there, and he will let us know what we are ought to do", Dorsey said.

Wilson nodded. When it was this group's turn, the clerk, who looked in his fifties and calmly dealt with this large crowd, looked at them.

"Much apologies, gentlemen. I have but one room left. There are only two beds in there-"

"We will take it." The clerk was caught before he said. "Very good. Whose name shall I-"

"Jefferson Davison."

"Very good." Wilson paid for the room. While the clerk filled out the register, Wilson continued.

"Sir. We have a business to attend to early and need to be woken at four. Will you kindly do so?"

He took the last of the confederate money he had left and laid it on the desk. "Indeed, I will, sir! Without fail."

The clerk led them upstairs and to the second floor. The room was cramped. No windows. Low headroom, and two small beds.

"Thank you," Wilson said to the clerk. "Anything else I can assist you, gentlemen, with?"

"No, sir, that is all."

The clerk left.

"Jefferson Davison, Alf?"

Wood smirked. "Hush."

Wilson threw his hat, coat, and boots on the floor. This was his first time sleeping in a bed since...He couldn't really remember. He thought about food. The train stopped for dinner at Dalton several hours ago, and he ate heartily. He was fine. It was agreed that Pittenger, Slavens, and Dorsey were to sleep in the same bed. While Wilson and Wood shared the other. It was either that or the floor. As the minutes and hours ticked by Wilson couldn't sleep, he lay in the dark with his eyes closed, but couldn't stop thinking about what was to come.

***

The door was knocked on at the designated hour, Wilson was ready for it. The clerk stood in the doorway, candle in hand as the five men rushed to put boots, pants, coats, and their hats on. Wilson had tied his things in a pile, so it was easier for him to grab everything, as opposed to everyone else who had scattered there's on the floor.

"Hurry up, or you'll be left!" Wilson hissed.

"Oh bloody 'ell, let us finish dressing up on the run, boys", Wood said. The clerk held the candle outward towards the hallway and the stairs, lighting the area dimly. He pressed himself against the wall as these strangers were rushing out, throwing their hats and coats as they thundered downstairs.

Wilson waited behind so he could ask, "Sir, whereabouts the Ma'ietta Hotel?"

"Just make a left along the track. You won't fail to miss it."

"Thank you, seh." Then he took off after his fellow raiders as the clerk welcomed him.

The air outside was cool and crisp. A welcome relief from the hot, stuffy air in the room. There was a slight drizzle. While running, Wilson remembered his knapsack, thought of going back for it, but decided against it. There was nothing in it besides a muddy blanket and worn map. They would be a surprise Yankee gift for the next rebel.

"Make a left!" Wilson hissed.

It was still before the crack of dawn, and the gaslight posts were quite dim. Still, they went left and found a nice square building and made out the words 'Marrietta Hotel.' They lowered their pace and entered. This lobby was considerably more spacious than Fletchers House. An elderly clerk was behind the desk reading a newspaper by candlelight when the bunch came in.

"Excuse me, she," Dorsey said. "We are awfully sorry for our intrusion at this hour. We have an appointment with our employer. He is in room three."

The clerk looked mildly annoyed. "Well, go on then. It is up the stairs, third to the left. There is a bunch in there already. Jus' be quiet about it."

The five went in. The room was cramped, lit by candlelight. To Wilson's relief, they weren't the last. After waiting two more minutes, several more stragglers came in. Everyone gathered close, as Andrews spoke in a low, hushed tone that was equally enthusiastic and determined.

"My lads today we go. After this meeting, we shall adjourn and go to the train station to purchase tickets for the nearest northern Georgia town for the five o'clock train. When we arrive at Big Shanty, that's when we move. Make sure to get seats near each other in the same car. Of course, say nothing to anyone of our businesses. When the train makes the Big Shanty breakfast stop, keep your places till I say so.

"If anything unexpected happens, look to me to lead. I require Mr. Knight, Mr. Brown, and Mr. Alf Wilson to join me to assist in operating the engine."

Wilson was surprised to be called for such a task. He nodded in agreement. Andrews continued. "The rest of you will go to the left side of the train, forward of where we'll uncouple it. Climb into the cars as quickly as you can when the order is given. If anyone interferes, shoot him, but don't fire unless you have to." He paused, then continued. "We must move on the double-quick. Any man not aboard when the signal is given shall be left behind. A delay of even thirty seconds could result in the slaughter of the whole party."

He let that sink in. "Now the difficult part will be getting out of the station. Once we are clear, our objective would be much easier. I have made this run before, and I am familiar with the signals used on the track, and what switches are to be made.

"We will use this ruse to our advantage when passing through the various depots. While we are in an open country, we will dislodge the tracks from the railroad and sever the telegraph wires. Thus, rendering them useless to the enemy. We shall proceed at a quick rate. So, my lads, we must work efficiently to accomplish this deed. I surmise we shall arrive in Chattanooga before dusk to a warm reception from General Mitchell's forces. Does anyone have any objections?"

They all nodded. It sounded simple.

Andrews' confident tone made everyone believe it was possible.

Except for Marion Ross. He stood up, cleared his throat, and spoke. "Cap, we've made this far into Georgia with the rebs none the wiser. We have all done well on that accord.

"Now, the rumors are coming that Mitchell is in Huntsville, and the rebs are moving everything they have here this way. I have seen it on my ride down. Also, the weather is not much in our favor. I only ask Cap, that perhaps you wait another day."

Ross also made the same points that Wilson had made. He thought of speaking up again, but the determined looks on everyone's faces in the dimly lit room made him think otherwise.

"Those are valid points. Sir, I must give a rebuttal. I had tried this before and failed. I will not do so again. The points you make will work in our favor. If the rebs are looking down. They will not look up until we have left. No one can suspect us as we have the element of surprise. Especially in such weather. Gentlemen, I am going. If any man doesn't wish to, you are free to leave. I am going to Chattanooga."

Everyone nodded and grunted their approval. Ross nodded too.

"Very well, my lads. Good luck and Godspeed." Everyone shook hands and wished each other good luck. They left the hotel, just as the train was whistling its arrival.

At the station, Wilson and Wood were in line.

"Say Marky, I am short of funds. Could you purchase my ticket?"

"Oh, God, Alf. When this is over. I expect a fresh quart of milk from one of your cows."

"We don't have any cows."

"Very well, then. A basket of eggs wrapped up in ribbon."

"Fair enough." They walked across the platform, just as the train pulled in.

The morning light began to shine and Wilson saw the main engine, but didn't see its number or name. They got on board and noticed the engineer looked at them and the other raiders closely. Both Wilson and Wood sat on the nearest seat. The other raiders also filed in. Andrews strolled in and sat in the first row.

"Oh, Alf. Your second train ride in less than a day. Aren't you a lucky boy!" Wilson smirked. "Say, did you notice we were short of several men in the room?" Wood shrugged.

***

Hawkins, who was the most experienced locomotive engineer, and young Porter, had asked the hotel clerk to wake them up at the appropriate hour. For whatever reason, the clerk didn't do as told. The men were awoken to the sound of the oncoming train. They rushed out the door, trying to put their boots on as they ran towards the station. By the time they got there, the train was leaving. They watched it leave dumbstruck. Eventually, they left the station and wandered around Marrietta, not knowing what to do next.

***

The engineer came into the boxcar. "All aboard! Next stop, Big Shanty! Big Shanty next stop!" He looked at the raiders and went on his way towards the next boxcar.

After he left, the whistle blew, the train lurched forward and started to move. It wasn't long after they had left the station that the conductor, a man with a boyish face, goatee, and receding hairline, came into the boxcar.

"Tickets! Tickets, please!" He went about collecting tickets while giving narrow looks to the men in the boxcar. Wilson gave his ticket and felt the conductor's stare at him before he moved on.

The minutes ticked by. Wilson felt a sick feeling in his stomach. His legs were jittery. He noticed Wood's were too, but he didn't say anything. He started to mentally prepare himself for the possibility of shooting someone. He looked out the window, the morning sky lit everything through grey clouds. The train was coming towards a gentle bend in the track. Wilson could see a white picket fence, a building that was perhaps a house, and a pond. He then saw the confederates. In a field surrounding the house, he saw a sea of tents, just like his regiment,

48

but these men wore different uniforms. He was able to make out what was happening through the window. It looked like the confederates were starting their morning drills, while the sentries patrolled with their muskets. He looked away. He did not want to see any more. He started to take deeper breaths. He wanted to be somewhere else.

"Big Shanty! Twenty minutes for breakfast!"

He was not aware of who said that, but it shook him back to where he was. The train slowed to a crawl and slid neatly into the station. Then it stopped. Wilson gained control of his breath. The other passengers started to file out.

Wilson, like the other raiders, stared at the back of Andrews' head. He sat there for the longest time. Then, without warning, he stood up and went for the door. On cue, Wilson and the other raiders got up and followed him out of the boxcar.

CHAPTER 7

Getaway!-First feelings-Stopping-An Unexpected Stop at Moons Station-The crowbar-Getting Away again-First damage-Telegraph pole-Jon Scott-The saw-Learning the brakes-Passing Acworth-Good progress-Passing Allatoona Lifting the tracks-The other train

The General was picking up the speed. Inside the rear side of the boxcar, the raiders sat in the pitch black for what felt like forever until they felt the jolt of motion of movement. Everyone stood slowly and gave an impromptu round of applause. To say Dorsey was the most excited was an understatement.

"Thank God, boys! We're done playing Reb! We can be blue-bellied Yankees again!"

George Wilson stopped him, "Don't be so fast at it now. We ain't out of the woods yet." The celebration still went on. That was it. The worst part was over.

The celebration suddenly turned to horror when they felt the train suddenly slowing down and came to a complete stop. In the cab, Knight was looking over everything to see what the issue was. Andrews and Brown stood silently, letting him work without interruption as precious seconds went by. Wilson came down from the very first boxcar to see.

"What's the matter?" Andrews and Brown gave him a look that he understood was to be quiet.

"Aw," said Knight. "It's the damper. Some fool did not close it properly." He shut it. "That should do it, let the steam loose, and restart the engine. Alf, stoke the fire to feed it, and we should be out of this snap."

Brown and Knight fed some more wood into the boiler. The engine let out a satisfying whistle while the engine slowly came back to life. Andrews called out to Wilson, "It's all good now, Mr. Wilson. Please return to your post." Wilson climbed back on top of the boxcar. The

General began to pick up speed. He made his way to the end of the roof and yelled out to the third boxcar, where the sliding door was open, and Wood, Dorsey, and Campbell had stuck their heads out.

"It's alright! We are fixed and going on!", Wilson shouted. He was not sure if they heard him, yet they nodded and disappeared into their boxcar. Wilson made his way back towards the front. It was dizzying, as the train went a breathtaking fifteen miles per hour. Wilson had never been on such a fast ride before. He rode in a wagon a few times, but it was nothing compared to this.

The landscape whipped by as the wind and the rain whipped him harder in the face. The whistle then blew. It nearly startled Wilson on how loud it was. He looked to see Brown and Andrews yelling something to him, but he could not hear. He climbed down from the boxcar, made a terrifying walk across the guardrail between the boxcar and the cab, and climbed into the cab.

"Mr. Wilson, if you can, please go back and release the brake. We are set to slow down over here", Andrews yelled over the noise. Having to go back, Wilson found the handbrake and began to pull back on it as hard as he could. He heard the screeching sound, but there was still some resistance required, so he put a little more muscle into it and pulled it more. The train blew its whistle and began to slow to crawl until it finally stopped. Now motionless, it was a little dizzying to see everything still. Wilson hopped down to the ground. His legs nearly buckled, but he caught himself immediately. He saw Brown walking toward something. He then saw them as a group of workers staring back at him.

***

Jackson Bond was the foreman in charge. His crew was charged with the repair of a siding switch at the place dubbed 'Moon's Station'. The work was going quite well. They should have been done by that afternoon, but he heard a train whistle, which was odd as his schedule said there wouldn't be one for quite some time. He had seen the General before, he knew the crew. But as the train pulled to a stop in the station, this time came two strange men looking back at him from the cab. Another man hopped down and spoke to one of his crews. The crewman nodded and then reached into his toolbox and handed a crowbar to the stranger. The stranger nodded and then climbed back into the cab. Another strange man glanced back at Bond and his crew before he climbed back on the boxcar. The train whistled as the wheels turned as it had started to move. Bond watched it pull away, further confused since there were only three boxcars behind it.

"What in the hell was that all about?", he asked the nearest crewmember.

***

No sooner had the General took off that it had slowed down again. Wilson had seen the boiler and decided to be in the main cab near to it, as his clothes now drenched from the thickening rain. He climbed down and replaced the cool, sweet Georgia air with the smoke-filled cab. After a coughing fit, he decided to alternate between standing by the boiler or by the open window nearby.

"Hey Alf," Wilson turned to Brown and Knight. "We are going to stop pretty soon. Get to the brake!" Wilson nodded and went out to work that brake again. The General slowed to a stop. There was nothing out there but rough wilderness and a number of telegraph poles.

Andrews asked, "Mr. Wilson, please gather the men and set to work on those telegraph poles." Wilson saluted, even though Andrews wasn't military.

"Yes, Cap'n."

Andrews turned towards the other pair. "Mr. Knight, Mr. Brown, please take a look at this engine and see if she has what it takes to complete our trip." Wilson scurried down and opened the third boxcar door to find his fellow Ohioans sitting, bored. "Alright, boys! We got some reb telegraph lines out here that need to be felled. Come on! Let's go get them!"

Finally! After all that patiently waiting and sitting, they could finally take it to the enemy. They had all piled out and gathered around the telegraph poles, only to stop.

"Who shall knock the wires down?"

"I cannot climb."

"Who shall it be then?"

"I will do it, my fellows." It was Jon Scott. Before anyone could agree, he already began to climb the pole like a squirrel in a tree.

"That boy got some injun' in 'im," said Campbell.

Scott kicked the insulating box off the pole and slid back down. The wires fell down with a wet thump.

"We still need to cut the wire!"

"Does anyone have a knife?"

"Did someone bring anything?"

"Wait, fellows, there was a toolbox in the cab!" Wilson ran across the wet ground. Almost nearly slipping twice. He scampered back up into the main cab. Andrews was talking to the engineers. "We need to keep this speed up for the sake of keeping up appearances." He turned to Wilson. "Is all well, Mr. Wilson?"

"Yes, Cap." Wilson went for the toolbox as he remembered it was placed near the boiler. He rummaged through it and found a saw. He ran back to the group, nearly slipping again. He went to work sawing the cables. It was tough work, nothing like sawing wood, but Wilson made short work of them. Wilson looked over his handiwork and felt good, like he had actually accomplished something. He felt the excitement in his fellow Ohioans as well.

"Alright, fellows! Let us not dawdle and get back on board so we can do more damage to the rebs!", Mason whooped.

Everyone whooped and got back on the boxcar. Wilson climbed back into the cab, where he saw Knight tying a red handkerchief to a pole on the cowcatcher.

"What's that for?"

"It signals 'danger', that another train is close behind or the track is damaged. Should buy us the time, you know."

"I see." They climbed back into the cab.

"Is all well, my lads?" Andrews asked.

"Yes, Cap."

"Yes, Cap."

"Very good, Mr. Wilson. Mr. Knight. We can be on our way then." "Yes, Cap." Knight brought the General back to life, and the engine was on its way back again. She began to pick up speed from the slight downgrade of earth and rumbled past the station at a small village called Acworth. Wilson poked his head out of the cab and couldn't help but smirk when he saw the people's expressions as the train they thought was theirs sped right on by. A few ran after the train to the end of the platform, but then stopped and watched it go in disbelief. Wilson looked away. Feeling embarrassed about his attitude towards them. Sure, they were the enemy, but they had places to go just like everyone else.

***

The General made a good pace as it winded through the country of Georgia. Wilson made himself useful, helping feed the furnace whenever required. Otherwise, he kept himself close to it and had started to dry off. Andrews was pleased with himself. He looked at the schedule and checked his pocket watch. "Very good gentleman. We are keeping good time. We should be passing through the village of Allatoona shortly." He watched through the window, as he was interested to see what these southern towns looked like. As the train rolled through the depot at Allatoona, he was disappointed to see a sad-looking train depot, a white building, and a few scattered buildings against the backdrop of a rocky looking ridge. He scoffed. Haskins was way more than that. As the locomotive chugged past the station, there were only three people on the platform. One ran to the edge. Wilson found himself waving to them. None of them waved back.

After a few minutes outside Allatoona, they were in a heavily wooded area, Andrews simply said. "Gentlemen. Please start braking. We can do specific damage to the rebs here."

Wilson was at the manual brake again. When the locomotive stopped, Wilson immediately moved to open the side doors to the boxcar, and everyone quickly piled out to breathe in the sweet air over the staleness of the boxcar. This time Andrews was before them to make a statement.

"Gentlemen, I am pleased to announce that we have the element of surprise still in our corner. As of yet, we are still on schedule. This right here will be a prime spot to cut down the telegraph wires. As well as take apart the tracks to deny it any pursuing train. In order to preserve our time allotment, I ask you to form two groups to achieve these tasks with ease. That is all. I shall leave you to it." He strode off back to the main engine.

Marion Ross, who is a sergeant major, and the highest-ranking person in the group of raiders, stepped up.

"Alright fellows", he said. "I will assign the telegraph poles back to Sergeant Scott again. He is capable of doing it himself. Sergeant Scott, please, commence your Indian act again."

"Yes, sir," Scott said before he climbed back up the pole.

"Now, this half will work the left side of the track," Ross said with a hand motion splitting the raiders in half. "While the other half should work the right side."

"I have a question," Pittenger said.

"Yes", replied Ross.

"How are we to loosen the track?"

Ross was caught.

"Here, this is all we have to give," Brown said as he approached him with a crowbar. Everyone glanced at him. "Then we use our hands, fellows. You have your orders."

The raiders pulled, kicked, and twisted the spikes out. It was rather time-consuming, they worked up quite a sweat, while several got nasty cuts on their hands. When they got one piece of track loose, they would pull up on the wooden cross ties to finally get it off. "Let's throw these away!"

"Keep 'em as a memento!"

Ross spoke up. "Throw the spikes as far as you can. Scatter the ties on the tracks to create a mess for any who may pursue. Load up the wood ties in the boxcar, less we have some use for 'em."

The men followed the orders. They had a moment to admire their handiwork of creating a big ditch in the tracks to stop any pursuer. They did a good job and were aware of it.

"Alright, men!' Ross boomed, all of the Sergeant Major he was. "Fall back to the boxcars so we may advance further!" The men whooped and went back. Wood fell in with Wilson.

"Ell, Alf, all the walk in the mud was worth this!"

"I'll see you at the next stop, Marky!" Wilson climbed back to the main cab, trying to contain himself even though his hands felt raw.

"Cap'n. The track and telegraph are reduced as ordered." Andrews was elated.

"Very good. Mr. Wilson. Mr. Knight, you may start the engine."

***

The General wounded through a downgrade before it crossed a bridge over a mighty looking river. Andrews said it was known as the Etowah. After it crossed the train passed by a stretch of buildings that went on for a while. Wilson had never seen anything quite like it. It was a mass of industry stretched out across five miles that included processing mills and ironworks. Coopers Iron Works is what the locals called it, said Andrews. The rain slowed down again to a light drizzle that blanketed everything in the wet mist. Wilson's attention was caught by another locomotive in the station across a bridge, adjacent to the track the General was on. It hissed and steamed, looking as if it reared to go. Wilson could see some workers milling about in the rain. They looked fierce. While the few who looked back at the General gave him an angry look. Wilson could barely make out the name on the locomotive as it passed. The Yonah.

Wilson said to Knight, "Do you see that?"

"Yes. Say, Cap, we better get out and destroy that engine and the bridge along with it."

Wilson felt for his revolver. He was ready for a fight. Andrews studied the other engine before turning back to Knight.

"It won't make a bit of difference, Mr. Knight. Press on."

Knight and Wilson exchanged a glance. Wilson's excitement slowly gave way to a dreadful feeling.

CHAPTER 8

William Fuller-Running along a muddy path for two miles-Plans-It Was the Work of Those Deserters-Young Fuller-Early Ambitions-New Horizons-Working the line-Early riser-Main engineer-War breaks out-Family-Lula-Governor Joe Brown's decree-That day

Two miles. For two miles, Bill Fuller ran. Without thinking, he ran. The rain came thick now, and the mud was also getting thicker. He just plodded through as best he could, while Murphy and Cain followed him behind. After he cleared Big Shanty, he was in the woods. He had overcome the shock of what had happened and started to analyze his next move. He was certain that it was deserters from Camp McDonald who stole his train, only to ditch it when they were away and flee into woods like the cowards they were. He knew these tracks quite well. He knew they would lead to Moon's Station. There he could send word of what had happened. Get a boxcar or horse to pursue. Or maybe those fools abandoned it before then. Either way, if they were determined to possess it, he was just as equally determined to get it back.

***

William Fuller was full of grit and determination. That was apparent from day number one. Born in Morrow Station in Henry County, he was quite tenacious and would not let anything get in his way. He would either go around or, if need be, though. He was modest and quiet as a youngster, as well as a dedicated student who had a decent appetite for anything dealing in science and technology. He liked reading tales of high adventure in far and exotic places. When he turned 19, he decided that Morrow Station was way too small and struck out on his own to the growing town of Atlanta. He signed on with the Western & Atlantic Railroad as a train hand, occasionally running ahead of a train for miles and miles to act as a flagman when there was an intersection that was to twist. He eventually made it to brakemen, and finally to a conductor after two years in 1857.

At the age of 21, he was one of the youngest conductors on the W & A. He had a diligent work ethic. Firm but fair. He never asked his crew members to do anything he wouldn't do himself. His account keeping was always found to be organized, he kept his train on schedule, barring any man-made calamity or act of God. He had even handled the hazardous job of keeping rowdy country folk coming into the city in line.

In 1860, he looked rather young than his twenty-four years, almost baby-like with his receding hairline, which had left nearly half of his head bald. He took to courting a Miss Lula Asher of Murray County. He proved to be the perfect southern gentlemen, but occasionally broke the rules and would take her for an adventure, as he let Ms. Asher ride in the main engine cab. In the fall, they got married. He was so preoccupied with his job and certain upcoming pre-nuptials that he turned the chants of secession and war and went down with Lincoln out of his head. It was only after the chants got too loud after Georgia had seceded, all that went away when he made the decision to join the confederacy.

He sat his wife down and told her.

"Dear wife," he said. "I have tried to keep the war out of my mind and our little home. Now I cannot. Not after that, vile Lincoln is raising an army to invade the south. For too long, I have heard tales of how the Yankees have been trying to put the south in their firm grip, and now they mean too at the end of a rifle. I cannot stand by and let it happen. I mean to enlist."

"Oh, Bill", she sighed. "I understand. I shall do whatever I can to aid your effort at home. I will also pray that this conflict comes to a swift resolution."

Even though he hadn't hunted for quite a while and would be considered 'city folk', he proved himself as a capable soldier and was able to keep up with the tougher men. His sergeant made a note of him making a fine commissioned officer until Governor Joe Brown made a decree. All capable railroad men were to best serve the state and the confederacy by staying with the railroad. Fuller initially wanted to stay in the militia, particularly after everyone had heard of the glorious victory at Manassas. His old employers wrote the governor and had personally visited and implored Fuller to reconsider.

He could better serve moving men and material to the front to help aid the fight. Eventually, he agreed and was back in a locomotive. He felt good to be back. At the very least, he was in charge.

"Well, my wife", he said to Lula. "My career as a soldier is at a premature end. Alas, I will assist the south the best way I know, and that is to run the locomotives filled with munitions for our troops. As such, I will be home more."

"Oh, too bad", she replied. "I was getting used to the notion of not having you here." She responded with a smirk.

"Very funny."

***

For over a year, he went up and down the line. Transporting troops and the artillery up north; while citizens down south. This day, he had been working since dawn; but never showed any signs of a tire.

He knew he couldn't now, not until the contest was decided.

CHAPTER 9

Moons Station again-Jackson Bond-Strangers a-comin'-Two miles
runners-Explanation-Yankees!-The handcar-Gathering the
handcar-The poles-Scattering-On track- Scattering the crew-Gaining
speed-Fuller-Cain-Murphy-The plan-Onward

The crew at Moons Station was milling under cover of a thin
veranda. In part due to rainfall, and partially because they didn't know
what to make of the incident with the train that had happened. Jackson
Bond was sitting on a barrel under the veranda. He checked his watch,
sighed, and sent it to his jacket pocket. He thought about calling it a
day. The rain poured steadily, he poked his head out from the veranda
and saw there was no end near in sight. The ground was pure mud. He
got up and was about to gather his crew around when he saw
something come at him. It took him a second look to focus and see it
was a form. He went to get his hat, wiped his eyes, and walked to the
platform to get a closer look. Sure enough, there was a hat, and when
it tilted back, he would recognize the babyface anywhere.

"Well, Bill Fuller. Have you lost your locomotive? Or is this the way
we are to move freight on the line now?"

Fuller ran right up to him. "Yes." He said, almost breathlessly.
"Have you seen it? How long has it been gone?"

"Right about thirty minutes?"

Fuller stopped to catch his breath. "Tell me, what had happened
when it came through?"

"It came through and stopped. There were fellers on the cab I did
not know them. One got out and borrowed some of our tools. A
crowbar. After that, he climbed aboard, and they skedaddled out of
here."

Fuller leaned back, sucked in some air, and drunk water. Cain and
Murphy came plodding along now.

60

Fuller suddenly exploded, "Damn it! I believed they are deserters! If they are taking your tools, they must be them Yankees! They stole my train, your tools, to turn this track to ruins! What a Yankee trick!"

Cain and Murphy looked at each other than at Fuller. "Yankees? Are you sure? Those fools do not have the sand to come down here and do a job like that."

"I'm sure." Fuller said, and then he asked Bond, "There is no use running after them. They are long gone. So, tell me. Do you have a horse to spare?"

"No horses. We do have a hand car."

"Show me."

"You, men! Get up off your asses and come help me!", Bond yelled to his crew as he located the handcar. It was sitting right next to the wooden station house. At once, they all got up and surrounded the handcar and lifted it up. Fuller was pitching in and helping lift it and carry it towards the track. "It works like a normal handcar, it rolls on the track. Yet you need two men to use poles to push off and gain its momentum. Except we're short a few poles. So, you'll have to get a running start to get going. There is a downgrade up ahead, that'll help plenty."

They set the handcar down on the track. Everyone grunted. Bond adjusted the handcar making sure it was even on the track. Fuller looked at Cain and Murphy. They looked in no shape to run any further. Even Fuller's feet throbbed.

"Say, my boys and I are about spent. Could you help us out here, Jackson?"

"Of course!" Bond thundered. "Yankees running wild in my woods? You'll bet I will do something about it! I'm your man. Get on and hold tight. Thomas! We are going for a little run."

Fuller, Murphy, and Cain climbed up on the handcar. Bond and a burly looking fellow, Thomas, got behind the car. Bond barked, "You men! You are now relieved. Get back to your town and spread the word that Yankee's had stolen a train and were heading north!"

The workers took off.

"Thomas. CHARGE!"

They pushed with all of their might and began to kick up mud before the handcar began to move. Fuller was able to catch his breath.

As the handcar hit the downgrade, it picked up speed, renewing Fuller's sense of optimism, he could catch his train. Had they not gotten the handcar, he didn't think he could have. He removed his mud-covered boots and wiggled his toes. His feet were beyond sore, but he could now let them rest. He looked at Cain. Cain had laid down, sucking in air and rain.

"How are you, Jeff?"

"Tolerable now, Bill."

Murphy looked back at him. "We are in much need of this rest, Bill. So, what are your intentions now?"

Fuller looked at him then at the tracks up ahead. "I know the schedule. There is no major traffic this time, and it is all southbound. I do know there is always a locomotive oiled up and ready to go. We have to aim to get to Coopers Ironworks and take command of the Yonah. I will use that to get to them."

CHAPTER 10

Moving along-Disappointed Passengers-Boxcar Conditions-Wood-Dorsey-Campbell-Slavens speaksPittenger-Boxcar rules-Wilsons job-The cab-The rain again-Cass Station-Refuel-William Russell and his suspicions-The story-The schedule-Andrews Charm-Off again

The General passed through the station for the town of Cartersville. It was ahead of its schedule, yet the people who waited for the next train got their hopes up that this train was theirs, only for them to be dashed as it rolled on by. Safely and out of sight, Wilson crossed over to the boxcar and bellowed.

"You may open the side door now. It is all clear."

The men inside were glad to hear the news. Save for a few holes on the side of the boxcar, it was almost pitch-black inside, and they were happy for the light, even if it was dark and grey from the outside. The rough, uneven track meant the ride was quite bumpy. Those sitting had to put up with the constant bumps, rattles, and twists. Those standing had to put up with the same hell, along with getting jerked forward or to the side when the brakes were applied. Wood and Dorsey pushed the sliding door wide open. The cool, wet air outside was a welcome relief from the hot, stale air inside. Dorsey leaned back against the door. Wood stood in the opening, as he watched the landscape roll by.

"Almost reminds me of my old 'ome." Dorsey asked, "Where do you hail from again?"

"Nottingham. In England. Before you ask. This is the same as the Robin 'ood story."

"What made you come here?"

Wood stiffened. "Oh, this chap had made a casual remark about my father that I found insulting. So, I proceeded to shoot the fellow. He was well connected in his bloodlines. So, I fled."

Dorsey looked at him saucer eyed. "Is that true?"

Wood laughed. "No. I was not content there and have always read magnificent stories about America, so I decided to leave. When I arrived there, I asked where the best place to start anew is, and I was told Ohio. So off I went."

Dorsey smiled. "It is at that."

"What are your plans after the war?"

"Go back and become a schoolmaster, I presume. Possibly see of practicing law. Yourself?"

"I've been stowing away quite a bit of my pay. Perhaps I shall strike out and seek my fortune elsewhere. Maybe the wild frontier. You ought to be a rough sort out there. I think I endured this. I can endure it all."

Campbell came barreling up and pushed his way to the open door.

"I ought to relieve myself", he said as he started to undo his pants. "Look away, unless you want to watch."

"Frightfully sorry, but no." Wood said as he and Dorsey moved away.

Slavens sat in the corner, enduring the bumps and rattling of the boxcar right against his back. He was enjoying the sight of the open countryside after Campbell had moved away. His moment of peace was disturbed when Pittenger came and sat right next to him. "Hello, Sam. What are you thinking about?"

"I was remembering days like this back at home. It would be raining, and my wife Rachel and I would sit next to each other. We didn't really need to say anything. We just sat together and watch the rain.

"That is just fine, Sam. I am not married yet. Perhaps when the war is over, I'll make it happen."

Slavens smiled and scratched his beard. "You are a lad. You have all the time in the world."

Buffum suddenly popped into view. "See, fellows. My hat is black. How couldn't you tell?" He held it up in the dim light. Everyone groaned.

"What is that about?" Wood asked.

"Don't mind him. He's been going on about that since the walk to Chattanooga", said Dorsey.

***

Wilson went back to the main cab. Andrews sat on a stool in the corner and was looking over a map. Wilson chose not to bother him.

He fell in with Brown and Knight, just by the boiler to get some warmth. "How are you boys holding up?"

"I am well as expected," Knight said. "I could use some coffee, though. Other than that, I am all good."

Brown said, "Are we still due to making Chattanooga by dusk?"

"Yes," Knight replied. "We are running low on both wood and water. Cap said Cass Station is right up ahead so we can gather their some more."

"Might we have you tell the boys back in there to close up? Then you may ready the brake?"

"Of course," Wilson said as he started to warm up back out on the boxcar. He then called out, "Alright fellows. We are approaching another station now. You know what you are to do."

Wood poked his head out. "You are doing a tremendous job, Alf, informing us of this, I will put in a recommendation so you may receive a promotion to corporal!"

Wilson shook his head and went at the brake.

***

The General rolled into the Cass Station. The stationmaster, William Russell, was in his office reading a newspaper while smoking his pipe when he heard a train whistle, as well as the chuff of an engine pulling in.

"What in all creation?", he asked. He checked his schedule and then looked at his watch from his vest. "There isn't supposed to be a train at this time."

As the engine came to a complete stop. Knight stepped off first, followed by Brown and then Wilson. "Gentlemen, there is a woodpile. Carry as much as you could and be quick about it. We have a schedule to keep onto."

Brown and Wilson went straight for the woodpile and gathered up as much wood as they could carry. The rain had softened.

Russell stepped out of his office and put his hat and coat on. He has a friendly yet curious demeanor. He knew the General and knew the crew. He was surprised to see the General manned by these strangers, and with such few boxcars.

"Morning. How y'all doing?", he asked.

Knight handed him a ticket. "I'm well, thank you." Russell looked at it and nodded as he pocketed it. A moment passed. Nobody said anything. Wilson and Brown now came back for some more wood.

Russell chewed on his pipe before he finally said. "I don't recollect ever seeing you fellows before around here." He pointed at the boxcars. "What's in there?"

Before Knight could answer, Andrews appeared through the mist and spoke for him. "You just drop a few sparks from that pipe of yours inside, and you will find out soon enough."

Russell's eyes widened. Andrews, making his point, just like an actor reciting a monologue, continued. "I have been ordered by the esteemed personage of General Pierre Beauregard, to impress a locomotive and load it with powder and ammunition. Then I am to make haste to his army and resupply his troops. You are aware that his forces were engaged in a desperate fight, are you not?"

"Uh...yes...yes, seh."

"Then you should realize the reason why this locomotive is not on a schedule. Why would you not recognize my men, and while we are in a hurry. This is all because if we fail to resupply our brave forces, the savage Yankee's could shoot them down for sport while we would have no way to respond in such kind. Do you realize this?"

"Yes, seh."

"Then, by my leave, we shall depart. My boys are almost done. I thank you for your assistance."

"For General Beauregard? I'd give him the shirt off my back!"

"There is no need for that, I am sure. Before we set off, may we be scheduled for the Western and Atlantic line for today?"

"Hell, you may have mine!" Russell ran back into his office. Andrews looked over at the cab. Knight nodded and climbed back up in it.

"There you are!" Russell walked up to him and handed him his schedule.

"Much obliged. I will favorably mention you to General Beauregard. What is your name?"

"Bill Russell."

"Mr. Russell, my humblest appreciation." They both shook hands. Andrews turned and walked back into the cab. The General came alive and chugged its way out the station. Russell watched it leave before he went back to his office. Going back to his newspaper, he could not help but feel he did something good for the troops today.

CHAPTER 11

Fuller-The discovery-Yankee destruction-Handcar troubles-No rest-Acworth-White Smith-Armed and ReadyHired Hands-Small Space-Back On The Handcar again-Break in the line-Fuller's determination-The Etowah-The Arrival-A better chance-The engine Yonah

As the handcar rolled on, Fuller peered through the rain that fell from the brim of his hat. He didn't say anything to his associates. Partly because he had finally started to catch his breath and while he tried to make a plan for what to do if and when they caught up to the raiders.

Looking ahead, something was amiss. The railroad track just ended. "Halt!!"

Bond and Thomas jumped and slammed their legs down to the ground, spraying mud everywhere before the handcar finally stopped. Fuller hopped up off the handcar to get a clear look. The rail ties were indeed gone for a considerable length of the track.

"What's the matter, Bill?" Bond and Thomas were winded from their turn running. Murphy and Cain got off and walked around it to see.

"With this, I have no doubt now that this is the work of those treacherous Yankees."

"That is not all; take a gander to the telegraph poles." Cain coughed. Indeed, the wires were cut and scattered about with missing pieces of rail.

Murphy started "For having doubted you I apologize-"

"There isn't time for that," Fuller said as he walked back to handcar. "We are to move this so we can keep pressing forward. Jeff? Anthony? Up and let's go!"

Murphy and Cain got on each side. When everyone was in position, Fuller boomed, "Now, LIFT!" Everyone lifted and moved gingerly. They had to move fast as their boots sank rapidly as soon as they would stop. Fuller was in good shape, but his arms started to burn as he moved. "We are almost at the end, men! Just a little more!"

"Bill, can we set it down for a moment? My arms are nearly gone." Cain said.

"We cannot. Or the mud will devour us." Fuller replied. They made it, and after some minor adjustments, they got it back on the track. Bond and Thomas preferred to sit for a moment, but Fuller wouldn't let up. "Onward, men!"

So onward, they went on through the rain and grey landscape. Fuller could see the station at Acworth at a distance. "Acworth is right ahead, men. Keep at it!" The station slowly started to grow in size.

"Anthony, you're with me", Fuller said. "See about gathering some help. I will question the stationmaster and see what he knows."

"Very well, Bill."

Fuller looked over at Cain. "How are you, Jeff?"

"I'm tolerable", he replied between coughs.

"Stay with the handcar." Fuller looked back to the runners. "How are you, boys?"

"We can keep going", said Bond, panting.

"Start slowing. We are almost there."

Fuller braced himself against his knee as the blurry world began to clear. When the handcar stopped right outside the station; Fuller leaped out of the handcar, bounded through the mud, and raced to the stationmaster's office, whilst careful not to slip. He burst into the stationmaster's office, causing the lone occupant to jump.

"I'm looking for the stationmaster! Where can I find him?", Fuller demanded without skipping a beat.

The man stammered. "He is...in the...outhouse."

Fuller got in his face. "Listen. I am Bill Fuller. I am a conductor of the W & A. My train was stolen by Yankee invaders. It is number 4-4-0. Orange. Has it come through here?"

"Uh. Yes. I believe so."

Fuller closed the gap between their faces. "It has been stolen. I mean to get it back. Do you know how many men were on board?"

The man thought. "Possibly three to four in the main cab."

"What is your name?"

"White Smith."

"Smith, do you have a horse available to you?"

"Yes."

"Take the horse and ride north to spread the word. The authors of this treacherous plot have not only stolen my train but have also severed telegraph wire and removed the track from its line."

"Yes, sir."

"Also, do you have any firearms about here?"

"We have two shotguns."

"Fetch them."

Smith disappeared and came back, wielding two vintage double barrel shotguns. Fuller took them. "Did you understand everything I told you?"

"Yes, sir."

"Then why do you still stand here? Off you go."

Smith saluted and disappeared out the back. Fuller stepped outside and walked towards Murphy, who was walking to him. Two men in tow. "Well?" Murphy asked.

"It did come through. Maybe three or four in the cab. I sent the boy to ride out ahead and spread the word. Who are they?"

"This is Martin Rainey and Steven Stokely. I told them of the goings-on, and they volunteered to catch the raiders", Murphy responded.

"We are eager to help," Rainey said. Fuller cast his glance at the rifles they were wielding. They were squirrel guns.

"Very good, gentlemen. We'll be off now." Rainey and Stokely walked off the platform, and Fuller handed Murphy a shotgun.

"In case it comes to it." Murphy nodded and took it. They stepped off the platform. Rainey and Stokely were waiting.

"Where are we off to, sir?" Rainey asked.

"To the handcar!"

"Oh."

They piled on the handcar and made introductions. With three, there was space. With five, they had to squeeze in. Bond and Tom had caught their breath, now they were to run again.

"Are y'all set?"

Fuller replied, "Yes."

The runners started to move. Fuller didn't say anything for the longest time. He especially didn't ask the newcomers anything. He was busy running estimates of how many men were in that boxcar, and if they were together. Twenty? Thirty? He noticed the handcar had slowed dramatically, and he was slanted at an angle. He recognized the location, the upgrade was the last obstacle before they went downhill and crossed the Etowah. Then to Coopers Ironworks, where the Yonah sat.

"Are you good, Jackson?"

"Yes, sir", was his grunted reply. They reached the crest. Fuller was upright. He then felt the handcar tilt down. Bond and Thomas hopped on the handcar, it started to slow, but swiftly picked up speed and flew down the downgrade. Fuller felt a whoosh in his stomach, but he could feel his heart leap as he saw the Yonah at a distance.

"The Yonah! God bless her. She is a fast one!"

"There is a break in the line!"

Fuller had just a moment before he saw the break. Reacting quickly, he leaped off the handcar, the mud broke his fall. Murphy, who shouted of their being a break, had a smoother landing. Bond and Thomas hopped off. Cain and Rainey rolled off, bounced off the ground, and landed in a ditch with mud water. Stokely couldn't get off in time and fly headfirst into a mud bank. Everyone was in a daze, trying to recollect themselves. Fuller was leading charge.

"We cannot bide any more time. Collect yourselves, and let's go!"

He stormed past the ditch where Cain and Rainey were climbing out.

"This is no time to swim!" He walked straight towards the handcar. "Help me heave this." Everyone staggered over to now lift the handcar. It took a few minutes to lift it and get it on the track. "Good." Fuller nodded at the work. "Now." He looked at his motley crew and pointed at Rainey.

"You, go back to Acworth and warn them of this treacherous gap. The rest of you, we shall keep going."

Rainey nodded. "Yes sir."

He ran back to Acworth. Fuller climbed back aboard. There was a little more room again. "I know you are quite tired, boys. It is just a little further." Bond exhaled, and then he and Thomas pushed off again. They slowed down considerably when they crossed the bridge. Bond and Thomas were extra careful to not slip on the track, as the Etowah had a fast current.

After they had made it to the other side, they were there. Fuller was already busy. All the station workers had gathered around when he called them over. They huddled both around him and Murphy in a circle.

"You, men! You know me! You know my locomotive! Well, I have some terrible news. This morning, a group of damn Yankees, who portrayed themselves as civilians, stole my locomotive and piloted it upstate. It has most likely passed this way, you all might have seen it go by, but did not think twice about who engineered it. So, my fellows, I aim to take the Yonah and get the train back. I need your help to do so. Who is with me?"

Everyone roared in agreement. Yankees? Stealing a train? Down here? That just would not do. That and the fact that Fuller had a shotgun.

The Yonah was on a turntable and had to be manually rotated to be attached to the tender so it could go. Nearly all the station workers swarmed it and began to move it. Cain approached Fuller.

"I feel fit, Bill, where do you want me?"

Fuller nodded. "I need you to tend to the engine making sure she is fueled and ready." Cain nodded and walked towards the main cab. Fuller said to Murphy. "Those scoundrels have most likely torn up more of the rail by now. We will need more ties, rails, tools, and men to use them."

"I'll fetch them," Murphy said. Fuller turned to see Stokely waiting. "Oh right, see about Anthony and what he needs."

Stokely nodded. "Yes sir."

Fuller went to the handcar where Bond and Thomas laid across. "How are you, Jackson?"

"Bill, Thomas and I are spent. We don't think we can go on further." Bond gasped. "You have done a man's job, Jackson. You brought me here and have given me a chance to catch those scoundrels. You have earned your rest." Bond coughed and waved good-bye.

Fuller turned and walked towards the main cab. The whole cab was tender and had been rotated. There was a line of men finishing loading the rear handcar with supplies. Murphy shouted out, "Alright, men! That is enough! We are off now!" He fell in with Fuller. "Bill, we have supplies as well as six men volunteered to assist. They are big fellows that can handle the work."

"Excellent."

They boarded the cab and found Cain waiting for them. "Well, Jeff, how is she?"

"She is ready."

"Let's be off then." The Yonah was a powerful engine. It started off slow leaving the station, but it soon took off at top speed right after the raiders.

CHAPTER 12

*Wilson-Conversation-Kingston-Wiley Harbin-Uriah Stephens-The
story-The Telegram-Must Wait-Reassurance-To much time-Another
train is coming-Tension-Suspicion-Hope-Stephens posse-An
Accusation-Diffusion-The Angry Old man-The Keys-Finally a
Departure*

Wilson's uneasiness had slowly dissipated and had started to feel
better after being out in the Georgia countryside. He rides in the cab.
He poked his head out of the window occasionally for some air. When
he felt a shiver, he returned to the boiler to help stoke the flame, and
to warm up. Brown and Knight watched him. "How are you, Alf?"
Brown asked.

"I am well."

"I don't suppose this trip made you regret to not become a railroad
man instead of a farmer has it?", Knight chuckled.

"It remains to be seen if I ride another locomotive ever again,"
Wilson responded. Andrews was in the corner, looking at his ill-
begotten schedule. He suddenly folded it and got in the middle of
everyone. "Look sharp, my lads. We are approaching Kingston. It
appears that the morning train has arrived. We must be prepared if this
stop to be hazardous then the last few. Mr. Wilson, the brakes, please."

"Yes, Cap."

Kingston was a much larger station than all the others. It held a
generous ticket station, a waiting room, and a structure that housed
luggage. There was even a restaurant in it. The main line of the track
curved as it came into the station, another line peeled off to the left,
forming a 'Y' shape.

The morning was busy with station crews going about their duties
as the locomotive William R. Smith had arrived and settled amongst
the heavy traffic. The main engineer, Oliver Wiley Harbin, walked over
towards the station agent's window. He was a big, bearded fellow.
Years of working on the railroads had served him rather well. He

tapped on the window. The station agent, Uriah Stephens, opened it. "Wiley, you keep smudging my glass; you better clean it!"

"Perhaps you keep it open so everyone can see you as acting the fool and not the station agent." Stephens laughed.

"What goes out there?"

"Oh, Bill Fuller and his boys are coming to bring me the mail and a few passengers to ferry over to Atlanta." They all heard the sharp whistle of an oncoming locomotive.

"Well, speak of the devil," Harbin said.

"Damn this weather. I guess it's best for me to get my coat", Stephens said.

"Well, go on then. A little rain never hurt me any." Harbin watched as the General pulled into the station. To his confusion, the train had only boxcars, no passengers, no mail car.

When it stopped and let out steam, a stranger wearing a fine-looking coat and top hat got off and approached him, carrying on as if he owned the place.

"That is Bill Fuller's train, but you are not Bill Fuller."

"It is irrelevant. I need to take the switch key, and I want to take the siding to await the freight train from the south." The stranger demanded.

"The hell you say!"

The stranger sighed. "I took this train by a governmental authority to run ammunition to General Beauregard, who requires it at once. Do you have the key? Or at least know where I may retrieve it?"

"Talk to the feller inside," Harbin said. "Hey, Uriah. This feller wants the switch key and-" He had to stop abruptly when the stranger walked past him and strode into the office. Stephens watched as this stranger walked right up to him.

"Sir, I have it on good authority to deliver this train up north to General Beauregard. It is filled with ammunition for his troops. As you may or may not know, he had been engaged in a desperate fight in Tennessee and was routed by the Yankees. Now the Yankees are chasing him, from the rear, and while other Yankees sweep through Alabama, he could be surrounded and cut off. His troops are very low on ammunition. They could be engaged already."

Stephens was astonished. "How may I help?"

"I need the switch key."

"I will get it for you."

"Why has the main freight train not arrived yet?" The stranger asked. Stephens was about to hand him the key when he stopped and pulled out a piece of paper from his desk.

"Seeing as you are in charge of Fuller's train, this applies to you."

The stranger took both the key and the sheet of paper, which was a telegram, and read it, His expression sunk. "The freight train is running behind. I am to wait for it and not take up the track."

"That is too bad," Stephens said. "I can wire down south to see if they are able to make an exception for you."

"No. That is alright. I am sure it won't be long." The stranger turned and walked out. "The main passenger train will be here shortly," Stephens said over his shoulder. He walked out into the rain and back towards his train.

Harbin, who stood by the open window listening, slightly nodded to the stranger, who returned it. He watched the stranger direct his crew to throw the switch and have the locomotive move towards the left side. Bored, Harbin decided to do something else while he was waiting. Andrews climbed aboard where the three raiders waited.

"My lads. It is no worry, but we must wait for the down freight trains to pass. It is the only way to maintain schedule and avoid a collision."

"How long do you think it will be?" asked Knight.

"Oh, only a few minutes," replied Andrews.

***

Nearly a full hour had passed. Wilson was waiting with the others out of the rain. There was nothing much to do. Brown and Knight made sure the engine was ready to go at a moment's notice. They made some small talk, but also kept an eye on the station workers around. Sometimes one or two would walk by, other times a group would stop and talk pointing at the General. Wilson would ready himself to fight, only to watch as the group went on their way.

Finally, they heard the whistle of an oncoming train. Everyone's spirits soared. They watched as a locomotive named New York rolled into the station, blocking the exit of the General. Before anyone could react, Andrews was already out of the cab and walking towards the New York's cab. With the chatter, engine huffing, and other noise, they could not hear what was said, but when they saw Andrews use the key to switch the siding, New York's engine started up. Their hearts lifted. This was it.

"This is it. Right?", Wilson asked.

"Be still. We go when Cap says so." Knight replied.

Andrews returned, shoulders slumped in defeat. "They have moved aside. However, there is another train right behind, and we need to wait a while longer. I promise it will be short. My lads, they have confirmed it. Mitchell has taken Huntsville and is now moving on to Chattanooga." Everyone was muted by excitement. Especially as the whistle of another train was heard.

"The only negative is," Andrews continued, "they are moving everything they can down south." The raiders nodded and turned their attention towards the second train as it rolled into the station, only to watch in disbelief as the last car had a red flag tied to it.

By now, a group of workers had formed on the station. They were lounging around mostly, chewing tobacco and smoking, but a few of them carried tools, like hammers, shovels, one even had a pickaxe. Stephens approached the cab, with Harbin close in behind him.

"Excuse me!" Stephens called out.

Andrews opened the cab door. "Yes?"

"It has nigh been an hour, and Bill Fuller's train has not yet arrived. It has held up Mr. Harbin, and now his schedule has ruined. I have tried to telegraph Atlanta but have not received any word back from them. I still have not received any confirmation of your special mission. What was your name again? Well? What do you have to say?"

Andrews just scoffed. "I am shocked and appalled by your behavior, sir. Along with your associates. I was told you ran an impeccable station here, what I have seen indicates otherwise. You run in constant delays; you are disorganized. But I am most appalled by the fact that you do not seem to understand we are at war. With an enemy army bearing down on us, and the only force that can stop them is woefully underequipped. I am the only means that can prevent the ultimate disaster; instead, I am here, dealing with a horse's ass of a station agent. When I see General Beaureguard, I will report you in the most unfavorable terms. What is your name?"

"Uh. Uriah...Stephens."

Andrews pulled out a pencil and a piece of paper from his coat pocket and started to write his name down. "That is all Mr. Stephens, you may go." Stephens sulked away than followed Harbin. Andrews walked back. "Mr. Knight. Can you please check on the cargo." Knight walked out on the platform, hands in pockets, all casual. He walked to the boxcar where the raiders were kept, leaned over to them and whispered. "Boys, we have to wait for a train that is a little behind schedule. The folks around here are getting uneasy and suspicious. Be ready to jump out if you are called and let them have it hot and fast." Inside the boxcar, the raiders were stuck. They had no way of knowing what was going or why they were not moving. They could hear the noises, and the crew people begin to talk now. They were hot. They were thirsty. Some had to go to the bathroom. It felt like forever. Now they had to get themselves ready for a fight.

***

The last train rolled into the station. Finally, it was all clear. Andrews promptly ordered to move to the side so his train could go through. While that one was moving, Andrews was already asking the elderly tender operator for the switch keys so he could move his engine on the mainline

"What? What in tarnation gives you the authority to be bossin ev'r'one 'round like you own th' road! Like hell, I will give ye my keys!" The raiders could hear of this exchange and were ready to jump out and start blasting.

Andrews laughed. "I've got no time to waste on an old fella like you" and walked past him, back to the station office, he went inside, and grabbed the keys off the peg, and walked back out.

Stephens watched him. Andrews returned to the old man hopping up and down, swearing up a storm as Andrews used the keys to flip the switch. "You goddamn sonuvabitch! I will report you! I'll see you behind iron!" Andrews puts the keys in his coat pocket, then motioned for Knight and Brown to start the engine. He climbed aboard waving to the old man, who still hopped up and down. The General finally chugged its way out of the station. After more than an hour of wait time. As they were chugging out of the station, Wilson felt that sense of dread again. He took place on top of the boxcar to get some air and try to clear up his head. As the General rolled out, he could see in a field right in the middle of the 'Y' a large troop of confederates drilled and practiced maneuvers. Wilson smiled and waved at them. It seemed to be the only thing to do. After the train cleared the station, Wilson turned and watched it fade from view.

CHAPTER 13

Fuller-Nonstop-Ties on the line-Brake Now-Clear the line-White Smith and his adventures-Continuing On-The Second Strange Kingston Arrival-Duncan Murchison and His Charge-The farmers turned soldiers-Commotion-The Story-Rousing speech-No go-Harbin's offer-Murphy's work-The William R. Smith-Off in pursuit again

The Yonah raced through the wind and the rain. Fuller stood on the front of the train absorbing it all. His hawk-like eyes served him well when he noticed something in the line.

"STOP!"

Cain threw all that he had into the brakes. The wheels locked and screeched. Everyone nearly tumbled over. It was too late; they heard the sound of the wheels crashing violently into metal. Once the Yonah finally stopped, everyone collected themselves. Cain coughed. "Damnation, Bill! I need more time to hit the brake!"

Fuller began to head out of the cab. "There is something on the tracks! Everyone out to clear them!" The posse piled out of the cab and began to clear the railroad ties off the track. Murphy approached Fuller.

"Say, Bill, this is the second time now that this is happening. Do you suppose the Yankees could possibly slow us down for an ambush? Take two engines instead of one"

"No. These Yankees are just raiders. Out for one locomotive to tear our lines. If they desired to ambush us, they would have done so already."

Murphy replied. "Just the same, when we arrive at Kingston, perhaps we should enlist some more men. Soldiers this time."

Fuller nodded. "Very well."

Just then, they heard the sound of a horse clomping swiftly through the mud. Fuller did not have his shotgun, so he grabbed Murphy's and drew a bead on the figure riding right at them. "Halt and state your business!" The horse reared back and neighed angrily.

"It is me! White-Smith! Do not fire!" Fuller rolled his eyes. Smith dismounted, tied the horse to a tree, and raced over to Fuller, slipping and falling along the way. "Sir! I have tried my best to warn others of the Yankees, but I was unsuccessful, I couldn't find anyone to warn.

"May I stay here and help you?" Fuller stared at him. "They need help."

"Go to it."

"Sir." He ran off to help others. Fuller looked at Murphy, who then shook his head. After a few minutes, the track was clear. "Let's go, boys!" Everyone piled back into the cab, and the Yonah started. Fuller was at the front of the Yonah again. His heart leaped when he saw the outline of the station. It sunk back just as quickly when he saw the main lines and the sidings packed with locomotives.

He wheeled himself around and made his way back to the cab.

Murphy was at the gears; Cain was already starting to break when Fuller got in.

"What're your intentions, Bill?" Cain asked. "It is going to take too long to move those locomotives out of the way. We will have to requisition one."

"A good one, this ole gal cannot go on. What would happen if you were refused?" Murphy asked.

"Then God help the man who denies me." Fuller snapped.

***

Duncan Murchison was the volunteer drillmaster of the troop in the field up north in the 'Y'. He was whipping these forty-odd recruits to good shape. Although with the lot them, it was hard to believe that these men were army recruits. They weren't wearing much of a uniform; many looked like they just came from working some fields or in shops. The weapons they carried were basically a hodgepodge of squirrel guns, shotguns, and some few old flintlock muskets. Murchison himself did not look army either, he had a straw hat, a brown overcoat covering a flannel shirt, and kept his revolver in a holster that he wore loosely at his side, accompanied by a large hunting knife. His veteran experience in fighting Indians made him an ideal candidate for a drillmaster, or at the very least, he had more experience in army affairs and battle than anyone else around here.

His men helped themselves to some corn juice, of which, leading by example, Murchison partook took part as well. With the rain starting to get heavier, the field turning to mud, along with the fact that some of his men did not even own shoes, Murchison was about to call it a day. When one of his troopers said, "Saye Seh, they are a doing's abound at th' station. Lookey yonda!", Murchison could see through the rain that a crowd was forming, and it seemed like much excitement was going on.

"Alright, boys, let's see what's causing a fuss over there." Murchison led the way. His men behind him buzzing with excitement. Rather than form a column or a line, his men were just a rabble. They walked through the station, up towards the platform, and made their way through the crowd. There was a man talking to everyone that Murchison had never seen before. He spotted Wiley Harbin in the crowd, shaking his head. Murchison pushed his way through to reach him.

"Wiley, what's going on?"

"Hell, you would not believe. Some Yankees had the sand to come down here and con us. According to Bill Fuller over there, they stole his train, then they came through here and spun some story about getting ammunition to General Beauregard to his station."

"Yankees?! Through here!?"

"Yes seh."

While Fuller explained the story, Murphy was in the New York cab, pushing the crew to get it up and running.

"Move double-quick men; every minute, the Yankees get farther away."

Murchison let out a whoop to get everyone's attention. "My fellow Georgians, this day is a black day if a pack of yellow-bellied Yankees came down here and made off with our trains? This proves their greed for what is ours is insatiable, what next? Our slaves? Our women?"

In the crowd, a woman suddenly fainted.

Murchison continued, "What are we to do about? Sit here and crow about it?"

"No!"

"No." "Send 'em to hell!"

"Yes! My boys will do the trick! Won't you, boys!" His boys let out whoops and cheers. "Let's go get them!" Amid the cheers, Stephens appeared and said in a much low tone. "I'm afraid you cannot do much. The train Mr. Fuller rode on is behind everyone else's. It will take half a day to clear this mess."

"Oh."

"No, it won't." Harbin appeared. "My engine is directly in line to go off to the siding. He may take mine. I have already directed my foreman to let the passenger cars loose so I can make up for the speed." Harbin turned to Fuller. "It is yours if you want."

"I accept it," Fuller said.

"C'mon boys! Let's go shoot some Yankees!" Murchison cheered and led the way onto the baggage car. His men followed, hooting and hollering. A few even fired their guns in the air. Cain, Fuller, and Harbin looked towards each other. "Those fools will wind up shooting each before they even get out of the station," Cain said.

"That would be too bad," Harbin said.

"Fellows, we must be off again", Fuller replied as he was walking towards the cab. Harbin and Cain walked briskly to keep up. Fuller glanced at Harbin.

"Thank you", he said in a soft tone.

"Do not think about it, Bill. I am in this now, same as you. When we catch them, I will be coming in hot." They climbed into the cab and started the William R. Smith on her way.

Murphy was still in the New York cab. The crew had just finished getting her all oiled and fueled. "Well done, men," Murphy said. He looked out into the station. "Now, where are Bill and Jeff?" He was startled by the whistle from the William R. Smith, as he watched it chug away. No, he thought. He quickly looked through the dissipating crowd. Then he looked back at the William R. Smith. "Oh, goddamn sonofabitch!" He leaped out of the cab and raced after the departing train. It was still picking up speed, so he managed to grab the handrail on the rear car and pull himself up. Safely on, he entered the baggage car, only to find himself facing a car full of rowdy soldiers. They all stopped and looked at him. "Howdy," Murphy said, managing a smile.

CHAPTER 14

Wilson-Hard Labor-Working On A Difficult track bar-Everyone Needs To Be All in-A new danger-Urgent-Adairsville-The Texas-Andrews and his fancy talk-Goin north-Need to Go Faster-Smoke filled cab-Never before-Calhoun-Watts and Renard-The Catoosa-Never again-Once more-A New Energy

The raiders dug the rails, they pulled the spikes from the oak ties with their hands. As the rain came down hard, it was easy to lose their grip; hence several of the raiders sliced their palms open. Andrews had decided it would be best to tear up more tracks to prevent any chance of pursuit from any train of Kingston. So out the raiders went, and by now, they knew what they needed to do. Remove the rail, scatter the cross ties on the track, and send Jon Scott up to sever the telegraph. Wilson and Wood helped scatter the crossties on the track. While the rain picked up, they had to keep on adjusting the front brims of the hats to keep their eyes from getting wet. The wind would blow it right in their faces, forcing them to repeatedly stop to wipe the water away.

"I must say," Wood said as they laid down some crossties. "It is delightful to be out and giving it right to Johnny Reb after waiting for such a long time." He tilted his head and opened his mouth to swallow some rain.

"Cap said we must fasten our pace to get to a place named Adairsville. We are behind schedule and must go at the double-quick to catch up", Wilson said.

"Is there any treacherous movement at this Adairsville you speak of?" asked Wood.

"No. Cap said there will be a southbound train that could delay us, though."

"That must be the best part then."

"Oh, no. The best part is once we are leaving Adairsville. We will be halfway to Chattanooga to a hero's welcome. You hear that fellows?"

"Yes!"

"Hurrah!"

"The day is ours!"

Wood chuckled. "Oh, jolly good! Just remember Alf, when they take our likeness to the papers, I get mine before you because the good readers would appreciate such a 'andsomness." Wilson just scoffed. They were headed back towards the train when he saw seven raiders struggle to lift a track out of place. Hurrying along, he rolled up his sleeves and fell in, right beside Slavens. Slavens nodded at him.

From up the line, Ross called out, "Once again men, on three! One! Two! Three!" Wilson pulled as hard as he could as if pulling out the track depended solely on him. The track did not budge. Everyone slacked. Ross called out. "Once more!" Everyone pulled again. The track still would not budge.

"It is no use, Sergeant," Slavens called out. "It is too deep dug into."

"You men are not pulling hard enough," Campbell growled from up the line.

Ross said, "No. We need to remove more spikes. It's the only way. Let her down, boys." Wilson helped lower the track and then wiped the rain from his eyes. He felt overheated from all the work. Just like back on the farm, he thought. Campbell came up with the crowbar to dig out some more spikes.

Suddenly everyone stopped when they heard a distant loud noise. It was the sound of a train whistle coming from the south. The whistle sent a chill up everyone's spines.

They froze for perhaps a minute before Ross called out, "Everyone once more! We need everyone to break the track! This is our only chance!" Everyone got back in line and lifted the heavy track. Wood, Pittenger, Dorsey, and Scott got on the other side of it. "Now. PULL". Wilson dug his heels into the mud and pulled again as if it was on him to dislodge the track. He gritted his teeth and dug his heels deep into the mud. His arms burned. His jaw hurt. He felt the track start to loosen, and that was when he knew he needed to dig in more.

Wood was on the other side, pushing as hard as he could while trying not to slip in the mud. There was a metallic popping sound, and the track came free. Sending everyone to the ground. This time it was Brown who shouted "Hurry! We must be on our way!" Everyone struggled to get back up while lifting the track and pile it into the last boxcar.

As half the raiders already in the boxcar, Ross called out. "Here, everyone inside. We must get moving."

Wilson nodded to Wood and ran towards the front of the engine. Brown was halfway inside and yelling at him to hurry. Wilson felt his feet slip out from under him, so he threw his arms out to slow his fall. He landed and made a splash but was already up and running. He saw the engine had begun to move, so he pushed himself to grab the handrail and swung himself in. He barely had a moment to catch his breath before Brown yelled at him. "We need more wood for the fire Alf!" Wilson deeply exhaled and got up to his feet.

***

The General rolled into the station at Adairsville. Andrews, Brown, Knight, and Wilson saw through the rain another locomotive on the siding.

"Let her off a little, my lads, this could well be the down freight." Wilson began to engage the brakes. The General slowed on the sidetrack, right alongside the other locomotive. They could see the brass plate with its namesake: TEXAS. Once the General had stopped completely, Wilson felt he could relax and began to breathe easier. Andrews stood straight.

"Be watchful my lads, I will sort this mess out." There was a canteen in the cab, Wilson took it, and stuck it out the window to catch some pouring rain. After a few seconds, he pulled his arm back in, sat down, and took a hearty swig. His arms felt numb. It took him extra strength to lift them. He forced himself to push his hat off and wipe away at his eyes. His hands were red and raw. Knight approached him with a handful of dry bread.

"Here, Alf I found this. Eat heartily." Wilson nodded and took the bread. It was dry and bland. It tasted good to him. "Cap here needs to talk these fellows out of the way." Knight continued. "You had to make a quick go of the track. How are you faring?"

"As well as I can." They heard Andrew's boom. "I'll do no such thing! I must go now at once! The fate of the army lies on me promptly, getting through with these carloads of ammunition! General Beauregard won't last through a three-hour fight!"

Everyone went for their pistols. This could be that moment. There was an uncomfortable pause before the raiders heard an unfamiliar voice saying, "Get through, by all means, you will have to run very slow and put a flagman out at every curve or you will collide."

"Thank you. I will report favorably of you to General Beauregard." After another moment of silence, Andrews stepped back into the cab and, without saying anything, gave the signal to go. General and Texas slowly started up. The Texas had twenty boxcars, so the General had to wait before it was all clear, so it may steam its way out of the station. Leaving Adairsville, Andrews checked his watch. "We are losing precious time and momentum; we need to start pushing this engine as hard as she can." The other raiders nodded. "Alas, my lads, after that fellow making usual inquiries of our mission, he spoke of another train on our way. I made an inquiry of my own on the status of Chattanooga and the current position of our army. He responded that lines of communication are down, and the rumor is that the federal army is gaining closer to Chattanooga as we speak." That statement lifted the spirits of the raiders present. "However," Andrews said sternly. "We must not let up. We need to push harder, even with the threat of another southbound train bearing down on us. Mr. Wilson, you must summon your strength to fuel the engine so Mr. Knight and Mr. Brown can fully resume their duties."

"Yes, Cap."

Wilson stood up. That little break was what he really needed. The feeling in his arms was coming back, and he caught his breath. "I am ready."

Andrews nodded. "Good. Boys, let's see how fast she can go."

Wilson had never gone so fast in his life. The landscape looked blur. They passed by houses and fields at an incredible rate of speed. Wilson felt the woozy feeling in the pit of his stomach. He thought he was going to be sick. That was interrupted by Brown's scream of "Give her more wood, Alf!" He promptly obeyed. Throwing the wood in, the heat instantly warmed him from the cold rain, but soon he began to sweat. The smoke soon filled the cab and burned Wilson's eyes, nose, and throat. There was no escape. The whole cab started to shake slowly at first, but soon it started to shake and vibrate more, almost violently. Wilson went to get some more wood. He almost tumbled over and had to catch himself. "More wood Alf!" He staggered over and grabbed a pile of wood, and threw it all in.

Outside, the wheels were almost on fire. Andrews called out. "Keep blowing the whistle, Mr. Knight! We must let the other engine know that we are coming." Knight blew the whistle. "The only way we have a chance is to get to Calhoun before the other train departs! Let out more steam and push her harder!", Andrews bellowed. Wilson staggered over to get some more wood. In the rear boxcar, the raiders were getting tossed and turned. Trying to keep steady and not to trip over each other, or on the rail equipment they had. All in the dark.

"This is a freight train to hell!" Campbell hollered.

"If that's true", Wood said before knocking into Shadrach. "Hopefully, it'll be quick if we are to be smashed to Kingdom. Frightfully apologize to whomever that was I tumbled into."

***

Wilson poured oil onto the wood to make it ignite hotter. He happened to look up out of the front window, and he made out that the station of Calhoun came up fast. Along with the southbound train that came out of the station. He felt a hand on his shoulder and looked to see it was Brown's.

"I think you better quit that and start braking Alf."

***

The southbound train, Catoosa, was finally chugging its way out of the station. The conductor, Frank Watts, was whistling of a tune, in a cheerful mood that they were on their way. When he looked out and noticed a train hurtling right towards them, he stopped.

"Say, Joe," he said to his engineer Joe Renard. "There's a rapture bearing down on us. Full brake, and reverse. Now!"

Renard took one look and slammed the brakes.

Watts cranked the gear in full reverse. In the General Knight closed the exhaust pipe to kill fuel to the engines. Wilson worked the brakes as hard as he could.

"Alf, you take the other brake, I got this!" Brown shouted. The world was spinning. Wilson staggered out of the cab; he could feel the heat from the sparks of the cab wheels. The screech was deafening. He almost fell on the handbrake, he shook his head and started to work at it.

In the Catoosa, Watts was watching as the General kept coming. It was slowing down, but it did not look like it would stop anytime soon.

"Keep in reverse."

"That is far back as she will go!" Renard called back.

Watts stared at the oncoming train. "Everyone out now!"

***

Wilson loosened his grip; the world was starting to come into focus now. He gritted his teeth and pulled the brake as hard as he could. He closed his eyes, expecting to feel the impact of the crash and be smashed at any moment. He could have given up and accepted his fate. Instead, he loosened his grip and pulled hard one more time. He slowly opened his eyes and was surprised to see that everything had stopped.

He blinked several times. The world was still. He staggered to his feet.

He moved across the guardrail towards the boxcar entrance, and he collapsed. Andrews was up against a fuming Watts and Renard.

"What in the goddamn hell are you doing? What are your intentions coming into the station like that? Who in the hell are you anyway?", Watts screamed.

Andrews was calm. "I am on a special mission for General Beauregard."

Wilson pinched himself. He felt it. The world was still spinning. He closed his eyes and started breathing deeply. "You are alive. You are alive", he said.

Andrews was calm and steadfast. He was gradually wearing these two angry southerners down, but he knew time wasted every minute he spent trying to get them to move to the siding, and out of the way. In a stern tone: "I must press on without further delay. Pull your engine ahead and let me out."

Watts looked up at him. Then he nodded.

"Very well." Wilson opened his eyes. The world had started to settle down. He struggled to make it to his feet. Making his way back to the cab, he moved slowly.

He arrived back at the cab just as Andrews did. "My lads. They are moving aside. It will be a moment." Sure enough, the Catoosa began to pull forward and clear the exit. The raiders could only look on in amazement at that sight and their leader, who had seemed to accomplish the impossible. After the Catoosa cleared the exit. The General was free to go. Andrews and the raiders waved at everyone in the station as they went by.

Clear of Calhoun, Andrews spoke in a more excited tone than anyone heard before. "My lads, we have done it! We have traveled more than fifty miles thus far. Our trip has been hazardous, indeed, but if all goes to schedule, that was the last scheduled southbound train until Chattanooga. Nothing else should be in our path except the bridges to burn! Hurrah, my lads, Hurrah!"

Brown and Knight both cheered. Wilson sat in the corner and drank from the canteen. Brown looked over. "You lookin might peaky, Alf. You alright?"

Knight chuckled. "He is just looking forward to when he rides a train next."

Everyone in the cab laughed. Even Wilson managed to smile a little.

CHAPTER 15

Fuller-Keeping Watch Outside-Obstacles-Collision-Moving slower-The crossties In the Track-The gap in the Middle-What to do-Cain's final decision-Harbin's contribution-Fuller and Murphy On The Track-Another long walk-The Texas shows up again-Peter Bracken-AccusationThe Train That Was Backward But going forward

Murphy had made his way to the cab from the last boxcar. Cain was about to laugh but coughed instead.

"Say, Anthony, it's good to see you join us" Murphy scowled, "after you and Bill had deserted me, I had to run much quicker to catch up with you, not to mention a crowd so wild that I had to wade through to get up here." He paused, then added, "Where is Bill?"

"He is on the running board, keeping a hawk's eye on the tracks," Harbin said as he ran the throttle. As if on cue, Fuller climbed back into the cab.

"There's something on the track! Slow her down!"

"Joe! Get it!" Harbin yelled at Joe Lassiter, the freeman. Lassiter slammed at the brake, causing the train to violently slow down, and emit the ear-piercing screech. It was too late, though; the engine struck the railroad tied the raiders left on the tracks. The whole cab shook and rattled as it plowed through the ties. After a few seconds, which felt like a few moments to everyone in the cab, the shaking stopped.

Harbin called out, "Bring her to a stop, Joe, we need to inspect the damage. Is everyone well?" Everyone replied they were.

"No!" replied Fuller. "Bring her to a crawl, Wiley! We are going around a bend. You ought to be at a low speed at this rate. I will check the engine!" Fuller crawled out.

"Do not tell me how to command my train," Harbin muttered. "See Anthony, you're bringing ill-fortune on us. You should have stayed at the station." Cain chuckled.

"Hush." Fuller cried out.

"The engine looks alive and well. Keep her going but at a much slower pace." Harbin grumbled. There was silence in the cab for a few minutes, save for Cain's coughing, when Fuller broke it with

"Wiley! More ties on the track! Slow her down!"

"Joe, release the brake this instant!" William R. Smith slowed to a crawl.

"Everyone, get ready!" Harbin bellowed. Everyone braced themselves. They felt a slight bump when the front of the engine struck the ties but was over quickly as it had pushed them off the track or dragged them under the cowcatcher.

"That's all, fellows," Fuller yelled out. There was a gap in the line. William R. Smith had stopped. Fuller, Murphy, Harbin, Lassiter, and Cain were looking at the gap. It went on to a foreseeable distance. Fuller nodded. "So be it. I will proceed on foot."

Harbin smirked. "You will never catch them on foot, Bill, especially this weather as well."

"I will not quit this, Wiley. Not until I see this through. I need to get my train back."

"You are stubborn as a mule, Bill. I say good luck to you. I will do what I can to repair the tracks and give aid when I am able."

Fuller nodded and extended his hand. "Thank you, Wiley." Harbin shook it. "Send 'em to hell." Fuller turned and walked. "Anthony? Jeff? Come along."

Murphy caught up to Fuller. "Gladly. We don't want those fools coming along. When we arrive at Calhoun, perhaps we will find some better company."

Cain, on the other hand, sat quite still. He could not stomach another run; the thought alone made his legs and feet ache. His cough had gotten worse. The rain-soaked through his coat and got him a cold. The boiler in the William R. Smith called to him.

"Bill?" The tone of his voice made Fuller stop and look back. "I am played out and cannot possibly go much further. I apologize, but I am done."

Fuller nodded. "So be it, Jeff. So long." Cain watched as Fuller and Murphy disappeared in the rain.

***

With the dirt now pure mud, the pair could not really run. They clomped along, still toting their shotguns. "Say, Bill, do you suppose we'll meet a southbound locomotive before we get to Calhoun."

"I believe so. I aim to take it over just as same as Wiley's. If they refuse me, I will use my iron to convince them."

"Ha-ha. I'm sure you would." Fuller did not say anything.

"When we get to Calhoun, we should inquire if there are any soldiers heading south that could assist us", Murphy said.

"We could double back and fetch the ones we've left behind." Fuller said.

Murphy quickly replied. "That will not be necessary." They clomped along in silence for a minute before Murphy spoke again. "Bill, I need to relieve myself. I have needed to for some time now."

Fuller stopped. "Go ahead." Murphy went to the nearest tree. After waiting for a minute, Fuller went to a tree to relieve himself too.

***

Peter Bracken was the engineer of the Texas. Trim build, a mustache, and a vest covering a grey flannel shirt. He was running the Texas slowly as he knew the track would eventually come to a curve, with the rain coming down, he wanted to make sure he had time to stop. He was looking out the cab and was astonished to see two figures walking through the mud, carrying guns as if they were out hunting or for a stroll. Eventually, they stopped and waved at him. Why it was Bill Fuller and Anthony Murphy! He called out to his fireman Henry Haney, a fifteen-year-old with a mature babyface and wood-passer Alonzo Martin, to tend to the brakes. The Texas came to a stop and hissed. Fuller and Murphy approached the cab. Bracken opened the door.

"Bill? Anthony? What in tarnation are you two doing out here in this drink?"

Fuller sighed. "Have we got a story for you."

***

"Bracken: They must be caught at all the hazards." Fuller said after he finished the tale. Him and Murphy were warming themselves by the boiler. They had walked another two miles and were now inclined to sit.

"I know you are a Yankee by birth," Murphy said sternly. "If you have not the means to assist us, I can run the engine."

"We need the Texas. We need your help. Will you help us?" Fuller asked.

Bracken sat and looked at the floor. When he heard the question, he looked to Fuller and said: "Indeed, I will." He then looked at

Murphy and said, "You need not worry about me. I have my home and livelihood in Georgia. My loyalty is to Georgia and nowhere else." He then stood up. "Let us catch those vile fiends. However, since we can't go forward, we will have to pursue them in reverse."

The Texas rolled back all the way to Adairsville. Bracken was quite skilled; he maneuvered the train onto the siding and had Haney pull the coupling pin to release the remaining of the train from the main engine. Bracken said, "Gentlemen, we have plenty of fuel along with determination. However, we do not have a turntable to turn around, so we shall make this chase in reverse. Now gentlemen, unless you say otherwise, let's go catch some Yankees."

CHAPTER 16

Wilson-Looking out-Moment of peace-Dirty Work-Clean hands-
Braking procedure-Stopping again-Halfway there-Celebration-Back
to work-Andrews distress-Digging at the track-Knights Dire
Warning-Some Bad news

Wilson was sitting at his post. Looking out at the terrain, he could see everything through the rainy haze. It was getting hot in the cab, and the danger was long gone, so Wilson felt like getting some fresh air. He took his spot and surveyed the terrain. The Georgia landscape was green and emitted a mist that looked like a painting Wilson had seen as a child. The mud on his hands had now dried, the result of being too close to the fire. He took benefit of the rain, rubbed his hands together, and wiped it away. Looking at his boots, they were all covered in mud. He rubbed his feet against the side of the boxcar to scrape as much as he could. Satisfied, he looked at the sole and noticed definite signs of wear and tear. He took a deep breath. Everything felt calm. The rain was starting to slack a little bit. His moment was interrupted by Brown:

"Say, Alf! Cap wants us to see to it that some of the track is removed. Start braking."

Wilson saluted. "Yes sir!"

The General rolled to a stop. In the rear of the boxcar, the raiders could feel the jerking motion starting and braced for it. They were used to this routine by now. The train would stop, and they would pile out to do the heavy work. Since they were crowded with all the cross ties, steel tracks, they were quite eager to get out. The boxcar stopped. They rattled with the stopping motion, but once when still, Dorsey and Wood pulled the sliding door wide open, and everyone piled out. "I must say that was exhilarating!" Wood said.

"It was not for all of us. I cannot recommend it again," Pittenger said. He looked like he was about to barf.

"Well, man up then, unless you get sick, then move away," Wood replied. Pittenger sucked in some air. "I should be well enough."

"Aw, there is our glorious brakeman. Alf! What's the good word?" Wilson came walking with the crowbar.

"Fellows, I have wonderful news! We are past the halfway mark of our journey! There are no more southbound trains to be had. What follows is us firing at the bridges! We are almost finished!" That set off cheers and hugs from all the raiders.

Wood nodded. "Splendid. To think Alf, you doubted us from the very beginning." Wilson shook his head.

Their celebration was cut short by a stern yell from Andrews.

"Do not do it, lads! We have many tasks to perform and still a great distance to go further. So, hurry up and get to it!" His whole demeanor seemed changed. He wasn't pleasant nor encouraging, but angry and agitated. His top hat was gone, replaced with a short cap he had gotten from somewhere. Rather than sit back and watch his men at work, he stormed past Wilson and grabbed the crowbar as he went. The raiders watched. Stunned. Slowly they fell in and began doing work. Andrews started cursing at himself, which only made the raiders feel more at unease.

Wilson noticed Brown and Knight slowly approaching. Both looked grim.

He walked toward them. "What's the matter, Brown?"

"It's too bad you told the other men that."

"Why?"

"We should have stopped when we could get more fuel, as now we are running short on it."

CHAPTER 17

Fuller-On the cab-Calhoun ahead-Blowing the whistle-The Captain-1st Georgia-Duty-Waiting for the train-A train pulls in reverse-The green private-A card game-The Announcement-New Mission-Volunteering-Taking over

The Texas raced along the track at nearly fifty miles an hour, and in reverse. Fuller was at the front (or back) hanging from the cab, keeping an eye on the track ahead for any possible obstacles. One hand hanging from the corner of the tender, while the other raised slightly to give a signal for danger, alternately adjusting his hat and wiping the rain from his face. His hawk-like stare was fixed, viewing everything as well as he could with the rain in his eyes and the wind whipping him in the face. His vision had not betrayed him, he could see the outline of the station at Calhoun. He pulled himself back up to the top of the tender and waved his hand. Murphy's head appeared from the other side of the tender.

"What goes, Bill?"

"Calhoun! It is dead ahead! Begin braking and have Bracken blow the whistle on repeat so everyone may know we are coming in hot!"

"I will!"

Fuller lowered himself down and resumed his watch. He was ready to jump off if he were to notice another train coming. With Calhoun coming in clearer, there was no one in sight, so that made him relax a little. The train's speed started to slow, and Fuller felt the motion in his gut. He swallowed and felt his throat dry from shouting. He tipped his head back and opened his mouth to catch some rain.

***

William Whitsett sat on a bench at the Calhoun station, watching the rain. He was under a veranda, so he held his hat in his hands. He waited. He was a captain. Commander of Company B. 1st Georgia Volunteer Infantry. A dedicated soldier. An effective leader. A son of Georgia. He had grown up not far from here in the town of Ringgold.

Like most soldiers in his command, they had gone home on furlough, only for it to be cut short on account of the battle that had occurred in Tennessee. Instead of being north to reinforce the army, they were sent south to garrison duty at the port city of Mobile in Alabama. His First Lieutenant, Jim Ferrer had already taken most of the company down south yesterday, now Whitsett took ten of his troopers down south. His first sergeant James Jenkins leaned against a pole, casually smoking a cigar. The other troopers were crowded under the veranda. Boredom was their greatest foe. There was some excitement when a train came barreling down the track while one man with a beard made another engineer move his train, but that was a while ago. Whitsett sighed. When the first reports of a battle came through at someplace called Shiloh, they said it was a great victory, but now the news suggested that it was an actual defeat. Whitsett was fearful. If the army was defeated, what would stop the Yankees from coming down to Georgia? To Ringgold? His regiment should be going to meet them. Instead, they were going to Mobile. Whitsett sighed. He did not realize he let it slip so loudly. Jenkins caught it.

"What's the matter, Cap?"

"Oh, nothing."

Jenkins blew some smoke. "It may be warmer in Alabama, but it's a damn waste to send us down there. Let the Alabamians defend Mobile."

"It is our duty, Sergeant. We go where we are ordered to go to and are needed most."

Jenkins shook his head. "I cannot abide by that. They speak of the Yankee navy coming to blockade us, but no one as if yet as seen any Yankee boats on the water."

A young private, Henry Rollins, barely 18, with a uniform that was a size too big, stepped nervously forward.

"Excuse me, sir. Uh, begging the captain's permission, but what's it like in Mobile?" Rollins had just enlisted.

"It is a city on the coast. Full of Alabamians. That's all." Jenkins retorted.

"At ease, private," Whitsett said. "It's hot and humid, and a wonderful city, with sandy beaches and lovely southern belles."

Rollins nodded.

"Go sit with the rest of the men. It will not be long before our train arrives and we all can sit for a spell on the trip."

Jarret Coleman and Jesse French, two privates who had set up a makeshift card game under the veranda, called out Rollins. "Come on, youngin! We got a game going here. There is room for a young pup who has never shown his teeth!" Coleman said. French laughed

"We promise not to tell your mother you had engaged in a vice with such low company!"

Rollins cautiously made his way to the group and sat down.

"Poker is our game fellows. Let me explain the rules to our young friend here." Coleman said. Whitsett watched and smiled, then looked back to the rain. He thought he could hear a train whistle.

"Say, Cap." He looked at Jenkins.

"Yes."

"I was pondering. What do you suppose-?"

"Wait!" Whitsett's attention was caught by a train whistle. It was getting louder. The people milling about the platform had stopped and watched for something. Whitsett stood up, put his hat on, adjusted his poncho, and stepped out into the rain to get a better view. What he saw was a train. Running backward. With a man hanging on the tender yelling frantically.

***

The Texas did not come to a stop; instead, it slowed to a crawl, and Fuller yelled out his story again. "Everyone! Yankees have stolen my train and are bent on destruction!"

The replies varied.

"Yankees? In Georgia?"

"Whatever shall we do?"

"Send them to hell!"

"Where are our brave soldiers?"

"What did the young whippersnapper say, and why is he leaving with that train?"

Frank Watts, stretching his legs, shrugged at Fuller and the people who looked at him. "Well, the fellow with the big beard told such a good story that I had to let him through." Fuller looked into the crowd and saw a familiar face. "Ed Henderson! Who are you making trouble for?" Henderson was a skinny seventeen-year-old wearing a black hat that covered most of his pale face.

"Oh, not today", he replied. "I am on an errand to find out why the telegraph is not responding further south."

"It is the work of those cursed Yankees. Hop on, I shall tell you the whole of it." He leaned out as far as he could reaching his hand out.

Henderson grabbed it while Fuller pulled him up aboard.

"Is the telegraph working at Dalton?"

"The last I heard it was."

"Very good."

"Say, Bill!" Fuller pulled himself up towards the tender to see what Murphy called him for. "This here is Fleming Cox. He is an able engineer and would be of great assistance to us." Cox was tall and thin, with a black goatee. Without wasting any words, he waved. Fuller waved and nodded back. He climbed back down and was about to talk to Henderson when he heard a voice from the platform calling to him.

"Excuse me, sir? Halloo you there."

He turned to see an officer walking in step with the Texas.

"I am Captain William Whitsett. First Georgia. What is this about some Yankees stealing your train?"

"It is true! The Yankees are down here. They stole my train under the disguise of civilians and are ruining the track and telegraph lines."

Whitsett slowed. Yankees. In Georgia. It had finally happened. They were down here. This bunch could be yellow bellies bent on theft or preparing for the rest to make a ruin of his home. No matter. He would assess that later. For now, it was all on this.

"My men are at your service to apprehend them. Are you able to stop so that we may join you?"

Fuller shook his head. "It's too crowded, and I want to keep moving. Perhaps you can borrow the Catoosa over there."

Whitsett was towards the end of the platform. "I will indeed, sir."

He watched for a moment as the Texas rolled out of the station and began to pick up speed. Yankees! In this country!

He turned to his men. "Men of Company B! At attention!" Compared to Duncan Murchison's militia, the men of Company B were much better trained and disciplined. All wearing matching uniforms of grey jackets, blue trousers, a mix of caps, or slouched hats, armed with Enfield muskets. They got up and formed a line Whitsett started to walk in front of them. "Men. As you are now aware, Yankees have come down here. Down here! They have proven themselves to be cowards by thieving a train. I aim to give pursuit and let them have it fall in so we can acquire that train."

Everyone stepped forward. Rollins nervously so. "Very well."

Renard and Watts oiled the engine making sure the Catoosa was ready to go. They did not say anything as they were both embarrassed by the fact they were swindled by a Yankee. The best they could hope for was Fuller to get the train back and that no one would say anything.

Whitsett suddenly stormed aboard the cab and took charge. "I am Captain Whitsett. Under military authority, I am now taking charge of this train to give pursuit to the Yankees." Without waiting, he motioned Jenkins to bring the rest of the men. Renard could not believe this.

"Now wait a doggone moment. I have orders to bring this train south-"

"My rank supersedes your orders." His men, with their knapsacks, canteens, rifles, and cartridge boxes, tried to make room wherever they could.

Renard nearly choked. "I need written orders."

Suddenly, Whitsett had his Navy Colt revolver out and aimed at Renard's head. "This is your written order. Now, will you obey, or will I have to find my lost 'mean streak'?" If that was not enough, the metallic click of the hammer being pulled back did the job.

"No, that will do. It would help if I uncoupled the boxcars to move at a much higher speed." Renard said.

"Go to it. At the double-quick." Renard did not require another warning. He was gone.

Whitsett turned to Watts, and slowly but menacingly released the hammer. "Are you able to pilot this engine?"

"Uh. Y–yes sir."

"Well? Go then."

Watts started the engine up. Renard came back, and the engine, now single, pulled out on the main track. As the Catoosa gave chase, Whitsett looked out of the window. He could make out the Texas at a distance, this was it. Everything seemed to build up to this particular moment.

CHAPTER 18

William Whitsett-Son of Ringgold-Gone to soldier Sergeant-Down South-Helping Savanahan's-The young girl-A nasty wound-Back home-The lumber yard-Tensions rise-Georgia secedes-Neutral no more-Rejoining the militia-Captain

William Whitsett was not much far from home. For as long as he could remember, he had always made sure to note the road that would take him back to Ringgold, Georgia. He was the product of a fire and a brimstone father who would have made an excellent preacher. Instead, he spread his homemade gospel to his children and instilled in them a sense of pride and devotion in maintaining and protecting their homes.

"This place, your homestead. Ringgold, Hell, all of Georgia is worth fighting for."

Young Whitsett took it to heart. When he was not attending church or going to school, Whitsett was off with his friends. He went from being a small runt to a tall, lanky teen. He became the leader of his group and led them on excursions deep into the woods. They camped and fished. When they were big enough group, they all got shotguns from their fathers. All of them bragged about being the best hunters, but the trees were ones who really felt their misplaced aim. Eventually, the boys were able to ride horses and would go off further into the woods and into the next town to explore, even if it meant a whipping from their fathers for taking the horse farther from home then promised. Even then, Whitsitt always made sure to know of the road that would take him home. Whitsett had many ideas for the future. He enjoyed the rough lifestyle that seemed afforded to the army. He initially wanted to enlist in the U.S. cavalry to see to the frontier, but his father talked him into joining the Georgia State Militia. "Better to serve your home, a nobler cause, than be shot by some red injun for nothin,'" he told him. He enlisted in the state militia and arrived for duty at Fort Pulaski, near Savannah. It was a world apart from

Ringgold. The heat, the humidity, and the mosquitoes. It was not all bad, he tried Gulf seafood, went out in the bay, and swam the ocean. In the meantime, he lived the adventurous life of a home guardsman, that is, drill, garrison duty, drill, the parade marches for any special occasions, and then drill some more. Whitsett made the 1st sergeant of his company, and his captain, Kinloch Falconer, recommended him to become an officer. He then received the opportunity to attend classes at the Georgia Military Institute, but the school was out early this time as the word was received that storms had flooded the gulf near Savannah. Whitsitt shipped out with his unit onto the railroad. His first time on a train. They arrived at Savannah and assisted with the evacuation of people living in the outlying areas. It was Whitsett's first time this far south and was an awakening for him. The heat, the humidity, and the mosquitoes. Oh, the mosquitoes. He had heard the cries of a woman calling desperately for her daughter. Whitsett was overseeing loading refugees into covered wagons that had requisitioned from Savannah. He heard her and felt the scared tone of her voice. She was coming out of the water with others to the bank, where the home guards guided people to the wagons. He approached her.

"Oh, madam!", he said. "What's the matter?"

"My daughter Rebecca!" she cried. "She's not here! She could well be still in the water somewhere! She cannot stay afloat!

"I will find her and bring her to you!" Whitsett dropped his rifle, threw his knapsack, brushed his cap off, and dove right into the water.

The cold water hit Whitsett like a fist to the gut. It was cold, really cold. It felt thick with debris everywhere. His muscles tightened as he sucked in some air when his head broke the surface. Without a sense of direction, he leapt paddling forward. He had swum plenty of rivers and creeks, so this was easy. He came across a large enough piece of wood that could have been a piece of someone's rooftop. He used that to float as he paddled, calling the name Rebecca intermittently. He was not gone longer than ten minutes or so, but to the mother, it felt like an eternity. The last wagon had left, but she refused to move along despite the pleas of the militia. Finally, through the bog, they heard a splashing sound of a little girl on a piece of wood being pushed by a man came into view. The woman broke into tears of joy as the militia pulled Rebecca (holding a small dog) on the bank. They then helped an exhausted-looking Whitsett out of the water. The woman ran to her daughter and could not have given her a big enough hug.

"Oh, Rebecca, I thought you had gone to the Lord!!"

"I am well, mama."

"Rebecca, I do not think Rufus will be if you do not let up on him," the woman laughed, letting her daughter go just enough for her puppy to breathe. She then looked at Whitsett, who was being tended to by his companions.

"Bless you, sir," she said.

"You are welcome," he said. He coughed and tried to get up, but a sharp burst of pain sent him back to the ground. His fellow militiamen tried to help, but he waved them away. He rolled up his right pant leg, and a stream of red flowed from his ankle.

Whitsett's eyes rolled back into his head as he slumped backward. He awoke on a cot in a hospital. Everything was fuzzy until his eyes adjusted. He could hear flies buzzing angrily about. He could smell the stale air mixed with rotten meat. He was in a closed room with one window that was closed. He coughed. His mouth was as dry as cotton. His head felt lighter than air. Shifting his legs, his right foot felt heavier. He had to force his head upwards to make out a bandage that covered up everything. He gave out and let his head fall back down.

"Help," he managed to get out. "Help."

Fever had set in. He was delirious at times. His foot looked worse. The doctor's initial inclination was to amputate, but Whitsett's commander and fellow soldiers vehemently denied. The woman whose daughter he saved had a brother who did quite well shipping cotton and offered to pay for any expenses. This was a good southern man, and a hero to boot. He had to be saved, along with his foot. The doctor did all that he could. He kept him cool. Fed him broth. Cleaned and dressed his foot. His captain told him he would afford him of accommodations and a promotion to lieutenant, even when he did not expect Whitsett to survive. Finally, after three agonizing days, the fever had broken, and Whitsett made an excellent recovery. It hurt to put his boot on for a few days, but eventually that too broke. His regiment had long since departed, Whitsett bid his adieus to everyone in Savannah, including Rebecca and Rufus.

On the carriage ride towards Fort Pulaski, he did some serious thinking. When he arrived at the barracks, he reported to Captain Falconer, who was his captain. He was shocked to see him alive.

Whitsett handed him a piece of paper. It was a statement requesting a medical discharge by the doctor who had treated him for reasons of ill health. His captain demurred, stating that he was a hero, he could have been an officer, maybe make colonel someday, but Whitsett had made up his mind. He almost died, and if he were to, he would want to die in the battle for a glorious cause, not because he got ill saving a little girl. He was glad he did it, but he longed for the simple life of a civilian who could come and go as he pleased, not the monotonous life of a militiaman. Besides saving the girl, there was one more thing he could say he was proud of doing during his time in the service. After some back and forth, his captain then agreed and forwarded the letter to the commanding colonel who signed it. Back home in Ringgold, Whitsett was greeted with cheers as a hero because word of his exploits had spread, but then there was the question of why he quit? He just said poor health and left it at that, not wanting to get in a quarrel over the question of honor and cowardice. His brother was pleased to see him, but his father grumbled. He could have been the next Zachary Taylor, he told his son. Taylor was his own personal favorite after he joined Taylor's army to do war down Mexico way. Whitsett held firm. What will you do now? His father asked. Whitsett shrugged and said he will figure it out. He had saved up enough of his pay to buy a small house on the edge of Ringgold with a horse. He would receive a stipend from the state, as a courtesy of his service. He got a job at the lumber yard to supply cordwood for the Western and Atlantic Railroads. The hours were long and tiring, but the pay was good, and eventually, Whitsett got promoted to foreman. He was also able to indulge in his childhood memories of hunting, fishing, and camping in the woods. He enjoyed the single life and decided not to pursue courting of a woman until he was thirty-five or so, as he had a few years to go. That was 1859. It was now January 1861.

***

Revolution was in the air. For a long time, Whitsett had only caught a small whiff of it, but it seemed thicker after Abraham Lincoln was elected as president. A lot of anger and passion boiled over at the local town meetings. The rich slave-owners felt Lincoln and troublemaking abolitionists would come down there and end slavery, forcing their way of life on to the south. The town fathers believed the federal government was growing too powerful, especially from the Yankee states, and would not respect the constitution, which they regarded as a contract between the states and the federal government that the government had broken, and the states could leave if they felt they should. Either way, secession was the common talk of the town, especially after South Carolina seceded in December. When the Georgia assembly called for a special session, the temperature soared. Whitsett had completed his whole day's work with two of his old friends and now coworkers James Jenkins and Jim Ferrer. They were walking along to the tavern for a drink before going back home. Jenkins was in a particularly jovial mood, he was looking forward to tomorrow, which was Sunday the 20th as it was his one day off.

"My particular favorite of going about the church and listening to the sermons as if we commit sin, then repent and ask forgiveness, it shall be granted," Ferrer snickered.

"Whatever are you talking about, Jim?" Whitsett asked. He licked his lips. The dust had started to kick up as they entered the main part of the town. He noted it was starting to get hot. Perhaps in part to the growing crowd outside of the telegraph office.

"Miss Rachel Myers, that girl I'm sweet on. We have sinned plenty, but always ask for forgiveness."

"You are a damned scoundrel; you better propose marriage to that poor girl," Ferrer said.

"Otherwise, you will find yourself at the end of a double-barrel... I'll tell you this much," Whitsett added.

Jenkins replied. "I want to, I just don't believe her father, and the good reverend will appreciate me."

"He is a man of God, of course, he would." Whitsett said, then he added, "Exceptions can always be made."

The trio laughed until a boy of no more than twelve ran past them nearly missing Jenkins. He grunted, "Why in the tarnation are you in such a hurry for a boy that you can't walk?"

The boy stopped and spun around. "The assembly is about to announce their answer on the question of secession!" He turned and ran for the telegraph office.

By now, the whole town had turned out. The three men quickened their pace as well. "I have never thought such an event would ever happen," Whitsett said.

"Well, this has been plotted for quite a while now. The damned fools up north have meddled in our affairs for too long", Ferrer growled. "If the politicians do it right, we should be able to secede. It is our right to do so."

Whitsett said nothing as they went and joined the edge of the crowd. The crowd was murmuring and getting agitated as they continued to wait. A hush swept over the crowd as the telegraph operator came running towards the doorway. Waving a piece of paper, he could not contain himself as he shouted. "It's official! Georgia seceded!" A blast of euphoria smashed the crowd. Cries, cheers, and whoops fully filled the air. Men with hats threw them in the air. Anyone with a pistol fired a shot or two. Ferrer and Jenkins rejoiced.

Ferrer: "Ready to fight!"

Jenkins: "We will show that Lincoln!"

In the tavern, drinks were free that night. It was a festive atmosphere as everyone was cheerful, broke into the song 'Dixie', or stated their opinions on the current state of affairs as though they were facts. It was too rambunctious for the three, so they stood outside and drank their milk punches.

Whitsett spoke. "I never thought this would occur. I believed a peace envoy would be sent to South Carolina to calm the angry voices."

"The Yankees are responsible for this treachery, bearing this down on us for some time now. Believing they can make us like themselves. Telling us what to do and what not to do with our slaves." Jenkins said.

"Do not bring up the slaves, Jim," Whitsett retorted. "None of us have the means to own one, and I am too self-reliant anyways."

Ferrer chimed in. "If it is not a question of slavery, then it is a question of economy. My cousin works shipping cotton to Savannah for trade. Cotton is the king, more so than cordwood. We all know about it. My cousin says the northern politicians want to impose tariffs on cotton so high that no southern man could afford them. The cotton would not be able to sell. Financial ruin would spread across the south like a plague. Then the northerners would be able to impose their will on us. Getting fat off our cotton while our women and children starve to death. Now that we are free, we can set our destiny without some fat Yankee interfering and telling us what will be." Ferrer finished his mini speech with a shot of milk punch.

Whitsett nodded. "You make a fine speaker Jim. It is too bad your chosen profession was in a lumber yard." They all laughed. After a short pause, Whitsett finally asked, "I have but one question. What will happen now?"

No one quite had an answer.

Whitsett still believed the situation would calm down and that a peace delegation would be dispatched to soothe the situation. None were sent. Instead, he read in the papers that Georgia, along with

Florida, Mississippi, Alabama, Texas, Louisiana, and South Carolina shall form a new government called the Confederate States of America with its capital in Montgomery, Alabama, appointed by acclamation a man named Jefferson Davis as its president. Whitsett's loyalties were indeed towards Georgia. His foot was healed, and he found himself spouting the same secessionist rhetoric that the younger men chanted. Guns were in shorter supply, selling like hotcakes. Ammunition was almost impossible to find. Everything was sitting on a powder keg.

***

It was April when it had happened. The air was much hot and dry. A rider on horseback came racing into town on a full gallop.

"It's war! It's war!", he cried, as he raced past the milling townspeople. When he reached the center of the town, he pulled back on the reigns, so his horse had to rear back. By now, a curious crowd had gathered all around him. He coughed from the dust he stirred and caught his breath. "It is war!" he cried again. "Our forces in South Carolina have opened fire on Fort Sumter. They have driven the damned Yankees out!"

"You mean we whupped them Yankees good?"

Someone in the crowd yelled back. "Your damn right we did! They sent the Yankees straight back to hell. Now the vile Abraham Lincoln has called for seventy-five thousand volunteers to come here. He seeks to seize our lands, pillage our homes, and force us back into line at the point of the bayonet. Governor Brown has called for all able-bodied men to join the State militia. Sons of Georgia, will you answer the call to defend your own lands? Your homes? Your wives?"

All at once, the crowd, which included Whitsitt, Jenkins, and Ferrer, erupted in cheers, threw hats, and pistols fired. The rider yelled, "Let them have it!" before he spurred his horse and rode off to the next part of Ringgold. Nobody had heard him. That did it for Whitsett. Georgia was his home. The reasons for secession were no longer much relevant. The state had acted on its own, and now the President of the

United States was about to send armed troops down here and force them back in? Well, not without a fight.

Whitsett packed his haversack. He grabbed his rifle. He sent away the possessions he had and shut the door to his house tight. He did not know when he was going to get back. When he stepped outside, there was a group waiting for him, including Jenkins and Ferrer. He had announced at the tavern that he was going to rejoin his old unit. His fame had preceded him, and he had managed to enlist twenty Ringgold men to join him. Everyone else debated how short this war would be and boasting how many Yankees they would kill in that time period. He had settled his affairs at the lumberyard and joined his twenty volunteers as Ringgold held an impromptu parade for its heroic sons marching off to fight against the impending Yankee menace. The streets were lined up with old men, young boys, and young ladies who sought the courtship of these heroes. In the street, the courageous fighting men walked in a loose mob towards the train station that would take them to their new lives as soldiers. For many, this was the first trip ever outside of Ringgold. The ones who appreciated their newfound fame, walked at the edge of the group to collect the well wishes and gifts from the crowd. Like Jenkins and Ferrer, the ones in the middle of the crowd walked with a sense of determination. Like Whitsett. Ferrer fell in with Whitsett,

"When I get my uniform, I will have my likeness taken away and sent to my sweet Rachel. When she shows it to her father, he will think more favorably towards me."

Jenkins fell in with him. "To do so, you must have your likeness taken on a glass. The glass will shatter from your face, Jim." Ferrer punched Jenkins in the arm. Jenkins responded in kind. Before Ferrer could muster a stronger reply, Whitsett hushed them.

"The two of you simmer down! Act like soldiers." They stopped. Whitsett shook his head. They were going to war. This was not a game.

***

It felt like coming back home when Whitsett rejoined the 1st Georgia Infantry Battalion. There were plenty of familiar faces there. His old captain was promoted to Adjutant General of the regiment. He told Whitsett this regiment would reorganize to a new unit, the 36th Georgia Volunteers, and would need some new officers to lead it.

Falconer got Whitsett an audience with the 36th's Colonel, John B. Villepigue. He was a West Pointer who had earned his stripes chasing wild Indians on the frontier. After talking to Falconer, Villepigue then met with Whitsett and talked about Whitsett's experience. He initially thought Whitsett organized this rowdy rabble to muster a promotion, but he was quite impressed when Whitsett said he only brought them to aid the defense of his home state. Villepigue gave him the rank of sergeant and tasked him to make soldiers out of the civilians he brought.

In time, William Whitsett had been elected as Captain Whitsett by his men, commander of Company B, of the new First Georgia Infantry.

Jim Ferrer had been elected the second lieutenant and promoted to the First lieutenant. James Jenkins had to settle for corporal and then as a sergeant. When the 1st was finally on the march to battle, his mind was on the struggles that were to come.

CHAPTER 19

Wilson-Tearing the track-Slow progress-The Engine-Panic-Raiders choice-Andrews decision-The fence post-Best Hopes-Resuming the trek-Uncoupling the boxcar Fuller-Keeping calm-Worst hopes-Spotting the prize-Renewed faith-Stop to see-Checking the track-The Need To Press on The boxcar-Keep the faith-A pair of notes

After burning adrenaline, tension, and anticipation, the raiders were moving much slower than usual to tear up the track. The mud was of no help either, it sucked the raider's boots in, and caused them to slip. Campbell tried to pry the spikes from the track. Pittenger was trying to help by adding extra weight but then slipped. Campbell stopped and yanked him to his feet.

"Move away, you are of no use to me."

Pittenger backed away, embarrassed, and not sure what to do next. Right then, a loud sound pierced the air, freezing the raiders where they stood and sending a chill up their spines. It was the sound of a train whistling. Everyone was stunned. They had torn up the track. The wires were severed. No one should be coming after them. Or, at the very least, everything behind them should still be backed up. Wilson ran to get Andrews, but he was already approaching, with Knight and Brown in tow.

"Cap! There is a locomotive coming in and-"

"YI hears it, Mr. Wilson." He stopped. The raiders stopped what they were doing and crowded about their leader. Out in the distance on the rolling plain, through the mist, they saw a locomotive. Except it was running backward. But it was running fast, and it was running right at them.

"What do we Cap?"

"Let us fight them!"

"We can hide in the trees and waylay them as they come out!"

"We are ready to fight, Cap! We'll give it to them hot!"

Andrews shook his head. "My lads, we cannot delay for a shooting contest. We must be on our way. We may give them some delay, can we not?" Andrews seemed awfully calm and cool in the circumstance.

Campbell shrugged "We bent the rail somewhat. We can put a fence rail under the track to dislodge it or force them to stop and inspect it."

"See to it and make haste. We have to leave at once."

Andrews headed back towards the engine. Knight, Brown, and Wilson followed. Campbell shoved the rail under the track. The mud was soft, so it did not give much resistance. Satisfied that did the trick, he joined the others back in the boxcar.

The General went at top speed. Andrews looked out the window, and then he looked to his crew.

"Mr. Wilson, it would appear that releasing the rear boxcar would slow our pursuers down. Kindly go back and request the other lads to do so."

"Yes, cap."

Wilson climbed out the first boxcar and made his way to the rear boxcar. He had to tread lightly as his boots were caked with mud while the top was slick with water. He eventually made it to the second last boxcar, the wind hitting him hard in the face, and the top speed making it much harder to stabilize.

"Say, Marky!"

The sliding door opened, and Wood appeared. "Cap says to bring everyone up to the front car and uncouple this one."

"Very well, Alf! Tell that bloke piloting the engine to be gentle now, we all were scattered about when he took off."

Wilson eased himself in the opposite direction and made the treacherous trek back. Only now, the General climbed uphill, so he knelt and gripped the edge of the boxcar to brace himself.

Wood spoke up so everyone could hear. "Well fellows, we need to move to a more spacious confine, and let this one go to slow Johnny Reb. Who shall be the unlucky chap to pluck the pin?"

Buffum appeared. "Once more into the breach, dear brothers!"

"Oh, the one who quotes Shakespeare, very well then. Off you go."

"He will need help", said Campbell. "I will lower him down.

"I'll assist," Slavens spoke up.

"I'll go along too," Ross said.

With the only light from the open boxcar door, everyone gathered up crossties, and made their way out towards the next boxcar, crossing the handrail, and settling in the boxcar.

"Right. Gentlemen?" Buffum asked. He went outside and knelt to uncouple the pin. Campbell grabbed hold of his overall band. Slavens and Ross took hold of one ankle and lowered him down. It was not easy, the pin was wet and took Buffum quite an effort to get a grip, and even then, the pin kept fastened tightly.

"Hurry up, will you!" Campbell growled.

Buffum ignored him. He used his left hand to grip the fin of the boxcar, and his right hand to grip the pin. He pulled as hard as he could. Finally, after a few seconds, it loosened up. He let go, shook his hand, and then went at it again. He unscrewed it fully. "Lift me up!"

They pulled him up along the pin. The boxcar shook at its sudden loss. Everyone watched as the last boxcar rolled away. They all cheered and clapped Buffum on the back. That should have done it.

Fuller was anxious. He knew if the raiders severed any more track, it was over. No other engine would head down this way for some time, and Fuller knew it was pointless to pursue on foot anymore. The Texas rounded at a bend. The rain splashed in his face. With one hand, he wiped it away and adjusted his hat. Blinking, he saw a locomotive at a distance and – wait for a locomotive? He rubbed his eyes and looked again. There she was! His locomotive! He would have recognized that beautiful red and black like it was his own children. His heart leaped as his eyes glittered. He lifted himself up.

"Hello? Murphy?"

Murphy poked his head into view.

"There she is! The General! Dead ahead!" Murphy let out a southern whoop and told the other crew members. Fuller set himself down. His eyes turned cold when he saw the raiders. It looked like they were scattering.

As a conductor, he was quite skilled at making a quick headcount and get their number at around twenty. He watched his locomotive started to move and pick up speed. Thinking quickly, he propped himself up again.

"Say, Murphy. Have Bracken slow us down to a crawl. I need to inspect the track now."

The Texas slowed to crawl. When they approached the approximate spot where the General was, Fuller made a mad dash ahead to inspect the track. 'Please', he thought. 'I don't have it in me for another run.' There were some spikes removed, but overall it looks serviceable. He kicked the track, then put his foot on it to apply pressure. It held. The Texas was approaching. He had to decide if it was safe. It was worth the risk. He hopped back onto the boxcar and waved the Texas forward. There was a slight bump, but the Texas continued on. It started to pick some speed until they rounded a curve and saw a boxcar. Just sitting on the track. Fuller climbed on top of his boxcar immediately.

"STOP! Boxcar on the track!"

He flattened himself on the roof and braced for an impact, feeling a whoosh feeling as the boxcar slowed dramatically. The impact did not come. When he felt the Texas slowed to a crawl, he climbed down, slid open the door of the boxcar so he could retrieve his shotgun. Holding it ready, he ran out to inspect the boxcar. He was alert just in case this was to be an ambush. He crept cautiously to the siding door, and with one quick motion, threw it open while he held his shotgun ready. Empty. Save for a few rail ties. Murphy then came running up with his shotgun, followed by Cox wielding a fire poker.

"What is it, Bill?"

Fuller turned to him. "They are trying to slow us down. I counted twenty".

"Twenty?"

"Yes. The regular soldiers will eventually be along. Until then, we continue to chase. Come, we can just push this along until we come to the next siding." He led them back to the cab. It was quite occupied.

"Bracken. How are we on fuel?"

"We can run all day at half speed."

"We are going to run at full speed. We are quite close to them. So, start it up and push that car along."

"Yes sir!"

Bracken released the valve. There was a jolt in the engine starting so suddenly, and a loud bump and tremor from connecting to the boxcar. Fuller sighed. His engine was close. He could not give up now. Even if the odds were against him in a gun battle. He set his shotgun down and reached in his coat pocket. He found a pencil and paper that was relatively dry. He then grabbed two sheets and pressed them against the wall, writing furiously as the train bounced and rattled. Finished and satisfied, no one looked; he turned to Henderson, who braced himself against the wall. He looked like he was trying to fight back against the urge to throw up.

"Ed," Fuller said softly. "I have two great favors to ask you. First, when we get to the next telegraph office. I need you to mail this." He handed Henderson a sheet. "Also. It is true we are not quite well acquainted, yet I will still ask this of you. If I should fall today, deliver this note to my wife. I have written my address on the front side of it. I know it is a great favor to ask. It is something that I need to take care of. Will you do this for me?"

"Oh, of course, Bill." He reached out and took the sheet of paper.

Fuller nodded and spoke to the others. "Very well, fellows. Keep at your post, and I shall resume mine." At the top of the new boxcar, Fuller paid no attention to the wind and the rain in his face. They were closing in on the General. He was going to get it back.

CHAPTER 20

Wilson-Andrews decision-His plan-Whatever it takes to Delaying
the other train-Target practice Fuller-DelayClearing the mess-
Martin's help-Running up and down-Off again Wilson-Request
again-Denied-Knight and Brown-The bridge-Only choice and way

Wilson climbed down to the cab. The atmosphere wasn't good. Andrews began to show signs of worry. So did Knight and Brown.

"Cap, the men, they request permission to take a stand and fight it out. They wanted to know what you propose to do." Andrews was silent. He stared at the floor. Knight looked back and forth at Andrews and his valve. He let it open a bit more to increase speed. "Cap. Alf is talking to you."

Andrews looked up. "Try to delay them in any way you may, Mr. Wilson. We have seen many soldiers today and do not know their number on that train."

Knight turned to him. "Throw out things on the track. That should get them to snap to stop." Wilson nodded. Andrews sighed.

"If we can make it to the Oostanaula Bridge and then burn it, we may have a chance yet."

Wilson arrived at the raider's boxcar. The side door was open, so the light shone in. Everyone gathered around him.

"What did the cap say?"

"Are we going to fight?"

"Are we not going to stop?"

"No. Cap says we ought to throw anything we have on the track to try and slow them down. That is all."

Everyone groaned. They were eager to end it with a gunfight, not running away, throwing things out the backdoor. There were not many cross ties left. Wilson grabbed one and headed out the door. Stepping outside, they were rounding at a curve. Just as they cleared it, there appeared on the other side of the curve. The yellow boxcar was coming right at him. A raw beast made from wood, running on steel, the hissing of steam. He froze, unsure of what to do next.

"Throw it, Alf!" He looked to see Wood was right in his face. "Throw it, damn you!", which shook him out of it. He leaned back and heaved the crosstie as hard as he could.

The General was moving quite fast now. The crosstie flew through the air, bounced off the ground, and hit the other boxcar. Wood threw his crosstie, which bounced off the track and hit the wheel.

"If you plan to just stand there, move out of the way!" Wood yelled, then to the other raiders, "We need more!"

Wilson stepped aside. Dorsey and Ross stepped out to throw more crossties. Wilson squinted; he thought he saw a man's head on the other side of the boxcar. He wished he had his rifle. He could make that shot. No problem. Could he do it with a revolver? He reached inside his coat for it. As if the man read his mind, he quickly disappeared.

"We are out of crossties," Dorsey said. "No matter. Look, they are easing back."

Wilson pointed at the train, which was now slowing down. "We can use the wood from their 'ere boxcar." Wood said. "I don't like Johnny Reb so close to me." Wilson nodded. Everyone went back inside. "Hack away at the car so we can use it." Wood said.

"Gladly," Campbell said. He started punching the wall with fury. Ross decided to go a bit easier, he grabbed the crowbar, and as a lumberjack, started to chop the wall. Campbell punched fist-sized holes in his wall but backed away as his knuckles were bleeding. A group of raiders piled in to start tearing pieces away. Once they had a piece, they would toss it on to the track. Wilson and Wood each tossed one. They were rounding another curve, and the other train had disappeared from sight. "How long do you suppose that would keep them away?" Wilson asked.

Wood scoffed. "Not long."

***

Fuller had to scurry down and get in the cab. "Bracken. Slow her down. The Yankees are crowding the track with crossties!" Haney worked the brakes, Bracken closed the valve, and Murphy reversed the lever. Cox and Martin stopped stoking the firebox. Henderson, who was safe in the corner, looked like he held on for dear life. When the Texas slowed to a crawl, Fuller looked over his new crew and picked one out. "Martin! Come on with me. I need your help." Martin nodded. They hopped out of the cab and made a beeline for the track. Working quickly, they grabbed the crossties and threw them off the track.

"You are doing quite well, Martin."

"Thank you, sir. Do you believe there will be a fight?"

"Yes. Keep your head down when it begins, less you have spare arms onboard, and want to join."

"I do not reckon we have any."

"Very well. Some of our soldiers should get by directly. Until then, I will fight them no matter the numbers. That looks about clear, yes?"

"Yes seh."

"Back onboard then."

Once they got back on, Fuller checked the map. "There is a siding up ahead past the bridge Bracken. We can leave the spare boxcar and a marker."

Bracken replied, "Very well, Bill." The Texas started again, only to be slowed down by more crossties.

***

Wilson staggered his way back in the cab. He was carrying some spare wood from the boxcar. The mood was rather grim. Andrews leaned in the corner, going over his schedule. He did not look much cheerful. Brown and Knight looked grim as well. Wilson's spirit sank. He could see through the front, a bridge was coming and coming fast. Wilson exclaimed. "There's the bridge! Can we slow down and fire it when we reach the other side?"

Brown scowled at Wilson. "Hush Alf and get that wood into the firebox." Wilson dashed towards the firebox and started breaking up the wood into small pieces. The engine gave a slight bounce when it hit the bridge. Wilson began to feed the firebox. He looked out and saw the swollen river. Knight opened the valve as the engine picked up speed. They hit the other side.

Knight spoke up. "I don't suppose it would not do well to fire the bridge, Alf. It is still raining, and the wood would be quite wet."

Wilson nodded and looked at Andrews. "Cap, the men still request to take a stand and fight it out."

Andrews looked over at him. "Their numbers may be greater than ours. Any attempt to make a stand would result in a massacre. No, Mr. Wilson, right now, our course is to try to arrive at Chattanooga. Please,

116

go back and tell the men that when we arrive at a refueling station named Tilton, I would need everyone to carry fuel for the engine."

"Yes, Cap."

***

After crossing the Oostnaula Bridge, the Texas had reached the siding, Bracken nudged the lever as the Texas eased the last boxcar onto it. Fuller released the coupling pin from the second last boxcar, then had the brakes hit. They went into reverse and nudged another lever, went forward, and was now one boxcar less.

Fuller was impressed. "That was some fine piloting Bracken." He poked his head out to see the track. "It's all clear for some distance. Release the valve!"

The Texas hissed to life and soon moved at a breathtaking speed. Bracken turned white; he had never gone this fast ever before. Murphy was calm. Used to this by now. Cox worked up a sweat, shedding his top clothes to his undershirt, and eventually shedding that too. Haney was readying his arms for when the next cry of 'BRAKE' came. Henderson was crouched in the corner, convinced that death could come at any moment. Fuller climbed back on top of the last boxcar and sat himself down with his legs hanging over the ledge, shotgun in lap. The speed, wind, and rain did not bother him as much. He could see through the rain, his train way off into the distance, His prey was before him, and he could smell blood.

CHAPTER 21

Wilson-Doing the hard work-Running back in treacherous conditions-Near fall-The Scene-Refusal-The New train Fuller-Dream-Closer now-Brackens reply-The new plan-Looking out-Wilson-Campbell-The obstruction Slowed down-Temporary victory-Raiders goal

Wilson was breaking the pieces of wood from the boxcar down and was throwing them into the firebox as fast as he could. Knight had the valve open as far as it could go. Wilson looked out the front window and, in a blur, he saw a rail station.

"Alf!" He looked to see Brown shouting at him. "You are low on fuel! Go back and get some more!" Wilson saluted and scurried out the cab. Crossing between boxcars, Wilson got the rhythm down of going easily and gripped the handrail to cross, but he ran so quickly that his feet slipped out from under him. His hands flew as he grabbed the handrail, catching himself. He pulled himself up, everything looked a bit blur. He entered the boxcar. The sliding door was wide open to allow light in. Half the raiders were working in shifts: kicking, punching, or using whatever means necessary to break pieces off the boxcar. Five raiders were acting as couriers and rushing pieces to the end to throw out by the remaining raiders. Wilson went to the pile and started to grab some pieces.

"Ey! What th' 'ell do you think you are doing?"

"We need fuel for the firebox Marky!"

"Come on out 'ere and see what we are doing before you leave!" Wilson sighed and walked out. What he saw was the other locomotive. Like a scene of a nightmare, the locomotive appeared as a mammoth apparition that came bearing down on them and seemed to stop just a few feet away.

***

Fuller saw his engine up close. He had a vision of dramatically leaping across the chasm between the two locomotives, landing safely, and single-handedly defeating the raiders taking back control of his engine. No. He could not drift. He climbed down out of sight. He was sure they were armed and could not take a chance of getting shot. Not now. Not when he was so close. He knew the Texas was well equipped with fuel. He was embarrassed to admit that it would outlast his little engine, but he will count on it. When they ran out of fuel, he was to strike. Fuller was a patient man. He could wait. They just had to keep the pressure on. Fuller went back to the cab.

It was an inferno. Everyone had taken off the top layer of their coats and vests and worked twice as hard to keep the engine at its speed save for Henderson, who crouched in the corner praying.

"Say, what town was that we blew through?" Fuller asked. Murphy and Bracken looked over, distracted.

"Say again?!"

"I say, what was the town past yonder we had blown through?"

"Resaca!"

Resaca. Fuller did some mental figuring. Tilton was ahead. If the raiders knew of it being a refueling station, they could use it to their advantage. No, he couldn't underestimate Yankee smarts. If they had made it this far, he assumed they knew what Tilton was.

"Do not let up on 'em boys!" Bracken looked back. Looking furious. "Bill! We are going to hit the downgrade. There are sharp curves and corners up ahead!"

"Just keep the firebox hot and the valve open!" He stepped outside and was hit with the welcome relief of cool, wet air. He peeked around the corner to see and saw the raiders going inside. He wiped away the rain, some were coming back, and holding something. It looked like a rear door.

Campbell had torn pieces off his shirt and bandaged his hands. With the crowbar, he, along with Ross and Slavens and Wilson, had pried the door off of its hinges. He dropped the crowbar, slanted the door at an angle to move out.

***

Fuller ran inside the cab. "BRAKE!" Having just been told to go on faster, everyone scrambled to reverse and stop the train. "At the very least, slow her down!" Everyone on the Texas felt a violent bump and heard a violent screech. Bracken closed the valve tight.

"What was that?"

"A door. May we press on?"

"We will need to remove it from the track first, Bill!"

"DAMN IT! Just keep it moving! Martin, get off your ass and come with me!"

Martin, who was quite dehydrated and overheated, moved as quickly as he could. The door had stuck under the wheel. Fuller held onto a handrail and kicked it until it was loose enough. All the while, the train was in motion. "Help me." He crouched down and started pulling on it. Martin got down and started to pull too. After a minute, it finally gave way, almost sending Fuller and Martin backward.

Fuller growled, "Back onboard, Martin!"

***

That sent some muted cheers between the raiders. Campbell received some backslaps and congratulations.

Wilson coughed and spoke. "I suppose I can take some fuel to the firebox now?"

"Very well, Alf. Off you go."

Wilson scooped up as much as he could and went back to the cab, careful this time when he crossed between the cars.

"What caused you to be gone for so long Alf?" Brown growled. Wilson told them what had happened. "Oh. I apologize. You are doing a man's job."

Knight looked back. "We are hitting tight bends and going on a downgrade. It worked out well that we are slowing down some."

Andrews: "Mr. Wilson, how are the other lads faring up?"

"They are well."

"Thank you. I have another errand for you. After you fuel the firebox, I need you to return to the boxcar and get the lads ready themselves. We will be stopping briefly to refuel at a station named Tilton."

CHAPTER 22

Wilson-Refuel at Tilton-Getting All the Water and wood-No time To Spare-Enemy Right Behind Fuller-Bracken's lament-Murphy's plan-Fuller relents-His plan Wilson-Approaching Dalton-Bad news-The switches-Andrews leaves-A wild turn Fuller-Dropping off-Leaving Dalton-John Scott-Ed Henderson-A race

The General raced for seven miles to the refuel station at Tilton, before it skidded to a stop. On cue, the doors of the boxcar opened, and the raiders poured out. Wilson led the raiders towards the tank. He grabbed a bucket and flipped the tap open and filled up the bucket while his squad formed a line right behind him. When it was filled, he passed the bucket down, and it moved down the line, some water splashed over until it reached the engine and Brown. Wilson started to look for another bucket when he heard the thunder of another train. He looked out; they had rounded a bend that was covered by trees. On the other side of the trees, he saw a cloud of black smoke. He was going to get some more water, but he knew they needed wood more.

"Forget the water! Get as much wood as you could carry!"

Wilson broke into a run to the woodpile, while everyone followed him. He grabbed two pieces and cradled them in his arms as he ran the best he could on a muddy surface.

***

Andrews could see black smoke coming around the bend. He sighed.

"Mr. Brown, how is the engine faring?"

"That water did the trick, we could use some more, and it looks like the fellows are going for the wood." He motioned to Wilson and Bensinger as the first to come up. Andrews looked at them as they climbed in to fill the tender.

"Lads that will do. Mr. Wilson, I want you here to assist." To Bensinger, he said. "You can return to the boxcar." Bensinger nodded and ran off.

Andrews said, "Mr. Knight, please prepare the engine for departure."

He stepped to the edge of the cab door and called out the raiders running up. "Lads, be swift when leaving the wood, we would be leaving immediately!" The tender was perhaps two-thirds full when the last raider, Pittenger, came running up. The Texas was coming up around a bend.

"Sorry, cap! I-" Pittenger started.

"Get out, you damned fool!" Brown barked.

"Mr. Knight. We may go now." Andrews said, his voice noticeably rising.

"Release the brake, Alf!" Knight yelled. Wilson did so. Knight released the valve and put the gear full forward. Just as the General left, the station master was leaving the outhouse, wondering what all the commotion he heard was about.

***

Behind them, the Texas was on the straight track forward now. Fuller stood on the boxcar, brake wheel in hand. He could see his engine at a distance leaving Tilton. It looked as if it was just departing. Confirming his theory, they knew what Tilton was and gathered some more fuel. He stomped his foot.

"Damn it!"

Climbing back down, Fuller went towards the cab. "Bracken, they have refueled! We need to pursue!" Bracken coughed and turned towards Fuller.

"My men are nearly spent! I will not force them to make another sudden stop like this again. We have more than enough wood and water to pursue them all day long. I doubt they had sufficient time to gather enough materials to keep ongoing."

Playing peacemaker, Murphy stepped in. "We can keep pace with them. Keep the pressure on them as much as possible. Their fuel would expire, and then we will have them."

Fuller nodded. He softened up. "You men are performing admirably. I admit that I am pushing you hard. When this is over, I will buy you all a decent meal in Atlanta."

"Only the costliest will do for me!", shouted Cox, which gave everyone a much-needed laugh. Fuller noticed Henderson still crouching in the corner looking almost dead.

"How are you, Henderson?"

"Tolerable."

"You are doing well." Fuller caught himself in mid-thought. "Say, Bracken, how much longer for Dalton?"

"I would say nigh on nine miles." Fuller then thought again. "How would you like to go off and return to your station?"

Henderson perked up. "I would enjoy that very much."

"Do you still have the message I gave you?"

"Yes seh."

"Very good then. Provided the telegraph line has not been severed. I have one more chore for you."

***

"My lads, we need to reduce speed as we approach Dalton. There are plenty of switches on the way, and I need to make sure we have the right ones set, les we go onto another path. I." His voice trailed off. "There is a real chance that the depot will be a crowded affair, and we will have to be waiting again." Wilson's heart sank. He was trying to give himself some hope, but with the supply of wood running out again, and the fact they would have to wait again. This time with an enemy hot on their heels.

The General stopped short of the depot. The tracks ran under the maintenance shed, and past a turntable right before going to the left. At that moment, it was all clear. Once it had stopped fully, Andrews bounded out of the engine and up towards the switch. Everyone else stood and watched.

"Do you believe he can accomplish this?", Brown asked.

"He has spoken well so far and gotten us out of plenty of snaps. I believe he will do so again." Knight replied.

"Come on," Wilson whispered. Instead of spinning his story to the station master or switch operator, Andrews ran up towards the switch.

Looking it over to make sure the correct track was set, and shouting "I am running this train through Corinth and have no time to spare." to anyone who may hear over the hiss of the engine. Satisfied, he then bounced back to the engine. "Very well, lads. We are all set to go. Let the steam be hot!" Wilson released the brakes, and Knight released the valve. The General regained its speed and rushed through the maintenance shed and sped past the platform. Watching on the platform, many passengers stared in amazement as this single engine, with a tender, lone boxcar sped past. One gentleman remarked, "If the superintendent could only see one of his men running a train like this.

He would discharge him. In fact, I shall take it upon myself to inform him of this. Did anyone see the number on that engine?"

The General was leaving the station at a breathtaking speed. Wilson held onto a handgrip, keeping an eye ahead, but ready to jump onto the brake. The track stretched ahead. Then stopped. Wilson blinked. There was no track! He was about to say something when Knight shouted: "Hold on!"

Wilson closed his eyes and squeezed the handgrip as tight as he could with both arms. The engine jerked violently towards the left. Wilson nearly felt himself get thrown away, but his arms were yanked rather harshly. The screeching of the wheels was particularly loud. He could feel that the engine still moved and not tumbling over. He slowly then opened his eyes. They were still on the track. Knight's whoop snapped him out of his stare. "The track went to the left! I did not see it! Cap, you are a rotten scoundrel for not telling me such!"

"You did not ask me if the track went any other way or not, Mr. Knight, so I did not say." That broke the mood. Everyone burst out in laughter. The Texas was a little under two miles behind when it rolled in the station, for everyone who was waiting had thought the earlier train was a bizarre sight and had to second guess themselves when they saw a train with a boxcar in front pulling into the station. The General was clear of the station when it came to a stop. Wilson went into the boxcar. By now, it was a mess with the front, rear, and sides all torn up. Everyone watched Wilson as he entered.

"I say Alf, a little warning next time? We all 'ad a bit of a tumble."

"John Scott! Cap wants you to go to work on the telegraph." Wilson ignored Wood.

"Are we all to work?" Pittenger asked.

"No. Just John Scott. And for everyone who was tossed around, I am sorry, except for Marky, I could not care less."

***

The Texas rolled to a crawl. Inside the cab, Fuller nodded to Henderson's jacket. "You do have my note Henderson?"

"Yes, seh."

"Jolly good. You may leave this train. Deliver the message to Chattanooga, and anywhere else. The line might be open."

"Yes, seh." Out of habit, Henderson saluted. The Texas had slowed down enough for Henderson to jump off it. After collecting himself, he tried to run, but his legs felt of jelly now, so he staggered to the station's telegraph, trying his best not to slip and ignored the crowd.

"What in tarnation is going on?"

"Why is that train running like that?"

"When is the next train approaching?"

Henderson nearly slipped but gathered himself quickly and kept going.

***

John Scott ran into the rain and started to climb the nearest pole. The wood was slick. He had quite a hard time getting a good grip. He slid back down. Sighed, then rolled his sleeves up over his hands, and jumped up. This time he caught a decent grip and started to climb.

***

Henderson ran into the telegraph office. The desk where the telegraph sat was empty, so Henderson made a beeline for it. In front of it, he stopped and took the note out. He had to go over it again to revise what to transmit.

***

John Scott felt tired. The anxiety, stress, and adrenaline had taken a toll on him. This and the fact he was hungry and thirsty. It took longer for him to climb up. He reached the top and pulled the hammer from the seam of his pants, hitting the insulating box.

***

Henderson figured the Morse code of the message and began to transmit. He started tapping as fast as he could.

***

John Scott paused, sighed, and started to take heavier swings at the box. His arms were heavy. Henderson finished transmitting. John Scott took one last swing, and the insulating box knocked off.

CHAPTER 23

Whitsett-On the Catoosa-Planning-What to expect-First Orders-Loading the muskets-Renard's thanks-Richard Bearden-Making Fun-Encouraging words Fuller-Open country-The Texas riding past-Tunnel Hill-Mystery-Possible Yankee trick-Entering-Murphy's Idea-Watchful eye-Spotted-Full pursuit now

Whitsett was staring out of the window. He could see the Texas through the rain. Because Catoosa was at a fair distance behind the Texas, it had much time to stop if need be. Which it had, many times now, when the Texas screeched to a halt, everyone was on a hair-trigger to get out and give chase, while only Whitsett and Ferrer had to stop them. But Whitsett wasn't sure of how many Yankees were there, and how they would have reacted. Would they flee into the woods? Or stand and fight? Where would they go? He decided the best way to decide was when the Texas stopped, and he could see their crew get out. He saw their conductor who appeared to be ready to fight a whole regiment just to get his train back.

Just like when he was a kid leading his friends in the woods of Ringgold, the time to take charge was now.

"Attention!"

Everyone had to maneuver into a tight space to face him. "When the locomotive in front of us stops, and the crew empties, that is when we will depart and pursue. Now, they are under the guise of civilians as a Yankee lie. Do not be fooled, they will most likely have arms of some sort and will battle if cornered. Just like we drilled, form a skirmish line and fan out to the trees."

Ferrer nodded. "Just like hunting them rabbits."

Whitsett looked at him, then to his men. "Load your muskets men, keep them at half-cock. I do not want any accidental discharge here." In the tight space, everyone had to squeeze their arms into their cartridge boxes to grab a wrapped cartridge.

Almost in unison, they packed the powder and bullet down the barrels, with their ramrods. Whitsett checked of his revolver to make sure it was loaded, and then he squeezed his way into Renard. Renard was still agitated at getting ordered about on his own train, not counting the fact he had never been threatened before, much less had a gun in his face.

"Just keep pace with the engine in front. Be prepared to stop when they do."

"Yes, Cap."

Whitsett could see his annoyance. "When all this is over, I will write to my commander and to the president of your railroad line, and it will be in favorable terms for you, requesting you get special accommodations for your actions today." That softened Renard up.

"Thank you."

Henry Rollins's hands shook when he packed the powder down. When he angled his rifle so he would put a cap on the call, he could not hold the rifle straight. Another soldier, Richard Bearden, looked over at him and smiled. He was going to have some fun,

"Say, fellas. Lookey here. This one can't keep his hand steady. Perhaps' it was a might early to bring him in from the drummer troop." His statement drew some chuckles.

"T'aint true! He makes it, so his money is easy to take at cards!" called out French.

"Eyes front, everyone!" Ferrer called out. Whitsett maneuvered his way to where Bearden and Rollins were. He gave Bearden an icy stare. "Keep to yourself private."

"Yes, seh." Whitsett looked at Rollins. "Be still." Rollins, embarrassed, stopped what he did. "Be still and breathe even," Whitsett said.

Rollins took a few breaths. The shaking stopped. "There. Now try again." He put the cap on. Whitsett looked over the rifle. "Half-cock private."

"Yes, cap'n."

"You have hunted before? Rabbits? Birds?"

"Yes, cap'n."

"This fight will be just like that. Take aim, shoot, and reload as fast as you can. Keep your breath even. You will be fine."

"Appreciate it cap'n." Whitsett gave a slight nod and made his way to the front of the engine to keep watch.

***

The Texas was in an open country now. It raced across the Mill Creek Bridge, went by Buzzards Roost Gap. They were approaching Tunnel Hill now, amongst the hills and ridges that dotted the landscape, engineers, with the use of their slave labor, had constructed a tunnel through one of the hills for the Western and Atlantic Railroad to go through.

Fuller climbed down in the cab, where Murphy met him. "Tunnel Hill is up the track yonder, Anthony. Perhaps we ought to slow down. It will be a nervous matter to enter until the Yankees leave. We have come too far to be delayed by any more Yankee tricks they may still have."

Murphy nodded. "I certainly agree. Here is where it gets good. I have noticed the thieves speed has reduced since departing from Dalton. If we may see black smoke, they have plenty of wood and water to spare. If it is clear, and they are short, and then by God, we have 'em!"

Fuller smiled. Probably for the first time all day. "Hot damn, Anthony."

Murphy went into the cab. "Reduce speed, boys! Cox let her off." The Texas slowly approached a tunnel. Fuller leaned against the entrance of the cab, shotgun close at hand. He could hear his engine rolling from the echo from the tunnel. It was going. That meant it did not stop to let the Yankees off to set up an ambush.

Fuller aimed his shotgun towards the dark tunnel. Cocking one hammer, he had a hawk staring at anything up ahead. The Texas entered the tunnel. It was pitch black. Fuller was ready to shoot at the first thing that moved its place. His finger itched at the trigger. "Say!" Murphy popped up.

Fuller was ready to at least club him. "Have you seen the track?" Fuller scanned the track; up ahead, he was able to see the light reflected from the track. The track was clear. "Look yonder at the other end." Through the other end's space of light, Fuller could see as his engine chugged away. There was no black smoke. Fuller and Murphy backslapped each other. "All clear! Let 'em have it!"

Bracken laughed.

"Boys, we've got 'em now!"

CHAPTER 24

Desperation-Anything for fuel-Last effort-Wilson's trek-
Make a fire-The Embers-Black smoke-Everyone out- That's it-
Council of war-Final decision-Andrews final order-Ringgold-Enemy
close behind- Wilson's plan-The General JUMP OFF!

The water tank was almost empty. There wasn't any oil in the cans. Everyone in the General's cab were exhausted. Wilson saw that there was only a tiny amount of oil in the can he held. He decided to stuff the whole thing into the firebox. Then he threw in the other one as well. He shut the firebox just as a plume of foul-smelling black smoke blew out.

"Mr. Wilson."

He turned to see Andrews staring back at him. His eyes were cold. "Please. Return to the boxcar and see about setting it afire to throw off the rebels."

"Yes, cap'n." Wilson grabbed the shovel immediately and used it to open the firebox. Releasing more foul smoke and scooped out some burning embers as he gingerly made his way out of the cab. As he crossed the tender, he happened to turn and see Andrews throw in his hat and saddlebags into the firebox. Wilson moved slowly. Partly because of his shovel, but it was refreshing to get outside and away from the smell. With the rain still coming on strong, his fiery embers had mostly extinguished by the time he had reached to the boxcar. He knew it was pointless to get more of it, so he decided to make do with what he had.

"Fellows. Our situation is looking more and more unpleasant at the moment. Cap wants us to fire this boxcar and set it a loose. That may be our last move to make", said Wilson, as he dumped the shovel's contents on the ground. "I need more kindling!" Everyone sprang into action, trying to find any scrap of wood they could. Wilson was pawing his embers by his boot, and crouched down, blowing on it, trying to get a flame going on. It was quite wet, and all he really was just blowing more of that smoke.

Everyone started to trickle around with what they had.

"T'was all I found."

"There's no more kindling to be had."

"I hope this suits you." The most Wilson had managed was a pile of scraps. He kept blowing and was joined by Dorsey, Bensinger, and Wollam. Buffum, Campbell, and Shadrach nudged the embers but were too wet. The smoke had filtered around the boxcar, and everyone had started to cough, some more severe than others. "The hell with this. I am going outside!", Campbell bellowed. Everyone then followed. The tender had more than enough room. All sixteen piled on. Wilson made his way past everyone to get to the cab. "Alf." He turned to look at Wood. Then he shook his head. Wood dropped his head. Wilson sighed. He hated to deliver bad news. Whether it was to his father that a crop had failed, or the livestock died, he hated doing it, but he still did it. "Fellows that would have been our last play. Our chances do not bode well now."

He went back to the cab. On his way, he noticed they were not going much fast.

***

"My lads, I have failed you. I was set on driving this engine to Chattanooga in glory as a rapid end to this war. Now, I have stranded us in enemy territory. Our dangers have only just begun." The mood was somber. This was it. Knight, half-closed of the main valve. "I may have stolen a few more minutes, but this locomotive will succumb for more of fuel."

"Thank you, Mr. Knight," Andrews said. "Mr. Wilson? How do the men fare up?"

"They are spent, Cap. This chase has tried them much, and they are in no mood for a fight."

"No," Andrews said. "To take a stand, with the enemy approaching fast, would only invite of a massacre of the whole affair. No, my lads, it would not be to get murdered in Georgia. I propose we break off and separate into the woods. Each man takes his own chance of trying to reach our lines."

Everyone nodded. They hated it, but it was the only choice they had. "Scatter in small parties and escape the best way you may," Andrews said to the raiders in the tender. "There are twenty-one miles between Chattanooga and us. God willing, General Mitchell has seized it, and there will be some friendly troops to receive us. Less you decide to try the longer and more hazardous westward route to Huntsville. Now, my lads, I can only say good luck and good-bye."

Knight stepped forward. "Brown and I will try to keep the engine running as long as we are allowed after we will set it in full reverse to try to smash the rebs' engine." Andrews nodded.

"Say, what town are we passing through?" Pittenger asked.

"The town of Ringgold," Andrews replied.

Wilson tuned everything out. He peaked right around the side of the tender. The rebel train followed close behind. Like a hunter who stalked wounded prey. He didn't like to take any chances. His father instilled in him the confidence to never gamble, never get involved with any sort of games that promoted chance, and to always stick with things that are known. With that, he decided to try for Huntsville. There was no way of knowing if Mitchell had taken Chattanooga, and he did not want to take a chance if he did or didn't. It didn't matter that this meant another long trek through the heavy rain. It meant he would be alone in a hostile country, surrounded by people who want him dead. No doubt, news of this escapade would spread, and the raiders were to be hunted. The General rounded towards a steep bend. Wilson looked to the town. It was disappearing. His view engulfed by the trees. Ahead he saw a steep hill and beyond that an imposing ridgeline. The

General began to climb the hill. Wilson looked to the west. It looked flatter. Easier. The General was coughing its last of chuffs. Wilson studied it. There were plenty of trees in the way, after an open area, but then it turned to a slight incline. That's where he would go. General coughed and slowly expired. Andrews shouted out his last order.

"Jump off and scatter! Every man for himself!"

CHAPTER 25

Fuller-Victory! -Fuller Goes-Empty train-Into the woods-Murphy's
orders Whitsett-Time to fight-Everyone out-Skirmish Line-Up the
ridge-Shot fired Fuller-Full Run-Up and down-Seeing his prey
Alerting the locals-Nelly Whitsett-Doc Patterson-No glory-The
prisoners-His Orders-Travelling

Fuller could not contain himself. He went down to the cab as fast as he could.

"They are running! The Yankees have finally run out of the steam! They are taking to the woods like the flock of yellowbellies they are!"

Murphy stepped out. "I wish to see this!" He climbed up onto the boxcar. From his vantage point, he could the General stalled on a hill, as the raiders dropped off the train and flee into the woods. Murphy let out a rebel yell.

"Hot damn boys! We finally got 'em!"

Everyone in the cab cheered. Fuller appeared with his shotgun. "We did it, Anthony! We have recaptured our train, saved the bridge. Now I want the raiders."

Murphy inclined to agree, they were getting closer to the General. There were fewer raiders jumping out and running for it. Murphy noticed the General. It was rolling towards them.

"Bracken! Go full reverse! The Yankees left our engine running right at us!"

Bracken swiftly switched the gear to reverse, in this case forward, while Haney and Martin worked the brake. The Texas then stopped and went forward at a crawl now. The General rolled, but never picked up enough speed. It simply came to a slow stop when it struck the even surface.

Murphy bellowed, "Alright, Bracken, it is over!" Fuller was already off the train and bounded toward his engine. A shotgun was ready, ignoring the cries of 'Bill! Wait!' from Murphy. Moving quickly, he inspected the torn-up boxcar. Nothing. He climbed up onto the tender. Nothing. He held his breath as he slowly made his way to the cab. One hammer cocked. Ready. He trod lightly. He was outside of it now. He exhaled and rushed inside. Nothing. Fuller climbed down.

"Have they all cleared out?"

Murphy almost caused Fuller to shoot him again. Murphy carried his shotgun. Behind him was Cox carrying the firebox shovel, Bracken, Haney, and Martin were bringing up the rear.

"Yes, they have. They won't get away." Fuller bounded to the woods. Murphy watched him go. Then he handed his shotgun to Cox. "Here Cox, follow Bill and see to it that the Yankee's aren't waiting in the trees. You as well, Alonzo"

"Yes, seh."

Cox handed the shovel to Martin, and then he took the shotgun and ran right after Fuller. "Come, boys, let's see what we have," Murphy said He led the group to the cab. Murphy inspected the gears and found everything to be in order, saved for the lack of water and wood.

"It all looks well and good." Bracken snorted, "Those damn Yankees can run a locomotive just as well as us. Let us get this coupled to your train and haul it back to Ringgold. Drinks shall be on me boys. You've earned it." Bracken smiled for the first time all day." I'll take it."

Murphy checked his pocket watch. "It is past one o'clock. We've been chasing them for six hours, he said to himself. He took a pad of paper and a pen from his pocket and wrote it down. He looked at a map on the wall. "We have stopped two miles outside Ringgold at Milepost 116." He put his article away and climbed out of the cab. Bracken was waiting. "We will not be able to leave right away. There is another train yonder."

***

The Catoosa came rumbling around the bend. Renard was piloting it when he saw the scene ahead. Two trains sitting on the track. There were some people on the side of the track who waved at them. "Cap, there's a doings ahead."

Whitsett looked out. This was it! That had to be.

"Stop the engine, conductor."

"Yes, seh." Renard was eager to be done with it.

"Alright, boys! Get ready!" commanded Whitsett. Jenkins elaborated. "Move out the engine as best you can. When you are out, forming a skirmish line. Remember, we are flushing rabbits out."

The train came to a halt.

"Everyone out on the double-quick!" Whitsett ordered. It took a minute or two for the troopers to maneuver themselves to get out, but once they began to file out of the cab, it took a few seconds for the cab to clear. Whitsett nodded to Renard and then ran out into the rain. It felt good to be in the open, breathing fresh, cool air. Whitsett held tight to the handle of his sheathed saber and made his way to the group walking toward him.

"Captain!"

"What can you tell me, seh?"

Murphy explained. "I counted about twenty of them. They fled into the woods. I have no doubt they have arms on them as well. They are dressed as civilians and will surely make a run for the north, lest they have a trap planned for us."

"Thank you dearly, my boys are more than ready and capable. You go on and return your engine to its rightful station. I do ask if you could send one of your men back to town and alert of the locals. Ringgold is my home. If my people know there are Yankees in their midst, they will gladly join the hunt."

"Very well," Murphy said. He turned and went back to his group.

"Now, boys." Whitsett barked his command as he drew his saber. "You heard the man. The Yankees are dressed as civilians. Form a skirmish line. Ten paces between men. Move at double-quick!"

His men all fell out and formed a line that expanded as it moved at a quick pace towards the trees and started up an imposing ridge. Whitsett fell in the extreme left of the line. He drew his revolver and half-cocked it. The rain was obscuring his vision. There was a mist that came from the ground. It was difficult to keep a steady foot on the uphill, muddy terrain. So, this was it. Everything he had feared and fought against was right here. Yankee invaders in his own backyard. Except they were not an army bent on conquering his people. They were thieves bent on stealing trains. It was both exciting and infuriating. His small command was going to fight them and whip them. They were to be heroes. Driving the dastardly, thieving Yankees away. No, concentrate on the current task. Especially as he navigated the treacherous, muddy slope. He stopped to sheathe of his saber, no need for that. His men were well trained and had rather deadly intentions, they didn't need to be rallied, and Whitsett had no plans to make use of it to skewer Yankee engine thieves. He did not intend to get that close. He put his revolver at full cock and at the ready. He moved slowly, in part, to concentrate on his footing and keeping an alert eye for what could be hiding behind the trees. Easy he thought. Take it slow. Be alert, if a shot comes, especially for him. He had to be ready.

His breath tightened. The air went still. A musket shot cracked through the air as well the silence. Whitsett stopped and gripped the revolver tighter. Sighting down the barrel, he was ready to shoot at anything that moved its place. Seconds passed. It felt like minutes.

"Who fired that shot?"

"Where did it come from?"

"Where are the Yankees?" Whitsett slowly began moving to the right.

"It was me! My musket discharged on accident."

"Are you well?"

"The boy Rollins has been wounded!"

Whitsett released the hammer. "Damn it."

"We need help!"

"Where is the captain?"

"I am coming!"

He broke into a run. Careful not to slip. Up ahead, it was not hard to spot a group of grey-clad men in a circle. Everyone looked to Whitsett as he came running.

"It is the boy Rollins," Jenkins said. In the middle of the circle, Rollins laid on the ground. Shaking. His right leg had an open wound that spurted blood.

"Do not stare! Help him! Make a tourniquet!"

Everyone moved to action. French pulled a handkerchief from his jacket and began to tie it around the leg. Coleman assisted. Whitsett turned to two other troopers. "Gather some sturdy sticks and fashion a stretcher with your blankets. We shall carry him back to Ringgold. Doc Patterson has a hospital there. He may tend to him. Go!" The troopers went.

Whitsett looked to Rollins. "We will get you to help privately. Stay with us."

Rollins did not reply. His shaking had slowed, and his eyes were glazing and on the sky. Whitsett looked to the rest of his men.

"Who has done this?"

Bearden, who was sitting away from everyone, slumped and looked ashamed, said softly, "It was not on purpose."

Whitsett walked over and yanked Bearden to his feet by his collar. "You better pray that boy does not die. You will bear the weight of carrying him down."

His troopers had returned with a makeshift stretcher of a blanket tied to two sticks. They placed it beside Rollins. "Gently lift him and place him on it. They did. "Be gentle when lifting him." Sergeant, lead the way. We will all go back down and see about rallying the citizens to continue the hunt."

Rollins was gently lifted. Bearden took the brunt of the weight.

Jenkins called out. "Form a single line behind me! Forward March!"

Whitsett fell in the right by Rollins' stretcher. "How are you, private?"

"I am thirsty." He said weakly. Whitsett put his own canteen to Rollins's mouth to give him some water.

"We will see to it that you get better. Stay with us."

***

Fuller was running still. He made his way through the trees and into the thick underbrush. It was bad enough that the ground would cave underneath his feet, he now had to struggle through a brush that clawed at his face and hands. He reached the end of the brush, and never saw a wide-open space when he came upon a field. He looked back for Cox and Martin, but they were not there. He cursed to himself and started about the field. In the middle of the field was a farmer working the land with his plow and plow horse.

"Hallo. You there! Mister!" Fuller cried out. The farmer, who was talking to himself in profanities, stopped to looked and see who was speaking to him. "I ask you kindly for your assistance," Fuller said as he walked closer and lowered his shotgun.

"Assistance!" the farmer shouted. "I am having the most damn time working my land in this foul weather. You ask for my assistance!"

"There are Yankee raiders let loose in these woods."

"Yankees! Why in the hell did you not speak up?!"

"They have stolen my train! I chased the devils until the engine quit, and now I am pursuing them on foot. I have intelligence that has saved three bridges, but I do, however, need your assistance."

The farmer was unhitching his horse. "What do you require?"

"I need you to spread the word far and wide that Yankees are in the hills and clothed as civilians, like wolves in sheep's clothing!"

"Say no more! I will ride to Graysville myself and send word!" The farmer mounted his plow horse and spurred it to Graysville. Fuller watched him go then was off and ran again.

***

Whitsett and his command had now arrived at Ringgold. The journey back to town was a long one, in part, to the need to adjust the tourniquet on Rollins' leg. They arrived at Doc Patterson's clinic, and he took Rollins in without question. That settled, Whitsett headed to the main part of town. It was Muster Day. Dozens of Georgians from the outlying towns and farms came in on wagons, horses, mules, or even bare feet. They carried squirrel guns, flintlock muskets, or even shotguns. Some showed up with wives and children in tow. They came to enlist or to hear the latest news of the war. A large group was now coming in. Whitsett stepped in the middle of the road and waved for everyone to stop.

"What in tarnation?"

"What is the holdup?"

"An officer!"

"Does he have news?"

"Was there a battle?"

"A battle?"

"Did we win?"

"Attention, citizens!" Whitsett acted as the military commander. "I have terrible news. The Yankee menace has reached down to Ringgold!" A gasp went about the crowd. "They have stolen a train and attempted to make haste with it to the north. Fortune was on our side as they ran out of fuel just outside of the town. Now they are on foot and trying to make it still. They are clad as citizens. They are also likely armed. I need volunteers to help round them up."

Instead of silently stepping forward, a giant fervor erupted in the crowd with whoops and rebel chants. "Whoo! let's whoop some Yankees!"

"Lahk a good time 'coon hunt!"

"Let's git 'em, boys!"

Whitsett tried to silence the crowd, but it was no use, the noise and excitement were much loud. He looked at Jenkins. "Sergeant, see about taking some men with you. Try to organize some sort of hunting party, spread out, and cover every inch. Let us see Private French." He looked to Bearden, then looked away to Coleman. "Private Coleman. Go with Sergeant Jenkins and see about my orders. I will try to organize more townsfolk until then."

"Yes seh."

Jenkins and the privates saluted and were left to try and form some sort of posse out of the rabble.

***

Eventually, word spread throughout the county. Yankee raiders were on the loose! Muskets were loaded, horses were saddled, and bloodhounds were let loose. The countryside came alive for a grand hunting party.

***

Fuller kept running. Going through thick bushes and muddy ground. He ran straight up a hill. He kept ongoing. When he reached the top, he looked out beyond, and a movement caught his attention. Looking across an empty field, he could see some figures at a distance moving fast towards the trees. That was them. He knew it was them. Or at least some of them. Oh, how he desperately wished he had a longer ranged rifle. They were quite far out of range for his shotgun, and he did not want to discharge it and let them know that they were being followed. He sighed; he could not just chase after them. It would take time just to get down the hill as they could increase their distance or just go another way. He decided he would cut left and go down a gentler slope that led to a dirt road. It looked easier and could potentially cut them off for now. Making it to the road, he needed to stop to catch hold of his breath. He just had to. The rain still poured, and he felt it running down his nose and mouth, so he wiped it away. Some men on horseback were riding in his direction. He pointed his shotgun to the ground and breathed slowly to catch his breath. The lead rider approached.

"Howdy stranger. What is with the shootin' ahr." Fuller gasped out the story.

"Damnation! We shall aid you in your pursuit frien'! Ride along, boys!" The riders whooped and spurred all their horses to turn around.

138

The lead rider turned his horse too. "We will git 'em. Say frien' you have blood flowing from your nose and mouth."

He spurred his horse and rode off. Fuller wiped his face with his hand. Sure enough, he bled. He grabbed his wet handkerchief from his coat and pressed it to his face. The day approached dusk. It was still raining. Fuller's legs just could not run anymore. He was cold, wet, thirsty, and hungry. Really hungry. It had to be called a day since he had a whole meal. He was not even walking, barely just dragging himself. There was a farmhouse off the road. In the window, he saw the light. He was drawn to it like a moth. He knocked on the door. He could hear voices coming from within. The door opened, and a middle-aged man greeted him with suspicion.

"Please, I am in need of help."

***

Fuller sat by an open fire. A blanket draped over his shoulders. His hat, boots, socks, and coat were drying by the fire. His feet were red and swollen.

"Yessuh. William Fuller. Conductor for the iron carriage." The man stated as he looked over Fuller's credentials.

There were two men and two women. They all sat at the table; the men looked at the papers. The women were watching Fuller. The man got up and handed them back. Fuller weakly accepted them.

"Thank ye kindly for obliging me. I can't be too careful afteh we heard what Yankee's was about's." Fuller just nodded. "Cai'n I git ye somethin' we jes' finished suppeh and cai'n have m'ah woman make you somethin'"

"Could I have some water?"

"Yeshuh! Wilbur, fetch some watah from th' well." Wilbur got up and went to get some water. "You ah welcome to stay on through the night. We kin fix th' place up."

"Thank you," Fuller responded. "I would like to return to my station at Ringgold. I must report to my superiors. I fear I cannot make it back on my own strength, so I must ask if I may have a fare to go. I will gladly compensate you for your time."

"Of course." Wilbur returned with a bucket. "Wilbuh. Put a blanket on Nelly and git heh ready to go ridin'. We awe gwyn' to give Mr. Fuller heah a ride to Ringgo." Wilber nodded and went.

The man helped in giving the bucket to Fuller. They both held it up to Fuller's lips as he started drinking. The water was cold. It was stale.

It was also delicious. Fuller nearly drank the whole bucket.

***

Nelly was an old mule. Fuller was sitting slumped over on a blanket on Nelly. His warm and somewhat dry clothes were a welcome relief. However, it still rained, and everything dry was all wet again. It was certainly a welcome relief to not have to walk, even on a bumpy mule ride. Fuller did not talk at all. The two men leading the mule through the dusk, seeing Fuller in this state, did not talk either.

Whitsett had made temporary headquarters at the stone depot, organizing half of his men to form posse's and hunt in the countryside. When they were all gone, he could only wait with the other half. He was busy at the telegraph operator's office, firing off messages and waiting for responses. His men were bored. Bearden sat by himself.

Whitsett felt like he sat for a long time, so he took his leave and left for Doc Patterson's. Doc Patterson was running his office for almost twenty years now. His hair was graying, and his eyes peered through thick glasses. Almost the whole of Ringgold had passed through his doors for one ailment or another. He washed his hands in his washbowl when he heard a knocking. "Come on inside. No need to stand there in the rain." He dried his hands on a towel. Whitsett cautiously entered.

"Ah William, how are you?"

"I am well."

"How is the Yankee hunt going?"

"We don't have word on much until my boys return."

"Ah," Doc Patterson went about to organize his tools.

Whitsett sighed. He knew Doc Patterson was blunt, so he asked, "How fares Private Rollins?"

"He is gone." Whitsett felt a blow to his stomach. "He was frail from a loss of blood. We did all we could, but he was too young and did not have the strength to make it-" He stopped when he saw the expression on Whitsett's face.

"William, I've known you since you were but a small babe. I have never taken you like one for going peaky. Especially from a fight." Whitsett nodded. "When this war ends, William, which it will, the numbers of boys like Private Rollins will continue on to grow. The final question will be how many before it's all over. Seeing how you and the fellows from the north can only solve your differences with musket balls instead of words."

"Yes."

"I have taken the proper arrangements to embalm the body. I suppose you may have arrangements to make as well. I will notify his next of kin. They would appreciate a note from your end."

"I shall write one."

Whitsett made his way back to the depot. A crowd was starting to run towards the edge of town. A small boy of maybe ten ran past them yelling, "Capn'! They caught 'em! They caught the Yankees!"

Whitsett followed the boy as a crowd formed. Boos and taunts were starting to get louder. Whitsett pushed his way to the middle of the crowd. Jenkins led a group; the five troopers were formed around three downtrodden looking men. The crow taunted them, but the troopers kept them back. Jenkins saluted.

"Seh! I present you with the prisoners! Not much to look at that. These damned men played false and claimed to be from Kentucky comin' down heah to enlist just before they confessed to their sins of being Yankees. Ohio. That's where they are from. They are Private Will Campbell, Sam Slavens, and Philip Shadrach. If that is the sort coming down here, we should have no trouble whipping them!"

Whitsett looked at them. They all had their heads hanging low.

"Sergeant, fix them up. See to it that they are bound together. I would see about our orders and inform the headquarters of their treacherous ruse if their comrades dared to do the same."

"Yes seh! I have told the other parties involved of this as well, and they have spread the word as it were gospel."

Whitsett received the telegram and then headed back outside. The three were bound and chained together now. The crowd had mostly subsided.

"Are we to hang them cap'n?" Jenkins asked.

"No, we're to take them to Dalton. Once you have secured a wagon, we will immediately depart. Unless you care to walk."

"No, seh." Jenkins saluted. He walked away, only to stop and turn towards Whitsett. "What of Private Rollins?"

"Dead. The wagon, sergeant?"

Jenkins had rustled up a wagon and a team to carry the full load of the people in the oncoming dark and rain. It was big enough to carry all of them, as Whitsett thought they would move faster that way, overriding Jenkins, who thought that the raiders should walk the entire way.

"No. They are Yankees, and it is true. It would only lead to us slowing down for them. I want to get to Dalton as quick as we can."

"What are our orders then after we are through with them, seh?"

"Mobile. We are still moving back to Mobile."

"Yes seh."

The troopers quickly loaded the wagon and set off for the long road back to Dalton. Whitsett sat in the rear of the wagon, looking out the open flap and watching Ringgold fade away to the darkness. Fuller, the Man, and Wilbur arrived at the Stone train depot. Fuller had begun to feel his legs at least. He would periodically tilt his head backward and lap up as much rainwater as he could. At the depot, the Man helped him down, and Fuller gave him some confederate scrip, thanked him again, and walked in the depot. Murphy greeted him. He looked well-fed and rested.

"Bill? What happened? Cox and Martin had lost track of you and returned to Ringgold! I bought everyone a round of drinks, it's too bad you could not join us. The General is on the siding. I am sure you have seen it. It has been refueled and ready to go. I have made sure of it. Oh, have you heard? They caught some of those rascals? Three of them, at least."

"Then, there are still some more out there."

"Oh, well, we are off to a good start, at least."

"Here, I purchased some fine Georgia brandy. Would you care to partake?" He handed a small flask over to him. Fuller took a generous swig. Murphy took it back. He followed Fuller as he hobbled into the agent's office using his shotgun as a cane.

"Say, you know the damndest thing? I checked my shotgun. It was never loaded!"

Fuller managed a smile. "I suppose I shall not check mine. I do not want to know the truth." He found a nice sofa in the office. Setting the shotgun down, he curled into a ball on it.

"So, what will you do now?"

"I will wait for the next train to Atlanta. I have to report on this."

"It should be along directly. What will you do in the meantime?"

"Sleep."

CHAPTER 26

A dream-Escape-The brush pile-Wilson's plan-On the road again-Rest for the weary-Unpleasant awakening-A Barn-Rude awakening-The Women-Wood's speech-An atlas for a pig-Floating down the river-Bridgeport- Destroying evidence

It felt like a dream. The exhausting walks through mud-lade country, the thrill of stealing a train engine in full view of everyone, the exhilarating and dizzying chases across Georgia. Everything was a blur after it.

Wilson made a beeline for the ridge he had spotted. Just letting himself go into a complete flight. He was going when he heard a cry of "Alf! Wait!" Stopping, he turned to see Wood coming running up towards him.

"Come on, Marky! Move your English ass!"

Normally, Wood would come up with a comeback, but he was also in-flight mode, and as soon as he caught up with Wilson, they started to run again.

Once they reached the ridge, they had to stop. They were hungry. Dehydrated. Out of breath. They could not run anymore. Wilson looked at the ground and saw plenty of soggy bush and leaves by the remains of a cut-down tree.

"Quickly! Lie down and make a brush pile over yourself!"

They both hit the ground and covered themselves as best as they could.

"Keep your revolver handy." No sooner had they covered themselves when they heard a group of unfamiliar voices approaching up ahead. Wilson tried to control his heavy breathing, but his heart pounded fast, he was sure they would hear it. The footsteps got closer. The revolver felt heavy. He was ready to lift it straight and start blasting upward at anyone who would challenge him. He nearly jumped when a foot stepped on some leaves inches away from his face. He hoped they would not hear his heart or stumble on him. He knew they would.

***

Chattanooga was much different now. They had all passed through when it was rather dark and cloudy. Now in the full sunshine, there were people and horses filling the streets and sending a cloud of dust over everything.

***

They waited. All-day. All night. All-day the next day too. All under a pile of wet brush and branches. All while in a cramped, uncomfortable position.

Finally, Wilson rose and fast. His back was stiff. He had to take it easy.

"Marky? Are you alive?"

"No", a brush pile responded. Wilson's legs were beyond sore.

"Come on out. There is no one but us in here."

The other bush piles flew apart. "Oh, that was a bit of a fix to be in. I shan't be doing an encore."

"It bought us an extra day did it not?"

Wilson was rubbing his legs down. "Quite right. Now what?"

"Cap said the best course was to pilot over towards Chattanooga on the chance that General Mitchell has seized of it. Less we take a chance and go for Huntsville. Which we know for sure that General Mitchell is in."

"I prefer the second object. So, we walked all this way to Georgia, and now we are walking out."

"Yes."

Wilson was staggering to his feet now. "Good. I do not care for such a state anyway." Wood said.

It was dark, with only a sliver of light. Wilson was facing leftwards. "Very well, Marky, if we head west, we can use the Tennessee to go west and to Alabama. If your all set, we can be off." Wood's dark form appeared from his right.

"All right Alf."

***

Wilson was headed towards a two-story brick building that seemed to be covered by a tall wooden fence. It did not look too impressive. He looked at Wood, who was walking in step. Wood shrugged. The front gate was open. The yard in front was unimpressive. Just dirt with rocks strewn about. Wilson did not pay attention to the yard. He was focused on getting inside.

***

After walking all night, they had found a barn at daybreak. Inside was a mow full of corn wrappings. They made a hole for themselves and slept in it.

The smell of the barn reminded Wilson of home and for a few hours managed to forget about the war and where he was. He was awakened by a female voice.

"Here is a hole. I wonder if a nest is down here."

He then felt something touch his hand. He looked to see a woman staring back at him. She let out a scream that would awake the deepest slumber, as she turned and ran away. Wilson scrambled out from the wrappings. Wood had jumped out of his hole and sleep. "Oh bloody 'ell! What has happened?"

Wilson coughed. "A woman Marky. She stumbled onto me and seemed frightened."

"Oh, perhaps because she saw your face?" Wilson threw a wrapping nearby at Wood. "Come on then. We need to make it right. We have enough enemies in this country already." After brushing themselves off, they went to the door, hats in hand, and knocked. It opened with a creek.

"I am awfully sorry to frighten you, ma'am. Of course, also, to sleep in your barn without your knowing. We are southern men out to pursue those scoundrels who stole an engine a few days back."

"Yes, I have heard of them. The awful thing it was." The door opened wider.

"Indeed, it was. Well, my friend and I were part of a search party and got separated on account of the rain and darkness. Seein' as how your barn was the only shelter, we took it. Again, we are truly sorry."

The door opened fully now. A fair woman with blond hair stood in the doorway. "Well, you are doin' your part. I suppose I can forgive you for giving me a fright."

The scent of food entered Wilson's nose. "Sorry to impose again, ma'am. It has been some time since we last ate."

"Oh, come on in then. We have some cornbread."

Wood and Wilson sat at a table. The woman served them up some cornbread. Her friend poured them some buttermilk from a pitcher. They both starved, but they had to restrain themselves when eating. "I can prepare something else for y'all if you could afford the time."

"Oh no, thank you, ma'am. We have imposed on you more than enough. We do not wish to be called on for an absence. We will be on our way. We thank you very much for your generous hospitality."

"You are very much welcome."

Wilson stood up and shortly bowed. There were two pieces of cornbread. "May I?"

"You may."

He grabbed them up and put them in his coat pocket. Careful not to open his jacket too much to show off his revolver. "Again, we have much appreciation for you. Perhaps we could repay with a coin? Mark, give the lady some money." Wood put a few bills for them on the table. Wilson got up and went to the door. Wood followed.

"You are welcome", she said again with half a smile. They were almost out of the door when the woman's friend said. "Your friend does not talk much, does he?"

Wilson had been caught. Wood, however, poked his head back in. "I ain' got much te' say on a coun' of being a might shy. I do mean business to git some Yankee raidehs", he said in a near-perfect accent.

She laughed.

"Alraht then."

"Yes 'um." They walked out and resumed their journey. Wilson smirked and looked at Wood. Wood chuckled. "To think old boy. I could have been a marvelous stage actor, but I gave it up to join the army just to walk through the south with you."

***

The inside of the building was quite hot. With stale air to boot. There was a shaky looking staircase. Wilson knew he had to go upstairs, but then he stopped. He wished he had some water. He knew it would be some time before he could get some more.

***

"Do you suppose our fellow cutthroats might have survived?" Wood asked.

"Cap said every man for himself. We must push on till we make it, and pray they all make it too," Wilson replied.

Two days they walked repetitively through the rugged country before winding up back to Tennessee. Wilson was a good hunter and a tracker, but he was beginning to doubt himself. When they approached the town of Cleveland, Wilson knew what he required. "Say Marky, how much of that reb money do you have left?"

Wood reached into his pocket and pulled out a couple of dollars. "This much." Wilson helped himself to it.

"I need a map." He started off. Wood followed. "Very well. When this is over, I expect the best cut of pork from your finest of pigs."

"Hell, Marky, when this is over, you can have a whole pig."

They went to town and bought an atlas. Wilson looked through to what he needed. Then he threw away the rest. They stayed at the home of a pro-union couple, and after being fed and receiving information, they continued on their way to a creek, and by chance, they found an abandoned canoe. They took it and floated up the creek until it turned towards the Tennessee River. For two days, they floated, no doubt it was easier going for now. Occasionally stopping to relieve themselves or trade places or to get information. They arrived at a bridge in the town of Bridgeport. Arriving in town, they heard a commotion going on that there were some Yankees in Stevenson. Only four miles away.

"Four miles. Can you beat that?" Wilson asked. "Alf, four miles for freedom is nothing at all." They walked the four miles to Stevenson, only to find the place full of Confederate troops.

"I must say unless our side has switched color uniforms, those gents will not be sympathetic to our cause." Wood said.

Wilson started to slowly tear up his atlas map, leaving the bits on the side of the road.

"It is sixty miles to Huntsville. Just be a natural southerner."

He tore out a large piece. Pretending to stifle up a yawn, he stuffed the piece in his mouth.

***

Wilson could feel the tension. When he heard the metallic click of the hammer on a revolver being pulled, it was enough to go.

***

Someone in the crowd yelled out that they were part of the Yankee cavalry that had come through earlier. They were detained by the soldiers immediately. They were searched. They took their revolvers.

They did not find the map. Wilson and Wood were taken back to Bridgeport. A stern-looking confederate colonel and major then questioned them. Standing before them in a house, they spun a story of riding down the river to visit some relatives, but they were instead lost and were trying to find their way. The fact that they were strangers and had guns was suspicious, but the officers did not really have a reason to hold them. So, they let them go.

A crowd had gathered outside. It was a small town as rumor had spread that two suspected Yankees were arrested. The colonel and major then stepped out. Wilson and Wood stepped out after. The colonel was about to say the pair was innocent until a short man with a rotten face poked his head out, then pointed at the pair, and cried out, "I know these fellows. They were on the train!"

If Wilson was ever at a point to kill someone, this was it. If he had the means. But the colonel was in his face.

"What was that story you spun?"

That was it. Word was sent out of their capture. General Danville Leadbetter, the commander of East Tennessee, had come down to interrogate them. Within days, they were taken to Chattanooga. It was not the welcome they had wanted. It was only from confederate sources they learned that Mitchell's advance had stalled as he never came close to Chattanooga. It did not matter, they said. They would drove him back north. The unlucky Yankee's were driven to the Chattanooga jail.

***

Wilson was at the foot of the staircase. When the sergeant escorted him, and Wood cocked his pistol, Wilson stiffened. The sergeant moved in front of Wilson.

"Ye betteh get on up their boy. Don' be givin me no trouble."

Wilson moved up the stairs. Down the hall was a rickety door. Because his hands were bound, he could not open the door. The sergeant was right at his side, with a smirk on his face.

"You wretched Yankees. Y'all come down heah. Don evin put up a fight. Y'all just steal a train and ruin ah railroad tracks. Y'all never did anything but cause some fuss and delay our goin's for a spell. Don' worry. We'll git our trains goin' agin. If thas th' way y'all wanna be. That jes' proves y'all a damned bunch with hell deep in your hearts."

Wilson stared straight ahead. The sergeant put the barrel of his revolver against Wilson's head and used it to push Wilson's face up, so their eye's met.

"It don' matteh none. We gwyn' a hang ye. You can count on that event occurin." He put the revolver back in his holster. He then opened the door. If Wilson was going to hell, he was about to meet the devil. An old man named Swims.

CHAPTER 27

***Old man Swims-Shackled-Down the hole-Reunited at last-
Dinnertime-Living Conditions-First days-New law and order-
Aleck's story-Parrott's troubles-Overcoming misery-Knight's
brilliance-The deal-Betrayal-A new deal-Peace***

"Well, well, well. We got some mo' of the engin' thieves, have we?
Well, seh, I kin make room fo' mo.'"

Swims was a wretched old man with dirty white hair, withered face,
and a stubble. He had a sneer-ish smile with a rather screeching voice.

Wilson and Wood were put off by the man and stopped in the
doorway. The guards jabbed them in the back with their rifle butts to
have them move forward. Swims pulled a pair of keys from his pocket
and got down onto his knees to unlock a trapdoor. It took effort, but
he pulled the door up while motioning for an attendant. Then he
motioned for Wood and Wilson to move closer. They were jabbed in
the back again. Swims got in Wilson's face.

"There is nuthin' I despise mo' thin Yankee's. You will do bes'
down thea until th' time cum's they hang ye." He then cackled
maniacally, pausing only to cough something up and spit it out. His
breath was the foulest thing Wilson had ever smelt.

Wilson did not say anything. He moved to the open door. He could
feel hot air and the smell. That putrid smell. Wilson had to step
back. The attendant came back and slid a ladder down the hole.
Wilson's heart sank. This was it. This was where the journey ended.

"Oh befo' I forgit. I have a gift fo' ye Yankees". He turned to his
attendant and made a motion. The attendant had a chain with a
padlock the size of an attached hand. Wilson and Wood were shoved
together as the attendant wrapped the chain around their necks. Swims
handed him his set of keys, and the attendant then locked the padlock.
The padlock weighed about two pounds. Wilson felt the weight and
the chain dig into the back of his neck.

"Well. Down ye two go."

Wilson looked at his handcuffs, unsure of how he was going to get down when he felt the point of a bayonet poking him in the back. He lowered himself down to the floor, only to feel the chain squeezing against his skin. He got up, so Wood lowered himself down at the same time. Down on all fours, he crawled and adjusted himself so he was on the ladder, only going as far as the chain would allow him to go. When Wood started down, Wilson started too. He could feel the hot air rising. The smell was the worst. He stopped to cough and try to stop himself from gagging. Each step was slow going. Wilson could hear voices below, like ghosts whispering from the shadows. His feet finally touched a hard surface. He could feel bodies pressed against him, and he had to move around to get some space. Wood finally stepped off, and quickly the ladder was pulled up, and the trapdoor closed. Everything went dark.

"Marky. I believe we are put in hell."

"Ell would be too kind, for we have to die first."

"My God! That is Wilson and Wood! Good heavens, they have got every one of us!"

They could feel bodies press closer around them.

"Yes, it is us!" Wilson called out. "Is everyone from Cap Andrews group here?"

"Yes!"

"We are all here!"

"We all had hoped you two had made it!"

"What awful luck had brought you here?"

The entire hole where they were kept was thirteen feet deep and long. There were two windows, but one was covered by dirt from the outside, and the other was covered by thick iron bars that barely emitted any light or air. In addition to all the raiders, there were twelve Union supporters from East Tennessee and also an escaped slave.

Wilson and Wood were responding to voices in the dark as they told the tale of their escape. They were the closest to making it. Some of the raiders were captured on the same day. The rest had made their way up north and had tried to bluff their way out of trouble.

"Halloo there! Mark? Alf?" It was John Porter.

"Porter? Is that you? How the devil did you wind up 'ere?", Wood asked. "Hawkins and I missed the train and the fun. We tried to join up along the rebs, they took us in, but soon word spread about all of you lads. The rebs, well, they took a closer look at us and decided they did not want us joining up after all; and sent us here."

Wilson nodded. "I believe there were still more of us. Were they not?"

He got a lot of unsure grunts as a response.

"Say, Alf, have you met ole' Leadbetter?" Knight asked.

"Yes."

"What do you say? Was he dead drunk? Or gentlemanly drunk?"

"I suppose gentlemanly drunk."

"Ha! He was the same. What did you tell that old buzzard?"

"I have tried to state that we are southern men on our way to a destination down further south. He did not take it well, as you may see."

"Ha! Since we are the rebs' guests, I decided to have some mischief with them. I told that fool that I was on my way to Chandler Springs in Alabama. When he asked why I told him that, I was considering buying it. After they took me away, I told him if that's how they had felt, I would take my money somewhere else." Wilson couldn't help but crack a smile. The first one in a while.

The trapdoor opened, sending a beam of light into the pit. "Oh well, its suppertime!" Dorsey said. Wilson looked up and adjusted his eyes towards the light. "Considering our lavish living quarters, I expect nothing but a king's feast", Wood stated as a bucket on a hook was lowered down into the pit.

"If your feast includes rotten pickled beef or pork with scant cornbread, then a king's feast is what it shall be," Knight replied.

The bucket was low enough. Everyone in the pit swarmed around the bucket, pushing and shoving it to grab at what was in there. Wilson moved towards the bucket; when he felt the tension in his chain, he barked, "Come along, Marky!" He had to push his way through to the bucket, and even then, he had to stretch out his arms sideways and put his hands in. His hands got scratched up quite bad, but he grabbed up what he could and got away. He moved further away from the crowd and felt what he had, careful not to drop any of it.

"Thank you, Alf. I will move more quickly the next time." Wilson separated what he had into two handfuls. "Hold out your hand." His hands were cupped palm to palm from the handcuffs, so he did his best to feel in the void until he touched Wood's hands and deposited a handful into his hands. Deciding it would be best to ration what he had, Wilson separated it into both hands and ate it. It was a little cornbread with some pickled beef. The whole of it tasted terrible. Wilson ate it anyways. The bucket went up, and then the trapdoor closed. The commotion died down immediately.

"What happens now?" Wilson called out.

"This. This is what will happen now. You are living it." Brown called back.

**

Whatever light from the barred windows turned to the night. Wilson felt tired.

"Where do we sleep?", he called out.

"Wherever you may find any room," Dorsey called back. "Marky, let us try to lie down here." They lowered themselves down like they were sitting. Then they lowered themselves onto their backs until Wood almost lay onto someone.

"Say, be careful there!"

"Quite sorry. Alf, push over a bit." Wilson did so until he was right against someone.

"Sorry."

"We are all packed in together like this. You should all prepare yourself. This is how it will be." Campbell said. Wedged in between Wood and Campbell, with his head against a dirt floor. Wilson closed his eyes.

**

Wilson tried to go to sleep. He awoke with a fright, both legs kicking. Something was nibbling onto his toe. His arms were burning.

"Let up on that, will you?" Campbell growled. "Something is biting my foot!" Several of the raiders were awake and grumbling.

"It is just rats and lice. It's best if you let it be." Wilson kicked again in the air and tried to scratch his arms, but with his arms shackled, it was close to impossible. Wilson groaned and tried to go to sleep.

**

He woke up with a headache, stiff neck, burning arms, as well as a bleeding toe. It took him several attempts to sit up. The hot, putrid air helped wake him up. Wood slowly rose as well.

"How did you fare in your sleep?" Wood asked.

"About as well as you would have expected."

Campbell moved away. Wilson scooted over so he could have some more space. The bucket came down. Everyone stampeded to the beam of the light again. Wilson and Wood were the last of them to move, and with everyone clamoring around, their prospects looked rather grim. By the time they pushed their way in, there was hardly anything left. After the bucket went back up, it was quiet again.

"Say, anyone with spare bones from Swim's rations ought to let me have at it," Knight said. Wilson and Wood did not want to waste energy, so they sat back down.

***

Spending the day in utter darkness until the door opened, and the excitement began again. When everyone squeezed in together, Wilson had to force himself to ignore the chewing rat on his boot and the various bugs chewing on his body.

A new day dawned. Wilson and Wood still ached all over their body. The door opened, and the bucket came down again. When everyone started crowding, this time, Marion Ross's voice boomed.

"My fellows! This shall not do! We can't continue like a rabid group! We must have order! I propose we elect a president and council to maintain rule and order!"

"Hear hear!"

"Well, said, Mr. Ross."

"Who should lead us!"

"Why Cap Andrews of course!"

"Of course!"

"Cap Andrews, will you take charge!"

In the light beam, Andrews appeared like a phantom from within the darkness. "My lads, I humbly accept. My heart is heavy for not speaking much sooner. We shall conduct ourselves accordingly. Henceforth, when the rations do arrive, we shall form an orderly line, and every man shall take no more than a handful."

"Yes, cap!"

"Hurrah for Cap Andrews!"

And just like that, the chaos turned to civility as everyone formed a line to take a handful of the awful food. After everyone was finished eating, Knight stumbled and bumped into everyone in the darkness, looking for any more bones.

***

"My lads, next we ought to make room and sit down. It does not do anyone well to stand and roam like this. That is what they do at a madhouse. We shall sit, and if the air is too stifling, then we shall stand.

"Next, we all have heard the tales of how we had arrived at this station. I would rather hear tales of a more light-hearted variety, as these would raise our spirits rather than let us bemoan in our miseries", Andrews said.

Pittenger piped up. "I have a tale to tell."

***

Random discussion of adventures and experiences of the past made the day go by swifter so that when the bucket was lowered, everyone was surprised by the time. An orderly line was then formed, and everyone sat back down. After everyone was done eating, Pittenger piped up again. "Fellows, who amongst you believes in the abolition of slavery?"

"I do" Buffum was the only one who answered. "That's a disgrace."

Pittenger continued. "The question of slavery is a rather cruel one with the only answer is to abolish it. I have read the Uncle Tom's Cabin and found it to be a horrid tale, only to be shocked when I found it was all true. My friends, these poor creatures are held in bondage and worked tirelessly less; they choose to be whipped mercilessly by their cruel masters, all due to their African heritage. Look to where Aleck, our fellow captive, is. Aleck, are you there?"

"Yes'suh", was the deep-voiced reply.

"How are you in this terrible place?"

"I took to runnin' I'se set ahn bein' free."

"How long have you been set in here?"

"I'se gwyn' ahn five months."

"How much longer is your sentence?"

"Seven mo' months they'sa say." Everyone grumbled at the thought of what that poor man had gone through.

"That is not all. They pry babies from their mothers and sell them as one did with dogs." Buffum added.

Wilson never thought about slaves or slavery, for that matter as much. He never dreamed of signing up to free someone else. "Marky, I want to stand up." Wilson stood up, then Wood behind him; he made his way to the window that was covered by the bars, emitting only a tiny ray of light. In the light, he could make out of Aleck's dark form.

"How are you, Aleck?"

"I be well suh."

"What will be your fate after this cruel punishment ends?"

"They'sa gwyn' put me back on th' mahket to sell."

Wilson sighed. "When this war ends, and the north succeeds, I suspect a great many changes will occur for you and yours."

"I ain' 'fraid. I 'spose when I am away frum dis place, and well enuff. I will steal myself and take to runnin' agin. Wilson grinned.

"There you go, mate. "Ave at again," said Wood.

"What are you doing there?", Wilson asked.

"Massah Parrott was whupped hard. I'se helpin' Massah Dorsey ten' t'e his backside." Wilson had to step a bit back and tilt his head to see Jacob Parrott lying flat on his stomach. In the faint gleam of light, he could see that his back was covered in vicious scars. He had never seen anything so terrible before.

Dorsey spoke. "Mr. Parrott and Mr. Robertson were caught and set upon a damned southern man who proceeded to whip Mr. Parrott."

Parrott added, "The man gave myself over a hundred lashes, less I gave him my part in our scheme, along with who was in charge. I gave him Nuthin'."

"It was Mr. Robertson who then finally spoke out. He said he did so to spare his friend any further suffering. Mr. Robertson was unable to tend to his friend, so Mr. Parrott asked me to do so." Dorsey added.

"He did not need to. I would not talk, even if I were near death." Parrott finished.

"You are a brave soul, Mr. Parrott, you need not answer to any other man of your bravery," Wilson said. He then moved away. He had enough of atrocity.

***

Everyone wedged together for bedtime. Wilson could not get that image of Parrott's back or Aleck's story out of his head. He sighed loudly and was abruptly startled when he felt someone grab his ankle and whisper, "It is Knight. Who is this?"

"It is Alf. What are you causing commotion for?"

"The rebs never got a hold of my jackknife. I have been using it to make a pick for the locks out of the old bones. Hold out your hands forward." Wilson did. He felt Knight's hands grip his wrists, feeling around until he grabbed hold of Wilson's handcuffs and began to pick them.

"It is about bloody well time", Wood said, sitting up.

"Hush. We don't want that old buzzard waking up."

"Very well." Knight worked at it for a moment, then there was the sound of a click, and the handcuffs sprang open. Wilson could not get them off fast enough. He rubbed his wrists; they felt all swollen and raw. Next, Knight patted Wilson's arm until he found the chain. Wilson felt some tugging before he felt the two-pound weight drop off his neck. He let it drop off. The feeling of that weight finally off his neck was tremendous.

"Thank you kindly, Will."

"Oh," groaned Wood. "This is tremendous. Bless your soul, William. Sorry to disappoint you, Alf, on account of being separated and all."

"You're both welcome. Just be sure to keep up the appearance that you are still wearing them when ole' Swims comes around", Knight stated, as he worked on Wood's handcuffs.

"Indeed, I will."

***

The next morning, Wilson and Wood were leaned against the wall near the slop bucket when they heard someone rustled in the dark and relieved themself in it. They could hear the contents of the bucket spill onto the ground.

"I must say", Wood said. "Do you suppose ole' Swims is getting on 'is years and forgets to empty our waste and refresh our water. Or is it just a cruel trick that old wretch is trying to pull on us?"

***

Everyone sat in a circle. They spoke about the war, home, and whatever else they could discuss to pass the long and hot hours. After a lull in the conversation, Buffum piped up.

"Fellows, I have long had an admiration for the good words of William Shakespeare. Allow me to recite some words from the story of Hamlet" He pushed himself up and delivered a masterful performance: "But that I am forbidden. To tell the secrets of the prison house. I could a... tell whose lightest word. Would harrow up thy soul, freeze thy young blood. Make thy two eyes, like two stars, start from their spheres. Thy knotted and combined parts to lock. And each particular hair to stand on end. Like quills upon the fretful propentine. But this eternal blazon must not be. To ears of flesh and blood. List, list, O, List!"

Everyone clapped and cheered. Listening to Buffum's rousing rendition, for a brief moment there, they were not prisoners. "Well done, old boy!" Wood said as the applause started to die down. "Your recitement of Billy Shakespeare was splendid. You have got quite an 'andle on 'im."

Somewhere from the dark, George Wilson called out. "I am truly sorry for inquiring if you have spoken of this before, the fellow who just spoke, what type of accent is that?"

Wood sighed. "Very well, then. This shall be the last time I speak of my ancestry. So, listen well."

***

It was nearing time for the trapdoor to open for the evening meal to be lowered down.

"Fellows. I have squirreled away some money from the rebs. A trick I learned back in Chicago. I propose that any man with any coin left may pool it together and use it to purchase real rations from ole Swims there."

"That is a fine idea!"

"Hear! Hear!"

"I have a few coins left!"

"Pass them forward!"

"Take mine as well!"

In the back, Wood said to Wilson. "Pity, Alf, we could have tossed in to contribute to the feast, but what happened? Oh yes, you tossed your money at a hotel room we barely slept in, and then forced me to toss mine to a pair Jane Reb's who fed us dry cornbread. Oh, what could have been."

"Oh, hush up."

"Very well, gents. I believe I have a fair amount of currency here. It is too late to request anything for now, but for the morning. What shall it be?" Knight asked.

"Real pork!"

"Real beef!"

"Eggs! Potatoes!"

"Now, fellows," Knight interjected. "We must extend our coin to the fullest. We do not know how long our stay in this hell hole will be. Perhaps something easy like bread?"

"Yes! Bread!"

"Bread by itself?"

"There must be something along with it!"

"But what?"

"Butter?"

"Honey?"

"Molasses?"

"Oh, yes! Molasses!"

"I favor molasses more!"

"Make it molasses!"

Knight broke up the cacophony. "Fellows. Fellows!"

He tried to calm everyone in the dark. "Molasses on bread shall it be." The trapdoor opened, and the bucket was lowered. Knight stepped in the light, shielding his eyes.

"Halloo up there? Swims?"

Swims's head came into view. He snorted. "What is it, yank?"

"We have a proposition for you. If we were to offer a few coins, would you purchase some actual food for us poor souls down here?"

Swims twitched his nose. Pondering. Finally, he said, "If y'all givin'me moneh. I s'pose I kin get ye somethin'"

"Yes. Kindly provide us with some wheat bread with molasses."

"Al'right then. Send up, whatche' have an' ah'll git yo feed."

"For tomorrow?"

"Yes."

Knight took his place at the end of the line, and when it turned, he took what was left and deposited some coins into the bucket. That night, they all dreamed of breakfast to come.

***

The next morning, everyone was lined up. This was all previous Christmas's in one. The door opened. They could hardly wait. The bucket came down. They were all salivating.

Andrews approached and reached in, only to pull his hand out with some more pork and cornbread. "My lads! We have been cheated! Swims played false and has given us the same rations!" Everyone's heart sank. There was minor grumbling before the volume turned up.

Swims smiled sweetly and sang out, "Oh, boys! I lost that money!"

Knight pushed his way into the front of the crowd. "The hell you did! You damned old scoundrel! You have spent it on whiskey. Your drunk now!"

Swims just cackled. "Aw right then. Y'all kin help yo' selves or I kin brin th' bucket up!"

Knight never liked losing. Especially to this old bastard. But he knew if they did not eat now, they would have to wait all day. Andrews put a reassuring hand on his shoulder and shook his head 'no'.

"Very well. We shall have what you have given us." Knight grumbled.

Swims nodded. "That's a lad."

***

The day's conversations were much tense. There was not any joviality or high spirits. Knight himself was agitated and did not have any funny stories or jokes to tell. When it was time for the evening bucket to come down, he was at the front again. The captain of the guards was up top, lowering down the bucket. He never introduced himself, and the raiders never cared to learn of his name.

"Excuse me, cap." Knight started. "We have a grievance. We were promised by Swims that if we provided currency, he would purchase us some real food. He gave us his word, and we believed him rightly, so as a southern gentleman, he would keep it. Sir, he played false with us and kept the money for himself."

The captain smirked. "If you believed him that was of your own doing."

"Sir. This was a grave injustice. Is nothing to be done? Are we not entitled to have our money back?"

"No! You are prisoners. Yankee ones at that. You are entitled to nothing. Git up and have your fill of the rations. I am tired of this conversation."

Knight could see he was losing. He had to turn the tide. "Well, cap, I can see that I was talking to the wrong gentleman. You appear to be much more honorable. If I could do business with you."

The captain studied him, "Speak yank."

"If I could persuade you to purchase much more suitable rations for us. Such as wheat bread with some molasses, we will provide suitable funds. This could be a regular engagement until our funds expire. Also, if I threw in a little extra coin, would you be persuaded to keep our water and slop bucket refreshed?"

The captain scoffed. These were prisoners. Yankee prisoners. He did not like the idea of giving them any extra comfort. But this Yankee had appealed to his southern sensibility, and if they had the money for it.

"Very well, yank. Put the money in the basket, and I shall see about your bread."

"Along with our buckets?"

This Yankee was pushing his luck. "Perhaps."

159

"Thank you kindly."

***

That night, no one thought about the meal because it might not be coming this time. They couldn't bear the idea of being let down again.

The next morning the bucket came down. There it was: A whole loaf of bread in slices, covered in molasses. Everyone cheered. Knight called up, "Thank you kindly, cap!" The captain scoffed and pulled the bucket up. "The water and slop buckets as well," Knight added. As everyone savored their bread, the captain had the guards empty the slop bucket and refill of the water bucket. He lowered both back down. He could not hear what they were talking about down there, but it was animated with a lot of laughter. He went back to his post. He did not want to ask what they were talking about. He also did not ask himself as to how these prisoners, who were supposed to be stripped of all their valuables and money, could afford to buy some bread.

CHAPTER 28

Plans for the court-martial-Andrews trial-Singing-Bad southerners-
On to Madison-Back to Chattanooga-New Quarters-Captain Law-
Outside-Wood's Cough-Escape plans foiled-George Wilson-A plan-
Cutting a hole-Andrews only chance

"Believe me, fellows. We shall not stray from our carefully laid plans. We must say unequivocally that we are United States soldiers and must claim the protection of the laws of war." George Wilson said. The passion instilled in his voice rang loud throughout the hole.

"Alas, we must state we are soldiers who were under orders for this daring raid." Pittenger chimed in. "We must not allow them to attempt to label us as common criminals. We must also state that we believed Cap Andrews was an officer of some sort. If this is too difficult, I propose I make myself available as a representative of the group to speak for us all."

There was some grumbling that continued to grow louder. Dorsey spoke out louder. "We all were in the guise of civilians. We walked behind the rebs' lines and got caught. That is what I shall say, we captured a train and made haste back to our lines, leading a charge of mischief along the way.

"The rebs will not look kindly on us no matter what story we try to spin. Boys, they are sure to hang us. That is all there is to it." Campbell said.

"Cap," Brown started. "Cap must order us to attempt an escape. Overrun the guards. Make a desperate bid for freedom."

Pittenger snorted. "There are guards everywhere as locusts, the fence has only one way out, while the people outside will not be friendly toward us. That is after you get out of this hole somehow."

Andrews spoke in a tone that commanded attention. "My lads. I fully appreciate your passions and rhetoric; I could not allow any action that could result in bloodshed amongst this group. Thank you, I believe the best course to take is the one provided by Mr. Wilson and Mr. Pittenger." As if on cue, the trapdoor opened as a ladder slid down.

"Oh-h, Andrews! It's time te face yer judgment!" Swims's voice called out.

Andrews put his handcuffs on, his chain tied to Martin Hawkins. Everyone gave their good wishes to Andrews as he got up and climbed the ladder to face his judgment. Everyone settled down and then broke off into separate conversations.

"There goes our brave captain. Suppose he might have a card up the sleeve that gets him and possibly us out of this mess? He talked up a good lot to get us past a lot of Johnny Reb's." Wood suggested.

"My father gave me some law books to read so that I could have a better grasp of the law. I'm afraid Dorsey is correct. They aim to hang cap, and this court-martial is all for show." Wilson said.

"I was merely trying to have a sense of hope, Alf." Wood retorted.

"It won't do. I let go of having hope a long time ago. Working a farm, hoping that you have a good harvest, only to be disappointed when it was a poor one who taught me a good one about hope." Wilson said.

"Say!" Pittenger called out. "This will not do, to have low spirits. We must attempt to raise it. Shall we sing a song?"

"Very well!"

"That would be best!"

"What song shall it be?"

"The Star-Spangled Banner!"

"That is a good choice."

"Very well."

"The Star-Spangled Banner it is."

***

As the days wore on, it started to get hotter. The money ran out, and the raiders had to go back to rotten food that Swims gave out. The water bucket was rationed before it inevitably ran out, and the raiders would have to wait for it to be refilled as the slop bucket emptied. Knight's bones that he had used to unlock the handcuffs and chains wore out as everyone had to go back to wearing them. Except for Pittenger, he was allowed to leave the hole and go outside.

"Do you suppose that fellow is in the cahoots with Johnny Reb?" Wood asked.

"Dorsey claims he is trying to talk the rebs into letting him be a witness of some sort to square the rest of us; however, I am not so sure now," Wilson replied.

***

The trapdoor opened, and the along the bucket was another familiar sight: A group of soldiers and civilians who peered down into the hole and stared at the shackled raiders as though they were studying something they had never seen before.

"Why look, Lincoln's abolition dogs awe lookin' mangeh and unwell."

"Y'all th' perfec' Yankee's, chained lahk dogs and kept hidden."

"Tell me, yanks. How fares that hole?"

Some of the raiders responded.

"Come down and see!"

"Be glad we're here! If we were to be set loose, I would chew your throat up."

Wood coughed, then he shouted above the rest. "There are too few ladies up there! Is that the southern gents 'ave to resort to fornicating with livestock to get by?" That shocked the ladies present and soon left, the men were shocked by this crude remark and had nothing to reply with, leaving. It did draw some praise from the raiders.

"Marky, under normal circumstances, I would disapprove of that vulgar tongue of yours, but I would say it's just right." Wilson chuckled.

***

That night the trapdoor opened, and Andrews came down the ladder after another day of trial. A guard followed and made sure he was shackled and chained with Hawkins.

"Well, Andrews, how did the trial go today?" Ross called out.

"I hardly know," Andrews replied. Then he nodded at Pittenger. "I am afraid the fellow has swatted me."

***

Wood had a cough that was getting worst now. His constant fits would jerk the chain that would then jerk Wilson's head. Making sleep an even more difficult proposition.

"Frightfully sorry, Alf", he said as they awoke. "A gentleman does not disclose his ailments. I shall make a more valiant effort next time to contain himself."

163

"Do not worry yourself. We are all in a bad fix. When that wretched old buzzard opens up the trapdoor, I will do my best to see that he gets us more water." Wilson said. Wood made a noise that started as a laugh but ended in a cough.

The trapdoor opened, and everyone fell in a line. Old Swims's head poked in. He coughed disturbingly before he started to talk. "Wal, boys, the Yankee Mitchell has advanced and 'eh taken Bridgeport. He has dun much harm to many good people. Now he has Chatt'nooga undeh his cannon and burn th' town alon' wit evwyn heah." This news caused some excitement for the raiders down below. "Now, befo' y'all git excited and believe yo' free'um is at han'." He paused then to cough again. "Y'all have bin ordered to be brought to anutha jail in Geo'gia."

That last part took a little longer to digest, but it did not matter; they were leaving the jail. Finally, leaving the hole. As long as it was away from this jail and Old Swims, it did not matter where they were taken.

After having breakfast, the ladder was lowered. Everyone formed a line and made their way up. Wilson's arms were much heavy. His head felt heavy. This was the most physical activity he had done in sometime when he went up the ladder. Each step and arm reach took a lot of energy. Bensinger was ahead of him and moved slow, so Wilson would have to wait for the next bar to be free before he moved up. He had to keep pace with Wood, giving him encouragement,

"There you go, Marky!"

"Keep it moving."

"Only two more!"

Besides coughing, Wood did not speak.

When Wilson's head broke the surface from the hole, the difference between the hot sickening air of the hole and the hot air from the cell room was immeasurable. There were guards waiting for them, looking stern. Wilson wasted no time to get out, crouching, so there was no tension in his chain until Wood got out.

Wood was barely out when one of the guards said, "Move on th' double quick yank, outsai. Y'all gwyn ahwn th' train. Yo' fellow devils ahw outsi'. Go and jine 'em."

As they passed by Swims, Wilson took what he hoped would be the last look. That dirty hair, nasty stubble, and blank looked complete with glazed eyes were what he got.

Wilson and Wood went out of the door, following Bensinger. There was another guard nearby the stairwell, eyeing them as they all came down. The prospect of going outside was much for Wilson, he never gave any thought about trying to overpower the guard and seize his rifle. When Bensinger opened the door, a blinding light hit Wilson's eyes so hard that he had to squint.

Staggering out of the door, the blinding light, the sweet smell of fresh air, the sound of people and horses going by; all hit him like a bucket of ice water in the face. He tried to cover his eyes, but the restraints wouldn't allow him to raise his arms above his head. Once all the raiders were outside of the jail, a group of confederate soldiers surrounded them with rifles that were fixed with bayonets.

A sergeant appeared right in front of the motley crowd and called out, "Prisoners fall in line. We are headed towards the train depot. If you fail to keep pace or fall behind, you will be prodded along with a bayonet. Now, forward march!"

The ghastly looking raiders, with tattered looking clothes, and slim frames did not march like soldiers; instead, they staggered like a bunch of drunks after a bar closes. It felt like a haze or a bad dream for Wilson as he tried to keep his pace. Everything beyond a few feet was rather blurry. He could make out people standing along the street stop to point and whisper at each other. What kept him going in an urgent fashion was getting further away from the prison and as fast as he could. Except Wood was constantly coughing and had a hard time keeping up with them.

The sound of distant cannon booming made everyone jump, then slow down, only for the sergeant's boom. "Keep a lively step 'less you want to git it!"

They staggered their way to the train depot. In the late morning, the depot was much busier, most of the people were going about their businesses. A few stopped to stare at them. Wilson's eyes had adjusted to the light now, so he took himself in, and was shocked at what he had seen. His clothes were torn up, his boots were chewed almost through, and he had lost much weight. Everyone else looked the same, if not worse. A train pulled into the station, the chuffs and hisses of the engine made Wilson feel as if he was back waiting for the train on that rainy morning.

All the passengers started moving off the train. Confederate soldiers began to come out. "This has the memory of our past deed. As though it 'twas a dream." Wood said.

"Perhaps you mean a nightmare. If you need further evidence of this all being a dream, look onto the engine", Wilson said. Sure enough, on the familiar looking dark green engine with red-orange accents, was the gold name plated 'General'.

"Johnny Reb sure does have a morbid sense of humor." Wood said.

"Say, look on the secesh there are. Plenty more than the last time." Knight said. A line of passengers then formed each, carrying a passport this time around. "Well, it appears we gave Johnny Reb a good fright. Perhaps we did some good after all."

***

The raiders were loaded onto the train and eventually departed on schedule. For Wilson, the train was still cramped, with hardwood seats. At the very least, no one was smoking, so no actual smoke loomed in the air. Some of the confederate guards were generous enough to let the raiders drink from their canteens. Wilson looked out of the window and made out what he imagined was the same terrain he and Wood traveled during their escape. Eventually, the thought of what he had been through turned to what lay ahead, and he decided he did not want to think about that, so he went to sleep.

***

The next day they arrived in the town of Madison and were taken to the stone made county jail. The jail quarters were not much better, but at the least, there was a window that allowed fresh air and light in. This alone raised the spirits of the raiders.

"Fellows," Knight said. "While waiting for our train, a kindly secesh slipped me a newspaper, I did not care to disclose the facts in the company of our enemies. Now I can. It states that New Orleans has been captured by our own troops. They emphasized the fact that the mighty Mississippi, as a whole, is almost in our hands. It also states that our general in Virginia that fellow McClellan is coming closer to Richmond. With Old Stars and Stripes nearing Chattanooga. This damn thing might be over soon!"

Everyone cheered. After a much longer journey and tortuous time in the hole, this was what the raiders needed to hear to buoy of their spirits. The food was not much better, but the water and slop buckets were filled and emptied regularly.

***

On the second day, everyone sat in a circle swapping stories when Porter, who was chained to Dorsey, jerked the chain rather harshly. Dorsey coughed, then huffed and jerked his end of the chain, but in kind. Then Porter jerked the chain again. Then Dorsey. Then Porter. Then Dorsey flew at Porter, and they grabbed the chain and tried to strangle each other. Because both their hands were shackled together and the best they could do was to jerk the chain, the whole show was made for a good laugh among the others. Hearing the laughter, Porter and Dorsey too broke into a laugh.

***

On the third day, the confederate sergeant strolled into the jail with that same stern look on his face. "It appears your Yankee friends were only putting on a show to threaten Chattanooga. Now that it is over, they have left for home. As for y'all? You are gwyn back te Chattanooga."

***

The train ride this time was in one of the boxcars. For the majority of raiders, this was a rather familiar trip, although at the very least they went at a normal speed and there were no real abrupt stops or starts. There was no merriment, no positive morale, not anything.

Everyone felt a sense of dread of where they were going back to. Walking back to the old jail, Wilson had a feeling of fear that he had probably never felt before. Before the raid he felt a sense of anxiety of what would happen. This time around, he knew.

When the prison came into view, Wilson's hands began to shake. When they approached the door, and the sergeant leading the detailed knocked on the door, Wilson started to feel sick in the stomach. "I cannot go back." He said to himself. The door opened, and the guard ushered them all in. Wilson decided to attack the nearest guard. Maybe it might inspire the rest to rush of the guards, but at the very least, he would provoke them into shooting him. He couldn't go back. The door slammed SHUT.

Wilson's attention was diverted by a kind-looking officer walking down the stairs toward them.

"Good afternoon, Yankees. My name is Captain James Law. Colonel Claiborne has instructed me to be the new captain of the guard. I am to remind you that you are prisoners and will be treated as such. I am a southerner, so I cannot condone your actions on the railroad. I am also a Christian, however, and have read the last report of your stay in the hole. It is a cruel business that we are engaged in here. Therefore, I decided to alleviate your suffering by directing a dozen, or so East Tennessee Tories be moved to the hole so you shall be moved to the cell upstairs."

A huge weight was lifted off the raider's shoulders. Wilson exhaled. The sick feeling began to slowly go away.

***

Once the raiders got situated, Pittenger spoke up. "That was a pinch we avoided, was it not? How about we sing a song to raise our spirits some more?"

The upstairs cell was not much bigger, and the sleeping condition was about the same. Because the guards made regular rounds, it was easier to get water and slop buckets taken care of on a more regular basis. The best part was there were three (barred) windows that emitted plenty of light and, more importantly, fresh air.

***

After breakfast, one of the guards approached the door holding a basket with some old books. "Here you are Yankees. Sum of the good folk' 'round here has let you have their books fer a time. I alsa threw in my pack of playin' cards. Now just so's y'all know. Y'all ain' gittin this on accoun' of any kindness. Y'all gitten this te keep yeh minds of mischief or any otheh foolish thoughts." He slung his rifle, used his key to open the door, slid the basket in, and then shut it back. Wollam was the closest to the basket and reached in to pull a pack of cards out.

"I was quite the fiend at cards. Perhaps I may shuffle with these irons on. Anyone care to play?"

"I shall."

"Cut me in."

Wilson thought for a moment. "I have never played before, but now I am interested."

"What? All this time later, and now you want to lower yourself? If only your father would see you now." Wood smirked. "To hell with that." Wood laughed, only to end with a cough.

"Shame on the lot of you", Pittenger scolded, as Wollam cut the deck. "Card playing is an immoral vice."

"Oh, bugger off."

***

Trying to play off the worries everyone had about Andrew's trial, and their own obvious upcoming trial, Pittenger and George Wilson organized a fake one and played a game of putting someone else up for prosecution for an imaginary crime. The more imaginative, the better. Campbell served as the judge.

"I accuse Alf Wilson of being a man with low morals and no redeeming qualities while consorting with the enemy. Twice he took a piece of my allotted bit of bacon. Twice! He is clearly in the graces with Johnny Reb." Wood argued.

"That is a lie! I have been a good Christian with many positive virtues. It is Mark Wood who has blazed the path to the devil's den. I merely followed it. As for the so-called bacon, I took it as I found no resistance." Wilson counter argued.

"Order, order!" Campbell tapped on the wall. "I move that both parties are found guilty. The main guilt lies in that both have abused our legal system by bringing such claims against each other and not allowing anyone else the chance."

"Hear, hear!"

"Guilty!"

***

"Come up here and take a look. The rebs are going about their drills. Perhaps we ought to have a bit of fun with them." Knight said excitedly.

"Oh, jolly good. Come along, Alf, some merriment at the expense of our 'osts is in good order", said Wood, as he stood up and tugged at the chain. Wilson would have preferred to sit down, but he obliged and stood up to go towards the window. Outside in the yard, there was a squad of confederates that were performing their drills. Several of the raiders gathered around the window, waiting for someone to say something.

Of course, it was Knight.

"You call that a formation? That is a very poor display. Even for rebs."

Then everyone joined in.

"Is that it? 'Eaven 'elp you when going up against our northern brethern!"

"You, you devil on the left. You are doing it all wrong. Do it better!"

"This is why the South is losing right here!"

The soldiers continued with the drill, but it was obvious some were losing focus and showed agitation.

"That is all wrong secesh!"

"You on the right. Does your momma know where you have been?"

The soldier on the right broke ranks, dropped his gun, picked up a rock and threw it hard at the window. It bounced off the stone wall, instead sent the raiders into a laughing fit, especially as they could hear the sergeant chew out the soldier.

***

The next morning Law appeared and approached the cell door.

"Yankees. It has come to my attention that some of your band has taken ill. It will not do well to start an epidemic, and seein' as doctors are in short supply, I requested permission from Colonel Claiborne to allow y'all in the yard. He has allowed this for today I am allowing two groups of y'all outside for an hour each." He waited as the raiders stated their various thanks. "Now then. I expect y'all to behave now. I do not care to hear for any foolishness on any of your parts. Understood?" Everyone acknowledged.

***

When Wilson and his group went outside, it felt exhilarating to be in an open area and not have to run into anyone. To feel the sun on their faces.

It almost felt-

"Alf! Slow yourself! I cannot keep up the pace!" Wood's comment and weight returned Wilson back to reality. He was almost running when Wood spoke up.

"I am sorry, Marky. This is marvelous."

"I know it, Alf. I do not want to spoil the moment, however-" he broke into a coughing fit before he could resume talking. "I am not feeling well. May we please sit?" Wilson wanted to walk some more, he also had the energy, but he knew Wood was not well.

"All right, Marky. I believe there is some more water in that bucket over there. We should get some and sit in the shade."

It was a nice spring day, sipping their water, and sitting in the shade, they paid no attention to the guards nor the soldiers drilling. They just leaned against the wall that had a tree looming over, which gave a generous amount of shade.

Wilson breathed it in. "This reminds me of Haskins. On a cool spring day, I would go for a walk in the nearby woods. I did not have anywhere in particular to go. Perhaps drink water from a creek. I would just enjoy myself." The memory made him think of past times.

"Go on then."

"Excuse me?"

"You had me believing I was somewhere else. Keep saying those fancy words."

Wilson smiled. He thought he was somewhere else as well.

***

Law was again in front of the cell. "Yankees. You have a guest today. Mr. Bill Fuller. He was the engineer of the train you stole and led him on a furious chase. He has requested to speak to you. Again, I expect you all to behave." He turned and walked out past Fuller.

Fuller stood in the doorway. He looked sophisticated. He never left his position. All the raiders stood up or scooted close to the bars to get a better look at the man. He spoke first.

"I wanted to see you Yankees in person. I had testified against Mr. Andrews, and I must say he is quite the individual. I understand why you would follow him on such a fool's errand."

Knight replied, "It was not no fool's errand. We got away with your train and ruined the particulars of your track."

"Yet it has been repaired where you sit here as common thieves. How is that view for you."

"You are welcome to come inside and see for yourself," Campbell growled.

Fuller smiled and shook his head. "No. I prefer this view."

"Did you mean, really believed that stealing my train and ruining a single line of track, could whip the whole of the south? Perhaps if your armies moved more swiftly, they would have split my country, true, but to whip the people of the south? That shall never be. No matter how many battles you win or land you conquer...hell, you might even win the whole war. It would not matter, as we will never accept you as our countrymen. This country will never be united. This is how things were, and this is how they will be." With that, he walked out.

"My, my! what a charming fellow." Wood said.

***

"My lads, I see that most of you have regained much of your strength, so now I must state the fact that we must begin planning our

171

flight from this place. My trial is coming to an end, and the outcome will surely not be in my favor", Andrews said. Everyone nodded in agreement. The guard had left to relieve himself. Andrews waited in case he could hear of the footsteps coming. When it was still silent, he continued in a hushed tone.

"I have puzzled over Mr. Pittenger's plan of using Mr. Knight's talent of relieving us of our shackles and charging at the guards, pursuing a bold rush to freedom. It will not do. I have no doubt of Mr. Knight's talent, it will take too long for him to make a suitable pick. While some of you are fine big lads and will, without a doubt, dispatch a guard at ease, I counted as many as thirty guards outside. Any bunch could turn the affair into a massacre. I believe my plan of using Mr. Wollam to hide away after he is brought back from the yard and quietly dispatch ol' Swims. After which, he will have the keys and may release us. Whence, we will proceed to the gate under cover of darkness and slip away together as the guards shall be none the wiser. Are you well for that job, Mr. Wollam?"

"To get my hands on that buzzard? I would enjoy that very much."

"My lads, what have you to say?"

Pittenger started, "I say, let your lawyer try."

"There are rumors of a prisoner exchange-"

"My lads. There is no time." Andrews snapped. The raiders have never heard him speak in such a tone before. "Are we in this together? Or are we not?"

Everyone nodded.

"Good. Therefore, I shall set a date for this coming Wednesday then. That will be sufficient time to smooth out the particulars.

***

On Wednesday afternoon, all the raiders were either anxious, excited, or both. Wilson and Wood sat in their usual spot outside. Wilson had found a heavy rock that he was using to work out his arms. He wanted to be ready. Wood grabbed a handful of weed and was chewing on them to calm his nerves.

"Do you suppose we all would leave" he said in a low tone.

"No", Wilson replied. "Some of our numbers will pay the penalty of escape with their lives. I, for one, am ready to make another attempt. I do not intend to hang in Tennessee."

"Such passions will get you so far. If we are to be murdered, at least we are in the good company of one another. Excluding you, of course", Wood smirked.

Wilson smiled and shook his head. A guard walked in the yard and bellowed, "Very well, yanks! Yeh, time is gone! Fall in and fo'hm a line!" The raiders staggered to their feet and formed up.

"Aye me. These spring days are far too short." Wood grumbled. As they started to walk back, they passed George Wilson, who was unchained and lied on the ground, coughing and looking miserable.

"Oh, come now. We cannot be having that now, Georgie. Come along with the rest of us." Wood cackled.

George Wilson groaned. "I will follow you. Once I regain myself." He sucked in some air. Wood and Wilson shrugged and then walked away. As the raiders rounded the corner, they saw Captain Law approach, George Wilson. The two saluted each other was the thing they saw before they walked to the front entrance of the jail.

"What do you suppose that was about?" Wood asked.

"I suppose we will find out."

***

"My fellows. I am being ordered to set for Knoxville to stand trial. This could be tremendous and might allow us to establish ourselves as uniformed soldiers who need to be tried as such. If the rumors are to be believed and exchange is imminent, we should plead our case to be considered for such an event.

"Now I was given the duty of selecting twelve of you to accompany me. I made my selection based on who has served with me in my regiment, along with those who have made the dangerous journey with me to get here in the first place. Pittenger, Ross, Shadrach, Campbell, Scott, Slavens, Robertson, Buffum, Mason, Brown, and Knight. These men shall go. I deeply apologize for the rest of you. I promise I will argue on all of your behalf."

"Oh, think nothing on it." Wood replied. Under his breath, he muttered, "Ass."

***

Three days later, the word came out that the raiders who were leaving were to get ready. All around, there were farewells, handshakes, hugs, well wishes, and the occasional promise of seeing each other in hell. Knight handed his penknife, and another bone he had fashioned into a lock pick, to Wilson.

"I leave these articles with you, Alf" Knight said. "For luck, and if by chance, you will require them more than I."

"Thank you."

The worst was with Andrews. The ones leaving had a sense of dread, as if they knew this was the last time they would ever see him. He knew it too.

"Boys, if I never see you here again, may we meet on the other side of Jordan."

"What are we to do now?" Dorsey asked after they all left. "Our numbers are less now."

"I am still able to try the plan we had agreed upon," Wollam said. "Perhaps we should slip away much better with so few?"

"There is not enough of us to bounce the guards. All the big fellows have now gone", Hawkins said.

Parrott, who was still lying on his stomach, his back a maze of nasty scars, turned his head and volunteered, "Perhaps those fellows will tell a good story, and we shall be exchanged?"

"Do not count on that," Andrews said. Then he sighed a tired sigh. There is no hope in believing the rebs will show us mercy."

"Cap is right. We have to find another way out." Wilson said.

***

It happened that afternoon. Everyone was outside now in a single shift. Captain Law approached Andrews with an envelope in hand.

"Mr. Andrews. This is marked for you." Law turned and left. Andrews put it in his pocket. He walked with Hawkins for a while before going back to the cell.

When the other raiders came in walking, he was sitting. He looked calm. Peaceful. He held up the letter.

"Well, my lads. The verdict is in. I've been found guilty and am to be hung by the neck until dead."

Wilson felt a blow to his stomach. He could not think of anything to say. He looked around the cell. Everything looked out of focus. He looked at Andrews. He smiled. It was the smile of a corpse.

When is this tragedy occurring?" Dorsey asked. "In seven days' time," Andrews replied.

"No. The hangman will wait. We will be gone before then," Wilson said.

"What are you proposing?" Wollam asked. "We obviously cannot dig our way out; perhaps we can saw our out through the roof."

174

"How do you propose to do this?" Andrews asked.

Wilson held up the penknife. "With this."

***

The next night, six of the raiders were in a circle and performed a nightly concert, mainly to keep up their spirits, and possibly to entertain anyone within hearing distance. They sang 'Do They Miss Me At Home', 'A Life on the Ocean Wave', and 'The Prairie Queen'. In between the songs, they would talk loudly or mock laugh at some unfunny joke.

Wilson, along with Wood, Dorsey, and Porter, approached the group as they finished. They had worked up a sweat, and their hands had blisters. Wilson gasped for air.

"We are weary of saw shoving. Who will be next to volunteer?"

Andrews was finishing picking the lock on his shackles. "I shall go."

"I cannot allow that, Cap," Hawkins said. "You will need your rest. Allow me to go."

"Thank you."

Reddick and Bensinger piped up. "We shall go." They got up and followed Hawkins.

"Midnight is nigh, my lads. We must work in hushed tones." Andrews said. Reddick and Bensinger stood together while Hawkins climbed on their shoulders and started to continue working on a hole with a pocketknife. He sawed as quietly as he could until his hands could not go anymore, and he traded places with Reddick. After the three men had their turns, the hole was wide enough for a man to squeeze through, and the knife was a thin piece of hot metal. The three men got a generous amount of water from the bucket and helped Andrews and Wollam up to the attic. There they started working, removing a brick from the end of the wall to create an opening. As they were working, the rest of the raiders used the little moonlight to make a rope of the blankets they had. All their hands were burning, but they pressed on.

"So, it will be Andrews and Wollam that get to go?" Wood whispered.

"Yes. It would be foolhardy for us all to make that attempt."

"Cap is a brave man, as any. If any of us should make it. It must be him." Wilson replied.

"If Johnny Reb does not murder us outright, it shall be Hellhole for us." Wilson paused before continuing. "We will endure it. We have endured much thus far."

***

The sun had started to rise. Andrews hissed out, "Be prompt, my lads! Our moment of opportunity is slipping away!" The raiders threw the blanket in the hole. Andrews caught it, and with only a sliver of light, tied an end to the rafters, and threw the other end outside. He could hear the sentry outside doing his paces. His heartbeat fast. His hair was wet with sweat. He didn't want to go. But he had to.

He heard the sentry walk past him. He took a deep breath, let go, and lowered himself down the rope, boots in the mouth to keep himself as quiet as possible. He did not get far before his foot dislodged a loose brick. It fell to the ground with the loudest THUD! The raiders jumped at the noise. There was some discussion as if they should try to sneak out as well, but the thud put an end to that.

When they heard the sentry yell, "Corporal of the guard! Corporal of the guard! Captain! Oh, Captain! Halt Halt!" They rushed to the window and could make out a figure running towards the wall and climb over it, followed by another one. The sporadic gunshots startled them momentarily, which gave way to a quiet celebration for the moment. The captain got away. "Do not let the festive spirit linger for too long, boys." Wood said. "For tomorrow, our troubles shall begin anew."

CHAPTER 29

Back again-Old routines new again-More Space-Swims-Andrews sad return-What Happened-Half to Knoxville Return to Atlanta-Fulton County Jail-Turner-Thor-New Routines-Wood's sickness-Trading-Old friends return-Captain Fry-Results of the court-martial-George Wilson betrayed-Swift and immediate action-Farewell

"Damn you all. Making merry while cuttin' meh jail to pieces! I might have known you that damned Yankees were up to sum devilment whilst singing hymns. Well. I have meh own merriment. No mo' time spen' outsihde. No mo' nuthin'. It is back in th' hole fo' y'all. Don' worry. It won't be long now until y'all ah hung. As for that loathsome, Andrews. We gwyn' to catch 'im and hang him on time", Swims stated in an irritatingly whiny voice.

***

"Well. 'Ere we are again fellows", Wood coughed. "Back in 'ell 'ole. It would have been a matter of time before we were back down 'ere."

"Perhaps we shall have another go at singing. Perhaps something to raise our spirits?" Bensinger suggested. The hot air was stifling Wilson's throat.

He coughed before he said. "Not at this time. As there are fewer of us in here, perhaps we could seek better arrangements by the only sources of air they have in here."

"Splendid." "That is a fine idea."

"How should we take care of this arrangement?"

Wilson continued. "There are ten of us now. That would allow for five by each hole."

After some shuffling, accidental bumping into each other, and stumbling around in the dark, the raiders split into two groups and formed around the two openings to breathe in what little air came through. It wasn't much, but it was enough.

Dorsey spoke up. "With our numbers less, we might have a chance to move about more freely. This will make our whole experience more tolerable until our fates are known."

"I believe we should sing another song, and forget about our troubles for a while," Bensinger said.

"Very well," Wilson said.

"I fear our best singers have gone on to Knoxville," Reddick said.

"That works in our favor. At the very least, our braying will bring some harm to Johnny Reb's ears", Wood said.

***

So, there they were, back in the hole. Back to getting eaten by mites, and clothes chewed by rats. Same dirt ground. Same pitiful rations. At least there was some more food to go around. By now, everyone had told the most interesting stories of their lives, so the raiders started making up stories or told a boring story whilst adding some exotic elements to make it more interesting to pass away the long hot hours. No one talked about what they would do if they got home.

***

It was during the morning bucket ritual being lowered that they heard from Old Swims.

"Heh." He coughed and then spit. "I told y'all we were gwyn' to catch the villain Andrews. Boy, did we! He'll be along shortly."

Everyone wanted to hope that Swims lied, but deep down, they knew it was true.

Later, the trapdoor opened, and Wilson felt a blow in his stomach when he saw the back of a figure climb down the ladder. When the figure turned to reveal Andrews, Wilson felt horror when he saw what was left of him in that dim light.

Andrews was emaciated, ankles swollen, barefoot, bruised, and bloody all over. As the ladder was being pulled up, Wilson could see his bloody footprints on each step. Andrews' face was haggard while his eyes had a blank look. Just as the ladder was pulled up, Andrews sank to his knees. Several of the raiders rushed forward, only to be caught up in their chains. Wilson made it to Andrews and helped him to the ground.

"Get some water!"

The trapdoor closed. Everyone scrambled in the dark to get to the water.

"There ain't much left!" Bensinger called out.

"Just bring what you can!" Wilson then told Andrews, "Hold on, Cap."

"Here." Bensinger and Reddick brought a handful of water cupped in their hands. Trying to find Andrew's mouth, they spilled plenty.

After drinking the water from their dirty hands, Andrews coughed and weakly said, "Thanks." The raiders did not dare move Andrews. They let him lay where he was, bringing him whatever water they had left. Finally, he was able to catch his breath, and little by little, he told his story of escape.

***

He was separated from Wollam as soon as they had cleared the fence of the jail. He made his way outside in the city and hid under a tree uncomfortably all day before resuming his trek at dusk, he tried to swim to the Tennessee, but the rapid current and a thunderstorm had exhausted him as he tried to cross. He wound up losing his trousers and boots. He wound up on a bank and got help from a local boy who took him to the home of a man named Williams. Williams then took him in, fed and clothed him, only to turn him into the authorities.

The trapdoor opened again, and the ladder was lowered. Swims was the first to come down. Holding a lantern with one hand. After him was a confederate officer who carried a sword. He got in between the raiders and Andrews, holding his sword out, pointing end at the raiders, daring them to attack him. Behind him came William Lewis, a colored blacksmith. He had brought along a hammer, shackles, and a piece of iron. Lewis nodded at the raiders.

One muttered, "Uncle Billy."

Everyone's heart sank as they knew what he did. Andrews was leaning on his elbow, watching as Lewis hammered the shackles tightly around Andrews' swollen ankles. Not a word was said by anyone. When he completed his work, Lewis stood up and slightly nodded with a sad face at the raiders and went back up the ladder, followed by the officer and Swims. As soon as the trapdoor was shut, Wilson went to the ground and started feeling in the darkness.

"Come along, Marky!"

"What in blazes are you up to?"

Wilson groped until he felt a parcel. "I knew it! Uncle Billy would not have left us empty-handed." His hands unwrapped the parcel as he felt something damp.

"Cap. Uncle Billy has smuggled across some lettuce. Here" Wilson reached out in the darkness until he felt Andrew's face, and then his hand found Andrew's mouth. Andrews chewed the lettuce slowly. Breathing through his mouth.

He finally spoke. "Thank you, Mr. Wilson. Please. Tell the tale of Mr. Lewis. For my sake"

"He was brought here as a younger lad. He was taught the trade of blacksmithing, and eventually made enough on his own to purchase his freedom and his family, and now he has his own shop here in Chattanooga."

"Thank you, Mr. Wilson."

The trapdoor opened. A sergeant poked his head through. "James Andrews. Yeh allowed to come on upstairs. It is less fowl up heah. We also brought a local minister oveh to talk with you. As the scaffold we ah plannin' to hang yeh with is almos' done."

Andrews dragged himself up the ladder.

***

There were no songs left to be sung. No jokes to laugh at. No stories to tell. No arguments to attempt to win. It was mostly quiet. It was Saturday. June 7th. The day Andrews was to be executed.

The trapdoor opened rather loudly, and the sergeant of the guard boomed out, "Up yanks! Y'all ah movin south on te' Atlanta. Get on up and get movin'!"

Everyone groaned and grunted as they got up and wiped cobwebs from their eyes.

"What if we need to relieve ourselves?"

The sergeant gave an annoying sigh.

"Be quick about it!"

***

Marching through the dusty streets, Wilson's eye's adjusted to the light much quicker this time. Everything felt like a fever dream. The heat, the choking dust. The people on the street were either moving at a fast pace or stopping to laugh and jeer at the raiders. Wilson finally felt like he had wakened up when he heard the train whistle blow and felt the forward motion of the boxcar.

Wood coughed. "I must say I am quickly tiring of doing these same paces."

Wilson shrugged. It took to much energy for him to talk.

There were guards in the boxcar, at both the ends. The raiders had scattered throughout. Andrews sat in the seat in front of Wood and Wilson. Two confederates walked through and stopped in the aisle right by Andrew's seat.

"There he is. The train thievin' Yankee sumbitch," one said. "Enjoy yo' las' rihde. Yank. They gwyn' te sen' ye te' hell where ye belon'."

The confederates giggled and resumed their walk towards the next boxcar. Wilson had to suppress his rage. It would not do him any good to burn over what they said. He looked at the back of Andrew's head. His head was lowered and let out a mournful sigh.

Wilson looked out of the window. He couldn't see much outside, but it was something to try to forget where he was, at least for a while.

"Mr. Wilson." Andrews' soft voice snapped Wilson out of his trance.

"Yes, cap?"

"I was wondering if I may persuade you to move to the water closet and make an attempt to pull the window up. I will follow you and attempt to jump out."

"Yes, Cap. Go along, Mark."

Wilson was on the aisle side. He stood up but had to wait for Wood's coughing to subside before he made his way to the water closet. Wood shuffled along behind him, guards in front eyeing him.

"Whar ye gwyn' boy?"

"The water closet."

"Don' give me a reason te cum in afteh ye."

Wilson just went straight in. Without wasting any time, he went straight for the window. With his hands clasped together, he did his best to pull the window up. His arms were hurt. He was tired. The window started to give. Because it was shuttered, it only opened six inches. Wilson took a deep breath and gave it one last try, only to feel his arms give out. He looked at Wood and shook his head.

Defeated, the pair shuffled back to their seats. As they were moving past Andrew's seat, Wilson looked at him and shook his head. Andrew's face showed much disappointment as he hung his head down low.

***

The train pulled into Atlanta. The sun was still high in the sky. The raiders were escorted under armed guards to a three-story building the locals called the Concert Hall. Andrews was the only one not chained to anyone else, and with his swollen feet, he did his best to keep pace with the others. They were marched to the second floor. There was an open space filled with wooden benches.

"Have a seat Yankees. Do not make much noise." Everyone shuffled to find an open space on the bench.

When Wood and Wilson found a spot, Wood said quietly, "Could I persuade you to allow me to lay down, Alf." Wilson nodded.

"I said, hush up!"

It took maneuvering, but Wood managed to lie down, as Wilson sat on the floor. Minutes passed. Wood's occasional coughing broke the silence. Wilson didn't know what to think. Maybe he didn't want to think.

The silence was broken again by the sound of someone's heavy boots coming up the stairs. Everyone shuffled and turned to see a man dressed in a black funeral suit.

In a calm, inviting voice, he spoke. "Come on now, Mr. Andrews."

Andrews stood up. "Could I have a moment to bid farewell to my men?"

The lead guard snapped "Well then be damn quick about it! We have no time to fool away here!" The Man in Black put his hand on the guard's shoulder, which quieted him down.

"Of course, Mr. Andrews."

Everyone stood up as Andrews went to each man and said his final good-bye. Wilson was near the back. He had time to think of something meaningful to say. He racked his brain. He wanted to say something inspirational or positive. Andrews was in front of him, hand outstretched.

"Farewell, Mr. Wilson." Wilson managed half a smile and nodded. He shook Andrew's hand. He watched Andrews walk to the door, past the Man in Black, and down the stairs, with the Man in the Black following. Everyone shuffled towards the windows. Wood struggled, but he made it. After a moment, Andrews appeared on the street as he made his way into a parked carriage. The Man in Black climbed in the right after him. The carriage driver whipped the reins, and the two reined horses started off, pulling the carriage away. After the carriage was gone, everyone sulked back to their benches and waited.

Time seemed to stand rather still. Finally, the head guard reappeared and yelled out, "On your feet, Yankees! You are now moving to your new station!" Everyone groaned and stood up. Wilson had to lean on one knee and wait for Wood to sit up. He felt the chain tighten against his neck, so he quickly stood up, only to nearly lose his balance.

The raiders marched downstairs to the fading of daylight and started to walk across a busy Atlanta night when Wood collapsed with a coughing fit, which stopped the whole group.

"Please, I need to rest for a while."

"You will do no such thing, yank. On your feet, now." A guard nudged him with his feet. Wilson helped him up, and they walked another block before Wood collapsed again.

"Please. I am not well."

"I do not care Yankee. Up to ye feet!" The guard started pushing him with the butt of his rifle.

"I will assist him," Wilson said. He helped Wood to his feet. They started again, barely making it past another block before Wood collapsed again.

"I have had it! On your feet Yankee and mean it! Less I bayonet you here and finish this!" Wood could only cough. Wilson went to his knees.

"There is no need for this. I will carry him and relieve you of your burden."

"Well, hurry it up then."

Wilson used the reserves of his strength and picked up Wood like a baby.

"Much obliged," Wood said. He would angle his head so he would not cough in Wilson's face.

***

After they had marched four more blocks, they arrived at the Fulton County Jail. The fact that they were going to the second floor perked Wilson's attention. He was ready to believe that they were going to another hole similar to the one in Chattanooga. Looking down the corridor, he saw four cells, two on each side of the hallway, and two of them had a smaller iron cage inside of them. They had oak planking for floors and iron bars on the windows. For the double cell doors, the inner one was made of riveted iron bars; the outer door was made of hardwood, hanging off the hinges completed with iron locks. The fact that it was better looking than anything in Chattanooga made Wilson feel better.

In the middle of the row right between the cells was a guard wielding a wheelbarrow with two elderly looking men in a dichotomy.

One was a kindly looking fellow, while the other had a rotten face, complete with a scowl. Behind them was a black man and woman.

Wood coughed. "I feel well enough to walk on my own now, Alf. Much obliged again." Wilson let Wood down. He felt that extra weight fall off of him immediately.

"Fellows", the kind-looking one said. "This is the Fulton County Jail. You may refer to me as Turner. Right here is my assistant, Thor. Behind us are the colored servants of this prison, John and Kate. They will tend to your rations and water. Now then, this is a prison, and as prisoners, you ought to be treated as such. You shall be fed twice a day. You are allotted time in the regular cell with the windows open. After dark, you shall sleep in the shorter cell. There are no exceptions to this rule. As for your stay here, I do not believe it will be for long. The rumors suggest that there will be a prisoner exchange coming along soon and that you will be a part of it. At the very least, paroled back to your homes."

"Bah!", said Thor. "Such a poor waste of resources. You damned men should have hung all together with that awful Andrews. I place money that y'all hang in time." Turner gave him a look that told him to be silent. Then he continued.

"As such, my jail is inaccessible to make a flight from. I keep it locked tightly, and the guards outside will shoot anyone tryin' to flee. Believe my word Yankees. They are quite the marksmen." He paused to let that sink in.

"Now then, since I have said my piece. I figure y'all have been tormented enough by the irons you were burdened with. I am going to unlock y'all, on the pretense that none of y'all would attempt to take a walk by yourself or bring harm to myself or any of the otheh folks hereabouts." Everyone nodded and said they wouldn't. "Alright, then." He introduced a set of keys and started unlocking everyone's locks and shackles.

"They ought to be saddled with more irons, not less." Thor growled, and then walked out. The news, along with the fact they would not be shackled together like this anymore brightened Wilson's mood. No more shackles. Forever. Exchange or parole? One, or the other, please. When Turner finally unlocked Wilson's hands, it felt extra good to not have that weight and to finally have full use of his hands.

***

Dinner was more the same. Rotten bacon, cornbread with the occasional cob ground in Negro peas, and some insects for good measure. Wilson had come to find that maggots gave food an extra flavor. At night, the guards herded them into the smaller cage that lined with hay. Wilson lay down and felt the floor was painfully cold.

"Say, boys. This ground is awfully cold and sore. Let's say we crowd around each other for some warmth?" Everyone agreed. They formed a tight circle. Wilson was not sure if he would have trouble sleeping, but not a minute had passed after he lay down and closed his eyes, he passed right out.

***

"Mark. How are you faring?" Wood sprawled out. He looked terrible and sounded much worst. Everyone had crowded around him. Wilson tore a piece of his sleeve and dipped it into the water bucket, rung it out, and put it on Wood's head. It was burning hot.

"He is in need of an immediate doctor," Wilson said.

"Do you believe the rebs will furnish one?" Bensinger asked.

"No. They are a wretched lot who would not provide any mercy to a dying Yankee", Hawkins said. Dorsey walked toward the bars as Porter closed in behind him.

"Say you there?", he called out to the guards. "May we have an audience with Mr. Turner? It concerns our ill friend in here."

The guards looked at each other before one said, "I shall go."

Dorsey walked back to Wood. "He is getting our jailer. Perhaps he shall do something." Wood's eyes were blank. He mumbled his thanks. Dorsey smiled and walked away. Porter followed. Dorsey stopped to look at Porter.

"Why are you following me so?"

Porter looked sheepish. "My apologies. I have grown accustomed to keeping pace with you less I want to be strangled to death."

***

Instead of Turner. They got a hold of Thor.

"What is this? You believe I should help yo' unwell friend? I do not have any concern fo' him. With them Yankee boats on the water, we cain' get no medicine anyhow. It is best to let him go to Eternity. Yo' friend Andrews? Frum what I heard, he hung, only he was too tall, and his feet hit the dirt as he was twisting all the while. Some folks tried to quicken his slow death. They say he died of strangulation. It might be best to let yo' friend pass on, so he is spared when the time comes for y'all to meet yo' end." He smirked and walked out.

Wilson did not think anything would happen with Thor. When dinner came, he would send for Turner. Looking at Wood, maybe it was best for him to go, Wilson thought.

"Mark, if I were you, I wouldn't try to get well. You can, by dying, save the rebels the troubles of hanging you. Why not be more accommodating, since all they do for us is done without pay." Wood's eyes came into focus, as he cackled wildly.

"What is that? Give the hangmen less work to do? Never. I shall get well just to spite ole' Johnny Reb."

***

That night, Turner went in to check on the raiders while John and Kate were doing their rounds to dish out the rations and take care of the water and slop buckets.

"Mr. Turner. My friend is in urgent need of a doctor. He is quite unwell. I am afraid he might pass on to us what he has."

Wilson thought for a second, then undid his belt and handed it to them through the bars. "My buckle. It is made of pure gold. The rest is worthless." Turner took it and looked it over.

"They have been halloing about their friend before. Mr. Thor did not care much to act on it", a guard said.

Turner nodded. "A nice buckle. Very well. There is a doctor roundabout I am familiar with. I shall request he come calling in the morning."

"Thank you."

***

The next morning the doctor came and looked at Wood. He instructed him to be placed closer to the window. He gave him a spoonful of medicine from a bottle of his. Satisfied Wood took it, he handed Wilson the bottle and a small package full of onions.

"Keep his head cool. Give him a mouthful of that a day. Be sure to feed him those onions."

"Thank you."

The doctor nodded and walked out of the cell. After he was gone, the guards walked out of the cellblock, Dorsey approached Wilson.

"Was that buckle really gold?"

"No. I told a lie to get some help."

"If only your father could see what you did."

Wood cackled. "Marky, you are getting well already."

***

Turner came in that night carrying a satchel. "I brought several copies of the Good Book. It is something y'all kin read. I also brought a pack of playing cards, though I believe I have missed a few. I also brought along some checkers, alas; I am missing a few pieces as well as a board so you will have to make do. I bring these for the purpose of keeping your thoughts from straying too dangerous paths."

He opened the cell door and piled on his gifts on the floor. Wilson had learned to play checkers from his father. He enjoyed playing it with anyone who played him. Turner shut the door and walked away, only to stop and turn as he had forgotten something.

"Oh, this may brighten your spirits. Your fellow raiders are arriving tomorrow. They shall be our guests along with three Tennessee Tories. Good night." He walked out.

"It would do well to see the old cutthroats again, eh?"

"Hell, I thought those boys were done for sure!"

"Perhaps they struck a bargain for us all?"

***

The next day everyone waited with anticipation when they could hear the cacophony of footsteps coming up the steps. Then the double cell doors opened wide, and there were the rest of the raiders. Looking rather well and not weighed down with as much as heavy iron as the first group was. Behind them were the Tennessee Tories, Captain Daniel Fry, G.W. Barlow, and Pete Pierce. Fry was put into the same cell with the others. Barlow and Pierce were put into a separate cell down the hall.

"Welcome to hell, boys!"

"Would not miss this for anything!" "What mischief have you been up to?"

"They held a court-martial for us!"

"No hanging for you?"

"They cannot hang us!"

"How have things fared here?"

"This is our palace. They have removed the beds but will return them soon. They come with satin sheets. Pillows. They feed us a feast every meal."

"Ha, ha! Very good."

Turner came up from the rear and hushed everyone. He opened the cell door right opposite the first group of raiders and unlocked the shackles from everyone before they had stepped in.

After he left, a stranger from the second group spoke up. "That was a much kinder reception than the one received coming here."

Dorsey asked, "I am sorry, who is this fellow?"

Pittenger piped up. "Excuse us. Fellows, let me introduce you to Captain David Fry."

"Captain Fry?"

"I have heard rumors of this man and his exploits."

"Was he not the one who burned the bridges in Tennessee?"

Fry was a large and imposing man. He had a manner that suggested a kind demeanor that could turn violent if threatened or provoked.

"I am a southerner true, but I am also a Union man first", he said. "I organized a band to burn the bridges and sever the telegraph. Until I was wounded and captured, along with my friends. Many good lads have been murdered up there, resisting these rebs. If that damn fool Buell would actually move to East Tennessee, he would find many receptive hands willing to join him."

"Ahh." Wood replied. "Ole Buell is quite the strategist. He plans to bring 'is army down here and bring Johnny Reb out, only to make him wait. And wait. Eventually, Johnny Reb will get so bored 'ee will retire and go home in time for the planting season, thus, ending the war without a shot fired. Quite a strategy. Wellington himself could not think of a better one."

Fry looked over at Wood. "That is a strange way of talking, friend. Where do you hail from?" Wood sighed.

***

After the excitement had died down, life returned to normal. The raiders passed the days playing cards with one another, a checkers board was scratched onto the floor from a loose nail. They passed the time reading, discussing the bible, or arguing about the course of the war. Wilson was changing another wet piece of cloth on Wood's head when another argument broke out.

"Oh, buggeh." Wood said. "I prefer to be in delirium then listen to this constant braying."

"We must attempt an escape!", Dorsey snapper. "They hung Cap in a rather cruel fashion. What do you think they have in store for us?"

George Wilson hissed. "Cap. May his soul rest in peace. He was a civilian. We are enlisted soldiers. We have been court-martialed. They will have passed sentence on us if we are to hang. As it were, they will not hang soldiers for going on a military expedition."

Dorsey shook his head. "They will say anything to keep us at ease until they deliver us to the hangman."

George Wilson felt impatient. "We are soldiers doing our duty. They cannot hang us for following the rules of war. You have heard it right from Turner. There is talk that an exchange shall happen. Or the court-martial board will approve parole for us. At the very worst. We remain here until the war has been decided, which suits me well. I would rather stay here then return to the care of that devilish Swims."

"The outcome thus far does not favor us much. The guards have been boasting about their general McClellan, who was chased out of Virginia by their General Lee. All the while, Mitchell and Buell sit idle and stare at their General Bragg." Campbell said.

Dorsey sighed. "What do you have to offer to this discussion Captain Fry?"

Fry was ready to jump in. "The southerner is a conundrum. He is capable of a Christian charity to his fellow men. He is also capable of unspeakable cruelties. I know this as I am a southerner. A union loving southerner. There is a place in hell reserved for me if you were to consult them. For us, we invaded his territory. We have all ruined his means on his property. We have insulted his code of honor by posing as his friends. For this, there shall be no mercy. Unless we break our confinement and escape. We will be murdered."

George Wilson scoffed. "I am growing weary of this dialogue-"

Ross, who had been quiet for some time now, spoke up.

"Cap'n Fry is right. None of us are leaving here alive."

***

Wednesday, June 18th, started off as another day. Cards, checkers, and conversations were the order of that day. Breakfast was awful and unfilling. In the afternoon, Wilson and Hawkins heard the loud clomping of a large number of horses racing up the street and stopping outside the jail. They got up and joined the rest of the first group of raiders who crowded the window to see a small troupe of cavalry out front. They all dismounted and walked into the jail.

"What is it?"

"Reb cavalry."

"What are they doing?"

"They are coming in here."

"Wait...Hush."

Everyone went quiet. They could make out the sounds of the cavalry sabers clanging against the stairwell. They got louder until the cell door flew open, and a group of confederate officers stormed right in. Right behind them were Turner and Thor. Behind them were several men dressed in black gowns. Wilson had a sick feeling in his stomach. The lead officer spoke to Turner. Turner moved to a cell door and ushered the Tennessee Tories Barlow and Pierce out and had them stand in the hall. The lead officer moved to the cell, where the second group of raiders waited by the bars, wondering what was happening.

"Are these the men?"

"Yes, seh," Turner said. He fumbled with his keys until he found the right one to open the locked cell door.

The officer held out a sheet of paper. "When I call your name. Step forward out your quarters! George Wilson. Samuel Robertson. John Scott. Perry Shadrach. Samuel Slavens. William Campbell. Marion Ross."

Everyone but Campbell and Robertson stepped forward. Robertson was ill, and Campbell helped him to his feet and out of the cell.

"Follow me." The officer turned and led everyone to the vacant cell. The raiders wearily followed. Turner and Thor waited with the Pierce and Barlow.

The door was slammed shut so hard it made the others jump up. The entire cell block was silent. Until they could hear of some muffled voices. After a few minutes, the door flew open, and the raiders walked somberly out. Faces pale like ghosts. Like death. Wilson felt even sicker. He knew what was going to happen before George Wilson had said, "We are to be executed immediately."

Tears flowed. Any personal objects were handed over with promises made of returning them back home to their loved ones. Wilson felt his eyes water.

"Wife...Children...tell them..." Slavens said before his voice broke.

"Boys, I am not prepared to meet Jesus," Shadrach said. "I have been deceived in my thinking of their intentions toward us. The rest of you will surely meet our fate. Pittenger, we had many disagreements about what lies beyond. I believe you may be right now. Try to be better prepared when you come to die than I am."

"God bless you", Pittenger sobbed. "Men. You are leaving this world of all your suffering and about to enter an Eternity of heavenly mercy."

Wilson's tears were flowing now. He tried to think of something to say. But he couldn't. It was too hard. If this was going to be the last time he was going to see them, he didn't want to waste it. So instead, he just stuck his hand out and shook theirs as they walked past. Sam Robertson was just nineteen. He had to hang onto Campbell to walk when he burst out, crying.

"Oh, I promised I would see my mother again! Now I never will! What will she think when she never hears from me again!" "We will write to her, Sam!"

"You will see her again in heaven."

Campbell had a half-grin. "Boys, this is damn hard. I didn't cry when my pa was struck and killed by a wagon carrying several barrels of beer. Hell, my brothers and I helped ourselves with the beer that was spilling over before we tended to our departed Pa."

"How was the beer?" Knight asked.

Campbell thought for a moment before he replied.

"Warm."

He paused before he spoke. "Well goodbye, boys," he said, as he shook everyone's hand and walked to the door. Ross was the last in line. He stood tall like the sergeant major he was, ready to march off to battle. His eyes had a gleam to them. Defiant almost.

"Boys, tell them at home, if any of you escape, that I died for the love of my country." He did an about-face and directed his attention towards the raider in front of him. "All right, boys. While we are destined to hang as criminals, we should do our best to die as proud soldiers." Nothing more was said as the officer in charge led the men out of the cellblock. The raiders crowded around the window to watch as their friends were put onto a cart while a crowd was gathering around. Once they were all loaded, their cavalry escort mounted their horses, and the entire procession rode away. The raiders watched until the procession, and their friends rode away for good.

CHAPTER 30

Turner's compassion-God's word in Hell-Summer activities-Knight's return-An old friend-Days gone by-Indian summer-The Letters-Captain Lee-New means of communication-New Threats-Fry takes charge-The PlanReady-RUN!

"It was a terrible deed that happened to your comrades. Two of them had a failed hanging, so the deed had to be done again. Seein' as how there is little I kin do to assuage your suffering for the rest of your time here, I s'pose the bes' is to put y'all in the same cell." Turner said.

***

The mood was rather grim in that cell. There was no joking or merriment of any sort. Time seemed to stand still. Fry spoke up.

"Come along, boys. It is times such as these when it appears the darkest that a fervent and solemn prayer to the Lord will bring us back to the light."

"I believe in the efficacy of earnest Christian prayer, but prayer in a Confederate prison would have less of an effect, I believe," Wilson said.

"I wholeheartedly disagree." Pittenger chimed in. "A good prayer will cleanse our souls and rid us of our despondent state. I believe that all of your wicked games of chance will ruin you further for your eternal Judgment."

With that, he stormed towards a card game run by Knight, Brown, Bensinger, Buffum, and Hawkins; he snatched up the cards and threw them out the window.

"You know, I am starting to dislike that 'orrid little man", Wood said to Wilson.

Over everyone's protests, Buffum jeered. "Pittenger. Pray in one hand and spit on the other and see which will get fuller the soonest!"

With everyone crowding and insulting Pittenger, Fry got in the middle and, with his immense size, calmed everyone down. "Hear me, friends. A prayer and a hymn will do us all well. Leave him alone.

Come, everyone takes a knee." Fry said. Seeing as how he was the biggest one, and a senior ranking officer, everyone obeyed. "Now then. Who wants to lead?"

"I suppose I should," Buffum said. "Lord, we are taught to pray for our enemies. Therefore, we pray Thee have mercy on these goddamned rebel sons o' bitches, for they know not what they did."

***

The days grew much hotter and longer. The raiders would remove some of their clothes and stay close to the ground. A Reverend George McDonnell, who had given comfort to the seven raiders before they were hung, would come by to offer spiritual guidance to the remaining ones.

"So long as it was in the best interests of the Confederacy", he stated. He also gave the raiders books to alleviate their boredom.

They would lively read out loud. Marathon games of checkers were played. Singing eventually came back with some more enthusiasm.

"Say, boys, I hear telling from the guards and from Turner that there is no word on what the rebs have in store for us," Knight said.

"Hanging is our fate," Fry said.

"It does not appear so. I have gotten over my dread of hanging and replaced it with boredom." Knight said.

"I must agree. It did not make a lick of sense that they sent away a random bunch of us for trial, and even then, they only hang half of that bunch." Brown said.

***

"Perhaps they have forgotten about us? Boys, I suggest we force the matter of our fates and implore the rebs to allow us in on an exchange or parole. To do this, I propose we write to Jefferson Davis directly."

Pittenger said. "Jeff Davis!"

"The rebel boss himself?" "Tis madness!"

"He will not listen!"

Pittenger waited until the furor died down before he would continue. "We write to him directly. Subscribe to his goodwill. Implore him out of Christian charity to spare our lives, with cap, and the rest hung and gone, perhaps he will show mercy. I will write a letter all you have to do is sign your names. It is the best chance."

"Perhaps."

"It could work."

193

"Let Pittenger try."

"Y'all can. I will never beg for anything from that vile treasonous snake. It is your death warrant if you sign it."

"How shall we get paper?", Bensinger asked.

"That is my portion," Knight said.

"I believe Turner will be more agreeable than that awful Swims. We might be able to trade with him."

"With what?"

"Coats, belt buckles, buttons...Cap Andrews left me his coat. I will use it to acquire paper and pen Pittenger. I have been craving tobacco for some time, as well. If anyone cares to throw in, I will share some, as long as southern tobacco does not give you a bother."

"Hurrah for Knight."

"Have my coat!"

"Hell, take my boots!"

Wilson wanted to chip in when Wood coughed. Wood's fever had broken but was still seriously weak and could only stand for a few minutes at a time. He looked at the brass buttons on his vest, grabbed the top two, and ripped them out. He handed them to Knight. "Will, we are in need of food. Better food."

"Very good, Alf."

***

Turner came in with the servants as Knight handled the transactions. The next day they were welcomed with a basket full of apples, onions, and bread. Along with a pen and paper. Pittenger wrote an impassioned letter, begging Davis that mercy be shown and that the raiders would agree to never bear arms against the Confederacy if they were set free. Or, at the very least, they be spared. Buffum wanted to add the line 'We are perfectly innocent', but he was voted down against it. Parrott was illiterate, so Dorsey signed his name for him.

It was another hot day. The raiders took to lying on the cold floor or at least sat on it. When Turner came in with a confused look on his face. He inquired, "Say, fellows, have any of you known a man by the name of Woolam?" That sent a chill up everyone's spine. Wollam! He must have been caught!

"Who is that?"

"No."

"Never heard of him."

They were discussing when a familiar, cheery voice called out, "Boys do not go back on me now!"

It was Wollam!

Wilson joined the others at the cell bars to cheer him on. Wollam strode in as if he had owned the place. He was followed by a guard who Wollam paid no attention to as he shook everyone's hand through the bars and made his way to the cell door. With his manner, he acted as if he was coming home instead of imprisonment. Wilson took insight. Wollam was shirtless, wearing black pants held up by suspenders, a worn pair of boots, and a straw hat to top it all off. What struck Wilson was Wollam was badly sunburnt. To the point that his skin was black and peeling, from his nose to his waist. But he just did not seem to care. He looked happier to be back with his friends in this cell than he would be free back home.

"All right, boys," Wollam said as he was led into the cell as the door shut behind him. "I will tell the tale of my glorious, failed escape. Hell, it is not as though you have anything else to do."

Everyone sat in a circle and listened with full attention as Wollam spun the tale. After getting separated from Andrews, he had made his way to the bank of the Tennessee and found a canoe and oars which he used to go down the river. He hid on the banks during the day and continued at night. He passed by a gunboat and believed it to be a confederate boat, so he hid from it. Although now, he wasn't sure if it really was a confederate boat. So, he continued, he kept going his way until he thought he was in friendly territory and continued on during the day now until he had the bad luck of running into a group of confederates and, "wouldn't you know? The same rebel bastard that caught me the first time was there, and he remembered me, so now I am here."

***

Eventually, the excitement wore off by Wollam's return, and he joined the monotonous activities. June turned to July. On the fourth, Dorsey sighed as he was looking out the window.

"I remember the fourth being a cause for celebration. There is none to be had in such a place. Even their flag seems guilty enough to not want to flaunt its face." The servants John and Kate brought up their meager rations.

"Say what do you have for us today?"

"Jes th' same. Massa Turneh says' some mo' peopeh cummin' to gandeh ach yeh."

"Oh, what fun? Did you bring the extras?"

"Yes, eh Massa Knigh'-"

"Please do not call me that. Will is fine."

"Will. Yessum."

Kate brought a tray with bowls of their rations. John picked up one and slid a week-old newspaper under it when he handed it to Knight.

"Anotheh thing," John said, as he reached in his pocket and pulled out a palm-sized piece of tobacco and slid it to Knight. They gave each other a knowing nod.

"Oh, what was that? The rebs are going to look at us again? They must be bored." Dorsey said.

"What a waste. I know how the livestock at the old fair feels when the people come over to judge them." Wilson sighed.

"Oh, is that what backwoods bumpkins such as yourself do for amusement? Go and gaze upon animals?" Wood said. "I preferred it when you were ill. You must be getting better."

***

The raiders were singing 'The Star-Spangled Banner' when a group of confederate officers showed up to see the infamous 'Train thieves'. They whispered amongst themselves. The raiders did not pay them any mind, except Knight, who hopped up and approached the bars.

"Say, mister", he said to a colonel. "Can't you let me go down the street? I'm patriotic and want to help celebrate."

"Well, hardly", the colonel growled.

Knight shook his head. "That's too bad. I intend to celebrate the next Fourth of July at home then."

"You shall celebrate it in hell!" The colonel snarled before he would storm out, his fellow officers behind him, all to the sound of the raiders roaring with laughter.

***

July turned to August. Turner offered his verbal kindness and suggested that he did not know of anything further of what was in store for the raiders.

"Perhaps, we shall know soon."

Thor would offer some verbal abuse. "Ol' Bobby Lee has gone and whupped your McClellan off the peninsula in Virginia. Maybe now that ape Lincoln would realize what a waste this whole affair is and let us

196

free. If that is the way, y'all should be grateful as we would surely let y'all go. Although I still do believe y'all, a bunch that's needin to be killed."

"Boys, this is a sordid set of days. Perhaps our letter fell onto the blind eyes. I propose we write another letter. This time to a humbler person. Perhaps their general in charge over here Bragg?

"No, Pittenger."

"Jeff Davis will not care. Bragg might."

"This will call too much attention to us."

"It might be the right kind."

Fry scoffed. "You are quite the odd duck, Pittenger. You keep pursuing this foolish line of thought. To hell with you", he said as he walked away to the other end of the cell.

"Let us have a vote to decide the course of this fate", Pittenger continued.

Votes were counted. The ayes for the letter won. After securing some more paper, Pittenger wrote again, pleading General Bragg and his humanity for an exchange.

***

August turned to September. The days were starting to get cooler. Thor raged, "All ye damn Yankee boats on th' wateh are thievin' away what we had left. All our food stores and supplies are gettin' to damn expensive! All y'all ah doin' is starvin' ah women and chil' ren." He paused as a sneer came across his face. "Y'all still a bunch of damned fools. Y'all jus' caught a whippin' at Manassas. Again! Lee sent the Yankees runnin' fo the secon' tihme. That and yo' Buell sits like a coward and does not move." Making his point, he walked out laughing.

"You gentlemen will have a special visitor whom you'll receive today," Turner said to the raiders. "A Captain G.W. Lee, the provost Marshall in Atlanta. He will grant you an interview for your case."

Lee was a meticulous, well-groomed fellow when he came forward stood in front of the raiders' cell.

"I am Captain Lee", he began. "I am hereby personal request of President Davis and the secretary of war, G.W. Randolph, to look into your case and ascertain its current status. I have received all pertinent information and have myself seen seven of your group being executed; exceptions were made for yourselves. So, I will ask plainly. Why?"

Knight stepped up to the bars. "It was a matter that was decided. Our ringleader, engineer, and brakeman, along with all the other prominent members of the party, were executed. Our fates were decided to be less guilty than the others."

Lee shook his head. "That will not do. I must have more information." He sighed and reached into his coat to pull out a watch. He sighed again and put it back. "I have quite some time before I depart. Perhaps I can stay for a spell and have a talk. So, Yankees. Tell me a story."

***

"Very good Pittenger. You have the rebs coming around, asking questions. Mainly why we have not been hung. You have done well for us."

Fry growled at Pittenger after Lee left.

***

A stovepipe in the corner of the cell was found to have a loose elbow which they could remove so they could speak to prisoners in the room next to them. They tied notes on a string and threw it across the hallway to the other cells there. With that and the old newspapers and information from the servants, the raiders had a good well to draw intelligence from. With some renewed hope that they might be exchanged or paroled.

"They say our blockade is tight along the coasts and that we have most of their rivers in our control!"

"Yes, yet they keep fighting."

"Our forces have taken large parts of Tennessee, Lousiana, Mississippi, and North Carolina."

"Yes, and yet we are not in Eastern Tennessee or Northern Georgia."

Then came some big news. "There was a great battle in Maryland. General Lee has ceded the ground and retreated!" Then, "President Lincoln had published an Emancipation Proclamation. He has declared that all slaves in the south shall be let free." Everyone was abuzz over the news. Wilson had changed his mind about slavery after seeing it right up close, he was glad to hear the news.

***

It was October. It had started well when the raiders heard of another victory at Corinth in Mississippi. It turned for the worse one day when they noticed Thor being a dash extra sinister and cutting their rations, saying "y'all won' need as much anyhow," and Turner being extra nice.

At dinnertime, it happened. John and Kate were delivering the evening meal. They both looked rather grim. When Knight asked what the matter is, John, swallowed hard before finally saying. "It is no good, Will. They're sayin' they g'wyn'a kill you and yo frien's." Wilson felt a blow in his stomach. He lost his appetite. He lost everything. Knight said his thanks.

No one felt like coming to receive their dinner, so John and Kate went inside and served them all. They retrieved the water buckets and then left.

"I am afraid it is true. Dorsey said. "The fellow in the other cell said they overheard the guards saying they that expect an execution order for us any day now."

Pittenger contributed, "Our friends across the hall have overheard Turner saying he expects us to be hung in a short while."

"Why in the hell did you not say so before?!" Buffum roared.

"I did not want it to be true," Dorsey confessed.

"I was beside myself with shock," Pittenger said. "So, what are we to do about it?"

"Let's make a run for it!"

"Jump the guards and make a last stand."

"Fight!"

"Escape!"

Fry stood up immediately and slammed his hand on the wall to quiet everyone down. "Simmeh down. I have been thinking about this for some time now. I always felt I knew that escape was our only choice. Now it is clear. You want to stay here and die in Georgia of all the places? Or do you want to follow me and take a chance of freedom?" Everyone agreed instantly.

"Very well. We do not have adequate time to prepare as the moment of doom could be at hand anytime now. So, no more singing or games. We must prepare at all times.

"Now then, Porter and Dorsey? You must save the bed tucking to assist in threading everyone's clothes together. Knight and Brown? You must make use of what we possess to ratchet up our shoes. Buffum and Bensinger? Try to make some sort of weapons. Hawkins? Keep up that circus horseshit you have us training to do. We must be fit to make this run. Everyone else must do what they can to assist."

Wilson spoke up. "Rations. We need rations to gather our strength and to take with us."

"Very good. Yes, anyone with anything remotely of value, toss it in. We will all share in what we receive."

Everyone moved with a single purpose. No more wiling away the time or waiting. It had given new life to the raiders. It also reminded them of what the stakes were at.

"I must say it is quite something to do such a thing. I was getting tired of singing the same old songs", Wood said, as he and Wilson sewed and patched up their clothes.

Wilson thought for a moment, then said. "There was a moment, I told Cap to wait for a day. I should have been more forceful to persuade him. I think of things and believe I could have done better. Maybe we would not be here. Maybe the cap would still be alive." His voice trailed off.

"No", said Wood. "Cap did what he thought was right. It was a series of unfortunate events that led us being here. Do not place any blame on yourself. It is all on Johnny Reb. The best course is to deprive him of the privilege of hanging us to death. To tell our story and Cap's story."

Wilson nodded. "You are correct. I want to be free. I am ready to be free."

Wood chuckled. "That is the spirit! What a cause for excitement this is! To think, the 'ole rotten lot of you wanted me to die."

***

"Our plan is rather simple", Fry said. "We wait until dinner time and rush the jailor, take his keys, and then unlock the doors. We form two groups and rush at both the front and rear doors. Overrun any guards in our way. Then make a break for the woods. After that, it's a matter of finding our way back to our lines.

"Now I have studied the fence, it does have pickets, and also has three stringers we can use to climb over. Everyone study those stringers and remember them when the time will come. It will happen in an instant, and we will not have time for dilly dally."

Fry sighed, letting it sink in. Then he continued. "There is a chance we all might not make it. Hell, there is a chance that we will all be murdered in the yard. I propose it is better to die on our feet on our terms than theirs. Tomorrow is the fifteenth. We will go then."

***

The fifteenth was a rainy day. Dorsey urged a delay as the rain could assist the dogs in smelling the raiders. He wore Fry down and agreed to postpone it for a day. Fry went to check on his fellow Tories.

"Are you still on, Barlow?"

"Hell, yes."

"Pierce?"

"No. I think not. I am too ill to be doin' all that runnin'".

Fry turned towards his friends when he heard a voice that called him. "Please, seh. I wish to jine yeh. I am in heah fer desertion. They all mean to kill me. I left the cause as my pap passed, my ma is all alone, and she be needin me. I kin help. I know these parts and kin poin' th' way." The confederate looks no older than seventeen. Fry looked at the raiders. They all nodded in agreement.

"Very well, then."

An idea popped in Fry's head. "We can use more men to create a fuss. There are some more deserters in that cell." He looked to another cell. "There are supposed murderers in there. Perhaps we ought to let them alone."

***

All day, they waited. No games, only an occasional song. It felt like the longest day of Wilson's lifetime. He wasn't scared, though, just anxious. He reminded himself that he was about to be free. No more fear. That was it. The hours crawled by.

Wilson wanted it to be night now. Pittenger read a new note. "It appears that General Bragg was in a fight in Kentucky. He did not drive our forces away, so I say it is a victory for us."

"Good. Except it means that more rebs in Tennessee when they come back", Fry said.

"They will not be back for some time," Knight said.

"Keep off the main roads and try to travel mainly at night", Brown added. "Head northeast. You will be in a friendly country",Fry said.

"It is bes' to head on wes.' That is the quickest way outta Atlanta", the confederate said.

"Stay near the river. You can use it to float away and perhaps catch a friendly gunboat", Wollam said. That comment made Wilson think of the story about Bill Withers and his escape in the Maumee.

"If you need assistance, try to catch a kind lady", he said.

***

"Gentleman, the time is nigh. I would like to shake all your hands and say, if this ought to be our last day on earth, I could not ask for a better company", Dorsey said. Everyone agreed and shook everyone else's hands.

After they finished, Fry said, "Gentleman, let us pray." He had just finished when Turner and his servants came in. They served dinner and left. Everyone ate a little bit and saved the rest.

Turner and the servants came back. This was it. Turner opened the cell door as John and Kate walked in to clear the dishes and change the water. After they came in, Fry, Knight, and Brown were first out of the cell. Wilson was on his feet and then after them. They walked past John and Kate while surrounding a surprised Turner in the hallway.

"Good evening Mr. Turner," Fry said.

"Good evening," Turner said. Unsure of what was happening. "A pleasant evening."

Fry looked to see more of the raiders coming out now. "Yes." Mr. Turner.

"We all feel like taking a walk this lovely evening."

"What? How? Where?"

"Well, we have been in here long enough, and you know that we will all be hanged soon if we remain, so we ought to go out."

"Yes, but you will have the guards to contend with," Turner said.

"We will take care of them," Knight said. They were closing in on Turner now. Buffum appeared as he reached for his keys.

"Oh yes, Mr. Turner, let us have those keys. The other boys want out as well."

Turner now stood his ground. "No. You can go out, but you cannot interfere with any of the other prisoners-"

Fry's hand immediately came over Turner's mouth. Buffum grabbed the keyset and began to unlock the other cells. "Go get it then!" Fry hissed.

It was on. Everyone made their way through the doors and down the stairs to a door that led to the yard. Knight was the first to the door. He paused only to swallow in some air, then opened it and rushed outside. Wilson was the fifth one out of the door. His heart was pounding. His legs were numb. He was alive.

The day turned to dusk. Everything happened so fast. His legs felt limp. He knew that he could not stop moving. He could see Bensinger was roughing up a guard. He could hear someone cry "Murder!" as he saw Wollam and Hawkins run to a trash pile and grab whatever they could. Wilson followed and grabbed two bricks. He went straight for the fence with the stringers. There were guards in his way. He aimed and threw a brick while on the run. It hit a guard in the face. He then threw the other one. It missed but sent the guard running.

He heard a familiar voice, "Alf! Come quick! The boys are getting over the fence at the back of the jail! There are guards coming!" He was gunning for it now.

"Bounce the fence, Mark!"

They reached the fence at the same time. Luckily, the stringers were long enough for the two people. They both climbed up as fast as they were able to. It was a blur still. Although Wilson heard an unfamiliar voice cry "Halt!" he decided to jump rather than gauge what was below him. Luckily, he just landed in some brush. He bounced and felt a nick of the brush right against his leg. Wood landed right beside him. "Are you hurt?"

"No."

"Then, run like hell!"

The open area, the dimming light, the unfamiliar surroundings, should have thrown him off, but he had spent hours studying not only the fence but the horizon beyond it.

He scanned for the tree line and formed a plan to head west and never to stop. It was easier said than done. In the fading light, and in unfamiliar streets, they raced and zigzagged through the streets, and sometimes yards, causing dogs to bark and people to yell before they finally reached the tree line to the woods. Even then, they kept running. Wilson finally allowed himself a thought.

"I am free."

They escaped.

Now the hard part.

CHAPTER 32

River creatures-Kind Strangers-River Wire-Wood's mistake-The mill dam-Hands and knees-Slipping past Columbus-In need of a bigger boat-Leaky Problems-Close Call-River Water-Pumpkins Make A Relief-Good news-In the bay-Oysters-A lot of trees

It was the combination of his stomach growling and a buzzing noise in his ears that woke Wilson up. His face and his arms were itching like crazy.

"Damn skeeters", he mumbled. He hit Wood's leg. That awoke him.

"What, what?" he said as he scrambled up to collect himself.

"Dusk is approaching. We need to move on."

Using his oar, Wilson began paddling out of their little bayou. Wood eventually helped. "I had a marvelous dream. I died, and then you awoke me." Wood said.

Wilson smirked. "Mine was much better. I was dreaming of wonderful things to eat."

"Oh, bother, why-" Wood started slapping at his face and arms. "What are these beastly brutes?"

"Skeeters. You had best get used to them."

They were on the river now, going with the current. "Such 'orrid things. And so large too!" Wilson could see a black mass buzzing above him and the canoe.

"Just keep paddling. The best we can do is to try to outrun them." They rowed for a few minutes. The sound of their stomachs growling was loud enough to hear.

"Alf. Might we try to gather some new rations? This alliance of dry corn and river water is doing best against me", Wilson sighed. He did not like it, but he knew they had to get food, they could not go on like this. He saw along the banks there were several slave houses and then a larger one. "We will go ashore and see what they might let us have."

After grounding the canoe, they approached the main house and knocked. They could see a soft light form through the window. The door opened, and an elderly man and woman stood at the doorway. "We ah awful sorry to disturb ye kin' folks," Wilson said in his best adopted southern twang. "We are sojers frum the eighth Geo'gia. We on Furla' and cummin' back to ah regimen.' We fell on hawd tihmes and are in need of a gud meal. We have no coin of any sort. Anything yeh kin spare will be much appreciated."

The pair were seated at the table. In the dim candlelight, they did look like a sorry lot, but the old man invited them in. His wife served them what was left of the evening meal. Chicken, biscuits, potatoes, and gravy. All Cold.

Wilson spun the story that they were beaten back at Corinth and that he and Wood had a hard time and lost many comrades.

"It don' surprise me none." The old man said. "The Yankees hired all sorts a' low down thieves and otheh awful bunches to come down heah with all the bad news of ah defeats. I feah the Yankee devil's will win. They gwyn keep on cummin.'"

"Oh, no, seh. We will triumph. One southeneh is werth five Yankees any giv'n day. We gwyn bleed 'em until they tire of fahting and let us alone."

The old man smirked. "I wish I had the same optimism as you, lad."

"Any further news?"

The old man glowered. "Those damn train thieves escaped! Sorry motheh for my words."

"The audacity of them all!" Wilson gasped. "They should have hung those bastards long ago. They made a-runnin' for it. One even threw a brick and broke a good southen soldier's face! They shoulda shot the sum' bitch!"

Wilson nodded. "Indeed! Any wurd if any of 'em was caught?"

"No. I suppose the feller that catches any of 'em will do the right deed and blow out their brains." His wife approached the table with a pitcher.

"I will have no more of such talk at the table", she said, refilling Wilson and Wood's glasses.

"Apologies, mutheh."

"Did yeh boys have enough?"

"Oh yes, ma'am."

"I am sorry that there was not anymo'."

"That was mo' than enough. We thank yeh kin'ly. My friend an' I must be off to citch the' ferry." The meal had provided a great boost to the pair, as they hit to the river again, and started paddling with more energy.

It was night when they went. The moon was bright enough for them to see clearly. Wilson forgot himself and stood up to see what was ahead. When he felt something strike at his face, the world suddenly went spinning, and Wilson was in the water. The cold was a shock. Wilson pushed his head out of the water, he was able to as luckily his right foot was hooked into the canoe. He waved his hands three times to grab the side, Wood reached over and pulled him in. He had a knot on his face.

"What in the devil was that?" Wood asked.

"It must have been a ferry boat wire," Wilson replied. "If it struck you the same, I do not feel much like a fool."

"At least I stayed behind in the boat." Wood smirked. Wilson wanted to say something, but with the cold air, he felt a chill coming.

"How long do you suppose until we reach the gulf?" Wood asked.

"Several days. We just have to keep going."

They went in silence for quite some time. Wilson pushed himself hard to battle the cold evening air. Eventually, he felt too fatigued to keep on going. "Marky, are you well to steer the boat." "I suppose so." "I am in need of rest. Please do so." "All right, Alf." Wilson laid down on the bottom of the canoe, curled into a ball, and went to sleep.

***

"Alf! Alf! Wake up!"

Wilson struggled to wake back up. "What is the matter?"

"We can't go on. We have come to the end of the river."

"End of the river?"

"Yes."

Wilson wiped the cobwebs from his face. True, they were not moving and were in utter darkness, save for a narrow gleam of light. "This is my due punishment for having left you in charge."

"I am sorry. I truly am."

Wilson grabbed his paddle and plunged it into the water. He felt the rocky surface and used it to push off and started paddling. He went towards the light. +

"We must be in a cave or under a mountain ledge of some sort."

Once they were outside again, Wilson was right as they had gotten trapped under a mountain ledge. "That was the final time I let you steer Marky."

"Perhaps that is best."

The river was getting rougher, with sharper rocks, and the dawn light had started to appear. Wilson called it. They went ashore, dragged the canoe with them, and slept, providing a perfect snack for mosquitos.

***

Night fell. They awoke and were back to the river. It was getting difficult to paddle and steer with all the water rushing. Up ahead, Wilson could make out a mill dam.

"Oh, hellfire."

"What's that, Alf?"

"There is a mill dam. We must maneuver around it!"

They tried to paddle around to see if there was another way to it when Wilson saw an apron that looked promising.

"There! Go to the right!" Instead of finding an apron, it was a break, and the canoe shot out like a cannon.

Wilson felt a woozy feeling in his stomach as he called out. "Hold Mark!" He closed his eyes and held his nose. After some moments, the canoe landed. Right side up. Wilson and Wood breathed heavily as they started slowly opened their eyes.

"Let's not do that again, Alf."

"I agree."

The dawn light was approaching. Wilson sighed. He did not like what he was going to say, but he knew he had to.

"Mark. We have to abandon our craft."

"What in blazes for?"

"It is too perilous going down in such a manner. Our little craft cannot manage these waters. We have been fortunate thus far, but if we stay in it, I fear we shall perish or be horribly maimed."

"Alf. I am far too tired to argue, so whatever you say."

They rowed to shore. Wilson stepped onto the sand. When Wood stepped out, he nearly fell. Wilson helped.

"I am fine. I assure you."

Wilson was tired and his feet began to hurt again. Wood was wobbling and weaving like a drunk person.

"Here, we are in need of some rest."

"Bless your soul." Wood crawled under a tree and laid down. Wilson gathered some cedar boughs and piled them right on top of Wood. Feeling cold, he lay close to Wood and fell asleep.

Daylight came. With no food and a hearty drink of river water, they began their walk. It was not long before the swelling and blisters on their feet had flared up, and it became too painful to walk, so they resorted to crawling along with their hands and knees. Wilson wondered again if it would have been better if they had not escaped. Or maybe it would be better if they just fell down and died on the spot.

No! He could not think like that ever again. He had to keep moving forward. Even if his arms were tiring and it was hard crawling across those sharp, shaky rocks. The hunger pains in his stomach were ever constant. Twice they passed by some cabins belonging to river workers. Twice Wilson decided to hell with all of it and knocked on the door.

"Please, seh. I am but a weary travelleh who is enduring a great misery on his way back home. Would you spare a meal?" Twice Wilson and Wood were fed. The next day they could see spires and smokestacks at a distance, coupled with the loud sounds of a busy industrial yard.

"That must be the great town of Columbus," Wilson said, a smile forming on his mouth for the first time in days. "After we get right below it, we have a clear course to the Gulf."

"What are we to do then?" Wood asked.

"Stay hidden until the cover of darkness. Then we try on the other side."

***

Darkness fell. They awoke and made their way. The detour around the town and the suburban area was long. They stayed low, crawling the entire way. They moved when it was clear, freezing when they heard a suspicious noise. Despite the cold, Wilson found himself sweating and nervous as they could be spotted.

It took the entire night to reach the other end of town and the riverbank. They crawled to a safe enough looking thicket and rested for the day.

"Alf, should we try for that lonely boat?"

They had crawled until they couldn't smell the smoke coming from the town anymore. It was time for another break, except the break, had lasted for about two days. Wood had taken to ripping his shirt for bandages on his feet. His sleeves were all gone. They had eaten leaves and grass and drank plenty of river water to keep them full.

"I have scoured the banks hereabouts," Wilson said. "I have found one, except that my difficulty has increased by the number of workmen about."

"We must try for it, Alfy. We cannot continue in such a manner."

"I will. You are in no means to be able for this. If I am not back by morning, or if you hear musket balls crackling. You are left to your own." Wood nodded.

Wilson stayed low, limping along the riverbank. He eventually came upon a large canoe. Sitting alone on the river, chained to a stump. Right above the bank were loggers of a sort. Working at night with gas lamps burning at full light. Wilson had to go for it. He found a large, sturdy stick. He made his way to where the chain was. He swallowed and very slowly crept over to the edge of the bank and propped the stick against the chain. The stick slipped. He then quickly propped it back. Sweat was pouring on his head. His heart pounded swiftly. He pushed the stick against the chain and tried to edge it upwards. It wouldn't budge. He exhaled slowly. He could hear the workers going about their duties and grumbling about this or that.

He then made a tighter grip on the stick and tried again. This time the chain began to move. Wilson was very gentle as he pushed the chain upwards. It slowly made its way to the top.

"Hey, you there!" Wilson froze. Seconds passed. Everything was quiet. Finally.

"Yeh damned lazy ass! Git up an' len' a han.'" The noise came back at a full volume. Wilson slowly exhaled. With a final push, the chain fell off the stump and landed in the sand, before he dragged it away. Wilson grabbed it and made his way back towards Wood, prize in tow.

"Splendid work Alf."

They crawled in and started floating down to the river and past the workers again. They had to keep their heads down, except Wilson noticed that the lights had dimmed, and there did not seem to be anyone around. Wilson was not sure if it was a meal break or quitting time. Actually, he did not really care. He grabbed the lone oar and started paddling.

"Alf." Wood whispered. "I believe this craft has a leak in it."

"Use your hands to bail the water. I am rowing."

Another day in the river. Wilson would lay diagonally, and so he could row and let his feet cool in the water. Wood was having trouble bailing the water out.

"Alf. I am too fatigued to keep this going." Wilson sighed. He risked his life to get this boat. On the other hand, he could feel the water underneath him, and the river did seem to get higher.

"Damn it all Marky, I suppose we can try for another boat."

**

Dusk was approaching when they spied down three boats against the bank tied to a tree. Wilson rowed over, and as soon as they were in the shallows, he soon hopped out. Wood followed.

"Just our luck, they are held down by a rope." Wilson's hands were dry and raw, yet he worked quickly to untie all the three. "See about a pair of oars. Set them in the middle boat. That looks the most promising." Wood started off.

"What's happening down there?"

"A bunch of goddamned thieves!" Wilson nearly jumped. He looked to see a group of men coming over a hill, with vicious looking dogs. He did not skip a beat. He yanked the rope free and waded into the water to help push the boats further into the river. When he was waist-deep, he hopped over to the side, landing on his sternum. Wood frantically pulled him in.

"Damn it, Alf. They are coming!"

Wilson righted himself and started paddling as fast as he could, first going for the middle where the current ran fast. He paddled hard for several minutes. Wood grabbed a spare oar and did his best. Finally, Wilson looked back and couldn't see them.

"We keep getting in a pinch Mark. Perhaps that should be the last one before our luck runs out."

**

The next day, after a long rest, they decided to look about to find more food. It didn't take long before they found a cornfield. They went to it and stuffed several ears into their pockets. There were also some pumpkins in the mix, so they each grabbed one and limped as fast as they could back to the boat to resume their journey. This time the corn was much ripe and was easier to chew. They broke the pumpkins open and ate the seeds. They filled their pockets with the flesh for later and kept on going.

Their schedule was back to moving in the night. Resting and sleeping during the day. This morning they drifted by alligators as they rowed to a smaller bend of reeds. The reptiles would sit on the bank or log as they watch the boat go by but did not pursue. Wilson would look back at them. He knew they were waiting.

Moccasin snakes would often swim right up to the boat and circle it. Wilson thought they were claiming their prey.

"Alf, these skeeters will be the death of me." Hearing that made Wilson itch. "We need to cover up. Follow me to the bank."

After nearly two weeks in the river. They had used up their shirts completely. They were hatless shirtless and bootless. Their pants were tatters. Their skin was a light brown covered with mosquito bites and sores.

When they were at the shallow end, they hopped out and dragged the canoe towards the bank. "Here is a snap I learned from the Black Swamp back home." He reached down and took a palmful of mud and began spreading it on his arms and chest and face before he got some more.

"I see."

"Then we will gather some moss to top ourselves off. The whole affair will be a pig's ear, yet we will be free from the skeeters torment."

"Very good, Alf. I see being a backwoods bumpkin does gain you plenty."

***

"I am back, Marky," Wilson stated as he approached the canoe.

"What did you find?"

"After skulking about, I found a lone cabin that appeared deserted. In its contents, I found several fishhooks and lines. I appropriated them so we may now dine on fish."

"Splendid Alf! Fish would be more delightful than the corn. I am afraid of soaking it in the river had done us very little."

Night fell and they were back onto the river. After rowing to the middle to ride the current, Wilson cast his lines and waited for a bite.

"When I was a boy, my pa taught me everything there is about fishing on the Maumee. The Maumee was not all that different from this place. When I grew older, I would go by myself. On a warm spring day, I did not even have to catch anything. Just sit in my canoe and enjoy the cool breeze as the day drifts by."

Wood nodded. "That's good. I believe you have a twitch in your line."

It did not take long for Wilson to land a small pile of catfish. With the little corn they still had, they had a small feast. Wilson's gums were bleeding, and his teeth hurt badly, but his stomach was hurting even more, so he ate the catfish as gingerly as he could. Wood, on the other hand, tore into the fish like a rabid animal, tearing it apart with his teeth and gulping it down, all the while making strange noises as he did. When Wilson had enough, Wood grabbed another one from the pile and tore into it. His eyes looked hollow and sunken.

"Enough, Mark. That is plenty after that first one." Wood just looked at him and bit into the fish some more. "Mark, it will not sit well to eat so much raw fish. Please. I promise tomorrow we will build a fire and cook them properly. Please. That is enough."

Wood gulped. There were tears in his eyes. He let out a long sigh and set his half-eaten fish down. Wilson turned back to rowing and watched the river. It was some time before Wood broke the silence.

"How...How do you manage...like you do?"

Wilson reflected. "It is not an easy task to live and work on a farm. If there is a poor harvest or livestock dies, or you are unable to raise hogs or cows for the smokehouse, then you will not eat. So yeah, I have gone without a meal or two in my life." Remembering some of those moments sent a chill up Wilson's spine. "You get some rest now, Marky. I'll keep post."

The next morning, they set the boat along the shore. After making sure that it was secure, Wilson turned to Wood.

"We're close now. The river is growing wider and faster. I must inquire about the state of affairs below us. It will be a nervous matter to cross into the bay with rebel picket boats about." Wood glowered. "We have gone too now far to be picked up. We shall make it. Keep the faith, Mark. I will be gone now. If its midday and I have not returned. Push off without me." Wood nodded.

***

Wilson hurried back with the information. To his surprise, he saw Wood coming from the other way as if he been somewhere else. He had his arms folded across his stomach. He was cradling something.

"Hallo their Mark. What have you got there?"

"Sweet potatoes", Wood said.

"Sweet potatoes? Where did you find those?"

"I nicked them."

"Where in hell-"

"Perhaps it would be best to push off Alf?"

After finding a secure canebrake, they set ashore. Wilson found some sturdy sticks and built a fire. Then he roasted the catfish and some sweet potatoes. It was a hardy feast.

"I found an old Scotchman. He informed me that we are about five miles above Apalachicola. Eighteen miles below is the federal blockading squadron. There haven't been any rebel picket boats about. We may yet reach them the next day. I want to go tonight, so we can slip past the town."

"Splendid, Alf."

Wilson was full. Wood still ate. "It would be best to sleep for a while. We need to store the rest."

"I am still hungry."

"Mark, we need this for later as well. We need to rest now." He started gathering up the roasted fish and potatoes and stored them into the canoe. He reached for the fish Wood was eating, but he pulled back.

"Mark."

"Please, Alf." Wood's eyes were starting to tear up.

Wilson relented. "Very well. Finish up on that one. Then we shall rest."

They set off that night. Crossing to the other side of the bay, they used the bright lights which came from Apalachicola and the moonlight as a guide. They kept their heads low and paddled gently, as they did not want to do anything to draw attention. When they were safely across, they picked up the speed. Except the night grew cloudy, and Wilson decided to call it if they could not see. They set ashore, tied up the boat, and went to sleep in a thicket.

***

They awoke and said quite little as they gathered their food. Wilson was looking for fleet across the bay. He was too busy to appreciate the orange, lime, and palm trees. Or the strong smell of the gulf water. US Navy ships were what he looked for.

"Come, Mark, let us eat what we have. I want to be moving back again."

As they rowed, Wilson realized that their canoe was smaller than he had realized. There were some large fish swimming alongside them, flapping their tails above water. If enough of them hit the canoe, they could capsize. '*No. Keep paddling. Don't think about that*', he thought to himself.

They had been out of sight of any landmass for some time when they saw a small island up ahead.

"What do you make of that?" Wood called out.

"We will go around it."

Wilson looked right and then to the left. To the left, there looked to be a mass of dead trees. "Let's go right."

Up ahead was a sand bar. As they got closer, it got bigger. "Wait up, Mark. I need to figure out how to best this bar." He studied a small channel that went through and looked to go to the other side. "Very well. Onwards Marky!" As they went through the channel, Wilson could hear the water splash as if something went into the water and was coming out. He looked back to see Wood pulling some muddy rocks from the channel.

"What is that, Mark?"

"May I see a fishhook?"

Wilson was curious. He stopped rowing and handed over a hook as he watched Wood use it to pry the rock apart and eat something from it. "Mark, you starving Yank! What in thunder are you at now?"

"Taste this." Wood replied. He pried open another one and handed it over to him. It was a brownish, clear mass inside of it. Wilson ate it. His mouth exploded in a sensation of sweet and salty flavor.

"That is delicious! What is it?"

"It's an oyster and-, oh, dear me, I forgot backwoods country bumpkins such as yourself are not used to the sheer delicacies of the sea." Wood smiled for the first time in a while.

After taking a small break for a mini oyster feast, they rowed through the small channel and crossed the island, except Wilson could not stop looking at the mass of dead trees. He blinked and rubbed his eyes vigorously.

Wait. Those were not trees. Those were ship masts and hulls. Ship masts. Ships! "Oh, thank the good Lord! Mark, do you see that?!"

"Yes! Come along now, Alf! No time for dilly dally! Row!"

They were tired. Their arms burned. They couldn't get across the bay fast enough. Wilson could not contain himself; all their misery could have ended if they reached one of the three ships stationed there. As they approached the nearest one, Wilson strained to see the colors of the ships, if it was actually a confederate ship. He squinted. The sight of the red and white stripes, with the blue field full of stars, made his eyes tear up and brought both him and Wood to their feet.

"It is ours! Ha, ha!" They hugged each other and screamed. "Perhaps we should swim for it?"

"No! We are too far! Keep to it!"

They sat back down and put everything they had in rowing to the first and largest ship. They got closer and passed by the bow, Wilson could see activity buzzing along the side of the ship as sailors either ran back and forth or watched the spectacle of a little boat coming right up their ship.

Finally, a young officer with a hardened face appeared and leaned over the rail. "Come there! Who in the hell are you, and what are you paddling under my guns in this manner?", he barked.

That command shook the pair, as they froze momentarily before slowly picking up their slack. Wilson had been dreaming of this moment for many days now, he could not think of what to say.

"Well? Out with it!", the officer snapped.

Wilson slowly stood up. "We are Union men trying to get back to God's country. Amongst friends." The canoe drifted toward their ship. Moments passed. The officer stared at Wilson. He realized, with his being almost naked, covered in mud and moss, and in a boat full of oysters, corn, and catfish made for a rather odd sight.

"You better offer up a better account of your strange conduct and appearances", the officer said.

Wilson cleared his throat. "We are enlisted federal soldiers of twenty-first Ohio. We belong to the command of General O.M. Mitchell in Tennessee-"

"Well, you are a damn long way from camp!"

"Yes. We were dispatched on a special raid by General Mitchell to ruin the enemy's railroad. We failed and were captured along with the rest of our team. We endured the worst of cruelties for many months until my friend and I escaped. We have been fugitives for several days and have tolerated painful hunger as we made our way through the rough country. Now, sir, I request, nay, I beg for your safety under the flag and your guns."

The officer's hard face rather softened as he heard their tale. "I have actually heard of this expedition, and of this General Mitchell. Very well. I intend to hear more of this story at a later time. Now, row your little boat to the ladder and come on board."

Both of their hands were shaking as they rowed the last few feet towards the ladder. Wilson helped Wood, who had trouble standing on his own, up the ladder. The officer wore a crisp blue uniform, but he did not mind letting it get dirty as he helped the muddy Englishman up. When it was Wilson's turn, he had to take his time, as his legs were wobbly, and he felt dizzy climbing.

When the officer extended his hand, Wilson took one last look at the canoe before he grabbed the officer's hand and pulled himself on the deck.

"Gentleman, I am Lieutenant Crossman", the officer said. "Welcome aboard the U.S.S Somerset."

CHAPTER 33

Safe at last-Rumors-Crossman's kindness-The Rowboat-Standing on deck-Wollam and Porter-Dorsey and Hawkins Brown and Knight-What happened to the rest-New Medals-Dreams-The Reunion-Seeing an old enemy-The Widow-Epilogue

It felt like a dream. Or perhaps a bad nightmare. Did it all really happen? The train chase? The trek to friendly lines? Swim's prison? The escape down the river? If it was all really a dream, Wilson did not want to wake up as he was scrubbing himself in a bathtub with soap. The first time he had bathed in almost eight months.

After they came aboard, Wilson and Wood talked a bit about their adventure. The sailors who crowded them were horrified of what they heard. Crossman's face hardened again as he let the loose, rapid stream of swearing, the likes of which Wilson had never heard before. After threatening to do such and such to so and so if he got his hands on them, Crossman exhaled and then requested the pair to join him in his cabin.

On his way below the deck, he directed his adjutant to have the ships prepare a large meal. "You poor fellows have suffered greatly. That ends now." He offered them a bottle of his finest brandy. They both accepted took hearty sips. "I will have my surgeon tend to both of you. You will be provided with navy uniforms. I doubt army men will refuse a navy uniform."

"No, sir", they both said.

"Tonight, I request you to join me for dinner. I long to hear more of your story. Before then, however, I must request you freshen up. I shall write dispatches to my commander to forward the war department. Informing them of your situation and inquiring if they can assist your friends who may be in captivity yet."

"Thank you, sir", said Wilson.

"Thank you, sir", echoed Wood.

Washing and getting clean felt so good. Wilson took his time and scrubbed himself twice. By the time he was done, the water in the tub had gone black.

They were taken to the surgeon's quarters. He cleaned and dressed both their wounds, especially their feet. They were given an extra pair of uniforms. It felt good to wear the uniform again. Even if it was of the navy.

They were taken to the ship's barber. He gave each of them a clean shave. Their hair, however, was a wild mess, and it took the barber, a while to give each a clean cut. Wilson was not a man in vain. He did not care to use a mirror, and only begrudgingly agreed to have his likeness taken. When the barber offered a mirror, Wilson only agreed to look out of curiosity. He nearly dropped it. By outward appearance, he looked ten years older than he was.

In Crossman's quarters, they stated further details of their plight over dinner. The conditions of the prison, the trial and execution of their friends, their fear of each day being the last of them, and their adventures down the river.

"You fellows are the bravest men I have known", Crossman said. "If you care to, you are most welcome to stay until you are recruited back from your starved condition."

"Thank you, sir. We appreciate this kindness. My friend and I agree; however, we wish to rejoin our old comrades, and if possible, do anything that might help our friends in captivity."

Crossman nodded. "If you desire to continue right on, let me assist you. I will send both of you on a vessel to join the other blockading cruiser that is bound for Key West. There you will find another vessel that would end your journey in Washington. While you prepare to depart, I will send you with letters bearing my mark to be delivered to the commandant at Key West and other points explaining of your situation and requesting that you both be given accommodations."

The sun started to set when the pair were on the deck, waiting for the rowboat to come alongside the Somerset. Crossman gave each of them a generously sized pouch of tobacco, along with the promised letters.

"You men have been to hell and back. I can only wish you a better fortune in the future as well as a safe voyage." He gave each a sturdy handshake.

"Thank you, sir", they both said, as they shook hands. Crossman nodded. Then he turned and walked away. The sailors on deck saluted. Wilson and Wood saluted back.

They climbed down the ladder and were assisted in the rowboat. Going across the blue water, they approached a smooth looking cruiser. Wilson saw this name on the hull, the 'Stars and Stripes'.

Wood chuckled. "We made it, did we not, Alf?"

"Yes, we did."

"What do you suppose became of our fellow cutthroats?"

"I don't know. Perhaps we will find out."

They were now on the deck of the 'Stars and Stripes'. They had been shown their quarters, but Wilson had gone back to the main deck, a blanket draped over his shoulders to ward against the cold. He was taking it all in, the sight of the golden sunset, the smell of the ocean, and the sound of the water crashing against the cruiser. The feeling that he was free. He did not hold it in anymore. He wept. Closing his eyes, he told himself it was all a dream.

***

He opened them again at the reunion. Everything that had happened felt like it was a dream and a lifetime ago. Twenty-six years had passed as if they were mere moments in time.

Wilson had kept in touch with many of his fellow raiders after the war ended. He found out that the men who made a break for it, only eight others escaped, the rest were quickly recaptured.

Wollam and Porter made it out and made their way to northern Alabama and eventually to Mississippi, traveling at night and occasionally breaking in empty homes to steal food. They reached the outskirts of the city of Corinth, where they were surrounded by the Union soldiers, who accused them of being confederates. They had to tell their story multiple times and to different people on the chain of command before they were fully believed and returned to their units.

Dorsey and Hawkins had gone a different way. Going north towards East Tennessee, they crossed harsh terrain, before they had found a group of woodchoppers and asked for food, stating they were confederates. The wood choppers said no, that they were in the Lincoln district, and should leave. They then told the woodchoppers the truth and found assistance readily available. They were sheltered and moved by friends to the town of Lebanon. They faced skepticism again, but luckily Dorsey's regiment was camped nearby, and his commanders backed up his story.

Brown, Knight, and Mason tried to get away, but Mason was very much weak and ill to move. He begged them to leave him and go on. They reluctantly did so as they made their way across harsh terrain before finding a cabin with two men who were good friends of the union. The men hid Knight and Brown in a cave with plenty of food for one week, before they were taken and passed along by union folks until they finally reached their own lines.

Fry had made his way back to East Tennessee on his own.

The confederate deserter, unfortunately, was recaptured and hung to death. For the rest, Bensinger, Pittenger, Buffum, Parrott, Reddick, and eventually Mason, it was a terrifying few odd days as they believed they would be executed in reprisal. In actuality, Captain Lee was angry but eventually had them moved to another barracks where they were given better food, much better living conditions, and the opportunity to bathe.

In December, they were informed that they were being exchanged. It took three months of moving and negotiations before they finally arrived in Washington, D.C. After several days of resting and eating, they were issued dress uniforms and taken to the White House, where they were given a personal audience along with the secretary of war, Edwin Stanton and Abraham Lincoln. There, they were given the newly made Medal of Honor.

Jacob Parrott, for enduring a savage whipping and not breaking the least, was given the first one.

Wilson nodded; indeed he would receive one too, along with the other escapees. He was wearing his own now. He spent another year in the army before his enlistment ran out and decided to be discharged rather than get re-enlisted. He had enough of war and had a grand enough tale to tell. He had also never ridden a train since. Wood survived the war, only to succumb to an illness a year after the war ended.

***

Wilson felt sadness when he thought of his friend, but he was amongst old ones now. His thoughts returned to happier times. The Grand Army of the Republic, the veteran's organization that was composed of Union veterans, held a reunion in Columbus, Ohio. Seventy thousand veterans had crowded in this town.

Wilson had kept his correspondence with his fellow raiders, and nine of the others had also shown up and held a private reunion for themselves. Bensinger, Brown, Dorsey, Knight, Pittenger, Reddick, Mason, Parrott, and Wollam had gathered near a house next to the railroad tracks and swapped stories as they reminisced about the past and what they had done since then.

Rachel Slavens, Sam Slavens' wife, attended along with her sons so they could hear more about their father. For the most part, they had all achieved some degree of success, and they had found out that some of their numbers had passed on since the end of the war.

The sharp scream of the train whistle startled them all as they headed outside to see a train come to a stop. The engine had banners draped all over it. They were all surprised and delighted to see the nameplate read 'The General. They were even more surprised when it gave its final hiss, from the cab, out hopped William Fuller.

"Hello, gents! Once I heard of this gathering, I could not have stayed away." He went into the group and started shaking everyone's hands. When he got to Wollam, however, he was refused.

"I do not care for you, sir. I will not shake your hand."

"Very well."

Rachel stormed right into Fuller's face. "I don't care much for you either. It is on you why my dear husband was caught and hung like a criminal, which he was not." Having said what she wanted, she walked back to the house.

"Fellows," Fuller said. "We have had our skirmishes and, yes, you took my train and ran me through in getting it back. I have felt anger towards the north after Lee surrendered. It took time, now in my older years, for me to lose those feelings. There is no point to senseless hatred. I wish to extend my branch of friendship, which is why I arranged to bring the General here. It has taken some time, but she has come home to the north, where she was built. Perhaps we shall all come together." The raiders nodded. This man, the one who chased them relentlessly, the one who vowed to see them all hang, was offering peace.

"Damn well said, Fuller," Knight said as everyone voiced their agreement.

"Thank you. I must see about that woman now." He walked past everyone into the house. They followed him and walked inside.

He sat next to her on a sofa. Speaking quite gently so they could not hear. She had tears in her eyes. No one really said anything. It was a moving moment. Finally, they all stood up. Rachel looked as if a huge weight had been lifted off her shoulders that she carried for a long time. She hugged Fuller.

The remainder of the day was spent at a mess hall where the mood was buoyant. Fuller told some funny stories that made everyone laugh, even Wollam. Finally, Knight suggested. "Say, boys. What do you think? Shall we capture our likenesses for such occasion. I have no issue because of my good lucks? What do you say?" Everyone agreed. Even Wilson.

They took a group photo while everyone stood around the General. Wilson made sure he was on the tender. Brown and Knight were inside the cab. Mason, Reddick, Wollam, Dorsey, and Pittenger were right in front of the engine. Parrott and Bensinger stood by the cowcatcher. Fuller was leaning on a post by the engine. After making sure everyone would get their copy, the group decided to say their good-byes until the next time they were to meet. There were guffaws, backslaps, and occasional tears of joy. Wollam found himself facing Fuller.

"Say, Fuller."

"Yes?"

"I can shake your hand now."

For the rest of his days. Wilson had kept a framed copy of that photo, to remind him that for one moment, frozen forever in time, two former enemies were friends.

ABOUT THE AUTHOR

Phillip Urlevich was born in a small town in California and moved along his family to a slightly bigger town in Arizona. After spending much of his time in the library, exploring history as well as science and crime fiction, he decided to try his hand at writing, first with short stories, before moving up with his debut novel *Beyond Earth* and the screenplay for the independent film, *Suburban Rebels*. He put his love of history, especially the Civil War, into his second novel, *The Georgia Express*.

Also available on DVD and BluRay from Director Phillip Urlevich:

Enticed by the proposition of easy money, long-time friends Jesse and Billy agree to make a new street narcotic for a mysterious crime lord.

Unfortunately, one of them is about to be betrayed…

Their lives hang in the balance as they are being closely followed by a hitman.

Time is against them as they struggle to mix the ingredients before it's too late.